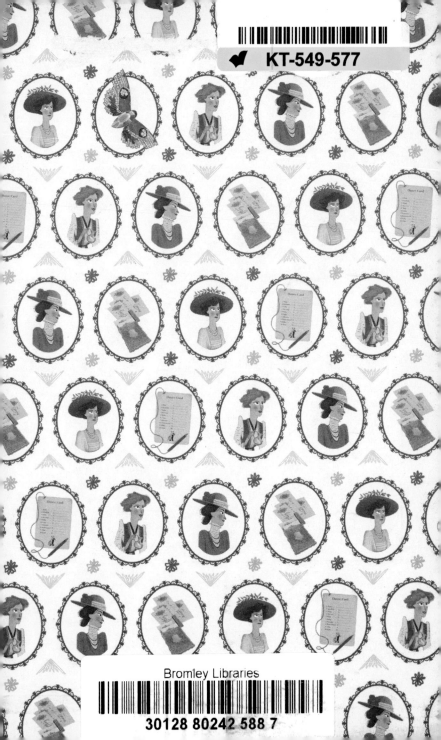

KT-549-577

The Mystery of the
JEWELLED MOTH

Also by Katherine Woodfine

The Mystery of the Clockwork Sparrow

The Mystery of the
JEWELLED MOTH

Katherine Woodfine

EGMONT

EGMONT

We bring stories to life

First published in Great Britain 2016
by Egmont UK Limited
The Yellow Building, 1 Nicholas Road, London W11 4AN

Text copyright © 2016 Katherine Woodfine
Illustrations copyright © 2016 Júlia Sardà

The moral rights of the author and illustrator have been asserted

ISBN 978 1 4052 7618 4

59403/1

A CIP catalogue record for this title is available
from the British Library

Typeset by Avon DataSet Ltd, Bidford on Avon, Warwickshire
Printed and bound in Great Britain by the CPI Group

For Duncan,
who read this first

the Season ahead, of which a highlight will be a grand ball at Hill Lodge, hosted by Lady Fitzmaurice.

A number of garden parties and fêtes are also fixtures of the coming months; it is to be hoped that the weather will be favourable. Lady Woodhouse will be holding a fête at Chesterfield Gardens: this is expected to be a remarkably pretty affair, attended by several members of the Royal Family. Lord Beaucastle will also be hosting his traditional garden party at his charming residence, Beaucastle Hall. The garden and the grounds are delightful, being very extensive, and entertainments of an outdoor nature are always appreciated there.

外
國
人

Another important occasion of the Season, which is certain to attract many members of the fashionable world, is the opening of the Royal Academy Show, which shall take place

PART I
The London Season

From the opening of Covent Garden to the Royal Academy show, from Ascot to the Royal Drawing Rooms, the London Season is rightly considered the finest and most elegant of any European capital. Young ladies preparing to make their debut in London society will feel themselves to be especially fortunate. However, they will enjoy the delights and entertainments of their first Season all the more by ensuring they are equipped with a correct understanding of etiquette: the rules that govern the proper behaviour of a young lady in society.

From Lady Diana DeVere's *Etiquette for Debutantes: a Guide to the Manners, Mores and Morals of Good Society*, Chapter 1: The London Season – Court Presentation – St James's and Buckingham Palaces – Who may be Presented – Court Dress – Rules and Regulations – The Drawing Room – The Levee

CHAPTER ONE

The green parrot was squawking downstairs. Mei rolled over and closed her eyes again, longing to slide back into sleep. She could hear voices in the street; the singing of the kettle; horns hooting on the river; and horses' hooves clattering over the cobbles outside: all the familiar sounds that spoke to her of *morning*. For a moment or two, she just lay there, letting them wash over her, but at last she forced her eyes to open once more. She could already feel the warmth of the sun streaming through the chinks in the curtains, falling in long stripes over the bedclothes. She had overslept again, and Mum might be in a scolding mood.

Hurriedly, she sat up in bed, and pushed aside the curtain that separated her corner of the room from the larger portion where her three brothers slept. Their beds were already empty: her eldest brother, Song, must have left for his job in the kitchen at Ah Wei's Eating House, and the twins, Shen and Jian, would be on their way to school.

At once, she hopped out of bed. It really must be late: why hadn't Mum called her? Only a minute or two later she was hastening down the stairs, still doing up the buttons on her striped frock as she went.

The stairs were steep and narrow and creaked as she went down them. The Lim family house was an odd little place, squashed right up against its neighbours in a cramped street in Limehouse, East London. It was all crooked angles and dark corners and patches of damp, but every square inch of it was friendly to Mei. She had been born here in the bedroom above the shop; she and her brothers had grown up here; she couldn't imagine what it would be like to live anywhere else.

As she always did, she jumped down the last few steps into the stone-flagged hallway. To one side was the door into the shop, which stood ajar, letting all the familiar scents of tea and spices and tobacco flood in. To the other was the back room, where the range was, and where the family spent most of their time. But before she pushed the door open and went in, she came to a sudden halt outside.

She could hear Mum and Dad talking in the back room. There was nothing unusual in that, but what was strange was the *way* they were talking. Their voices sounded hushed, even anxious.

For a moment, she hesitated outside the door. Dad was

saying in an urgent tone: 'We've got no other option, Lou. You must see that.'

'But if we give them what they want, we'll hardly be scraping by! And what if next month, they ask for more? I'll not be intimidated like this,' said Mum indignantly.

Dad's voice was tight. 'Do you want to lose this house, the shop, everything that we've worked for?' His voice dropped lower. 'Remember what happened to the Goldsteins. Is that how you want us to end up?'

The Goldsteins. Mei felt a little shiver run along her spine. Mr Goldstein had been a pawnbroker: his little shop was just a few streets away. He and his wife had been a quiet old couple, though Mrs Goldstein had always said good morning when Mei and her brothers went past on their way to school. But just a couple of months ago there had been a terrible fire: the whole building, including the pawnbroker's shop, had been burned to the ground, and both Mr and Mrs Goldstein had died. It had been a dreadful accident, Mei had thought, but now it seemed suddenly far more sinister and terrible. *Is that how you want us to end up?* What could Dad possibly mean by that?

'Of course not! But –' Mum began.

It came to Mei suddenly that she was eavesdropping; something that she had always been taught was a low-down thing to do. She pushed the door open and went through into the back room. Immediately, both her parents stopped talking.

'Well, here she is at last, the Sleeping Princess herself,' said Mum in her ordinary voice, just as if nothing out of the usual way had been happening. She was rolling out some pastry, stopping occasionally to stir or season a pan of broth that was steaming at her elbow. Whatever she was doing, Mum always seemed to be doing something else at the same time. More often than not, she was undertaking half a dozen things at once.

'Hope those boys have left you some breakfast,' said Dad, tweaking the end of Mei's long plait, as she slipped into a seat beside him at the well-scrubbed wooden table.

'You'd sleep the whole day through if we let you,' Mum said, shaking her head at Mei, but her eyes were twinkling. 'You must get those lazy bones from your Dad's side of the family.'

Dad made a shocked face, as if he was mortally offended, then jabbed playfully at Mum with his newspaper. She pretended she was going to retaliate with the rolling pin, then shrieked and dived behind Mei's chair, laughing, as Dad got to his feet to give chase.

Mei couldn't help laughing too, and in the corner, the green parrot squawked happily as though he were joining in. It was quite as if the tense conversation she had heard through the door had never happened, and she almost began to wonder if she had imagined those serious, fearful voices. They hadn't sounded like Mum and Dad at all.

Mei knew that her parents weren't quite like everyone else's. They were always laughing and joking, and doing what Mr Walker, the schoolmaster, would call '*playing the fool*' in his most disapproving voice. Mei had once been invited to tea with Jessie Bates, and her family had been so different: Jessie's father was so grim and strict that everyone sat around in silence, not daring to say anything more than 'pass the salt'. Mei had scarcely been able to believe it. Imagine being frightened of your own father! Mei's Dad was one of the kindest and gentlest people she knew. And to think that Jessie and some of the others had actually turned up their noses at her family, just because her mother was English and her father Chinese!

Happily, she did not have to worry about that kind of thing much any more. Now that she'd turned fourteen and left school, she rarely needed to step outside the little network of Limehouse streets that people called 'China Town'. Here, there were just as many Chinese faces as there were English ones – most of them merchant sailors – firemen, seamen, stewards, cooks and carpenters, who served on board the steamers plying between China and the Port of London, and would pass a few weeks at one of the lodging houses before working their passage back home on another steamship. But there was also a sprinkling of families like Mei's own. She'd heard people say that China Town was dangerous and sinister – a dark place of opium dens and gaming houses, but that wasn't the Limehouse that Mei knew. The streets might be dirty; the people might be poor; but here, she felt at ease. Here, no one turned up their noses. On the contrary: Lim's shop was at the very heart of China Town, just down the street from Ah Wei's Eating House; across from the laundry and the Seven Stars Inn; and around the corner from Madame Wu's Magnificent Magic Lantern Show. Everyone came to Lim's shop, and everyone knew Mei and her family.

'You'll run some errands for me this morning,' Mum was saying now, bouncing Mei suddenly back out of her thoughts. She realised that the clock on the mantelpiece was striking the hour and that Dad was going through to the shop. 'I need you to go to the baker, and the fish shop, and the cobbler. And for mercy's sake, don't come back without the fish like last time!'

Since Mei had left school, it was her job to help around the house and in the shop. Her older brother Song went out to work, of course, but as the only girl of the family, it was up to her to help Mum and Dad. She knew she was lucky to be able to do so. Most Limehouse families didn't have the luxury of keeping their daughters at home, and half the girls in her old class at school were now working in the white-lead factory, or at the box-maker's.

'But take this upstairs before you go,' Mum went on, handing her some folded linen, smelling soapy-clean from Monday's wash. 'I've got people coming to see about the room later.'

Mei took the stack of linens carefully up the steep stairs to the attics. Up here, little windows in the roof let in tiny glimpses of sky and patches of sunshine, and she almost tripped over their white cat, Tibby, who was sitting on the attic landing outside Uncle Huan's room, basking in one of the squares of yellow light cast on to the floor. She opened her green eyes at Mei, blinked at her disdainfully, and then closed them again as Mei stepped over her, into the other attic bedroom.

She still could not get used to the idea that this room was not Granddad's any longer. It was empty now, ready to be let to a boarder – and yet somehow, Mei still saw Granddad here, sitting in his upright chair. At this time of the day, he would have been reading the newspaper, Tibby curled in his lap, his own special pot of tea placed carefully at his side on the brass-bound trunk where he kept his treasures. Most of his days had followed the same careful, quiet routine: tea, books, the newspaper, writing in his notebooks, the occasional slow stroll down to the eating house for a game of mah-jong with his friends. Unlike Mei's father and uncle, who kept their hair short and wore English clothes, Granddad had believed in maintaining traditions and insisted on wearing his hair in a pigtail almost as long as Mei's own. He had painstakingly taught each of the children Mandarin – something that he had been especially proud of – and to Mei, who loved stories, he had told endless legends and folk tales that he in turn had been told by his own grandfather. Mei always delighted in Granddad's stories, even those that she knew Song believed were silly nonsense, although he was much too polite to say so.

But just as much as the fairy tales, Mei loved to hear Granddad's stories of their own family, and his life in the faraway village in Henan, China, where he had grown up, where Mei's father and his brother had been born, and where the Lim family had lived for countless generations. Indeed, that peaceful country village, which stood beside an ancient temple, seemed like a place from a fairy tale itself to Mei: she could never quite reconcile it with the dusty, busy, smoky Limehouse streets that she knew.

The most important of all these stories was Granddad's own: the tale of why they had left the village to come to London. It was also the saddest of all his stories, Mei thought. Granddad had told it so many times that she could recall almost every word. As she went back down the stairs, she repeated it to herself, imagining that it was Granddad's soft, quavering voice telling it.

'The greatest treasure in our temple was the Moonbeam Diamond,' the story began. 'An oval-shaped stone, as silvery as the moonlight for which it was named. The diamond had divine powers: it brought us good fortune and prosperity. It was famous for hundreds of miles around. Pilgrims came to see it, and many stories were told about it. Some said that a real moonbeam was trapped within it, and that was why it shimmered so strangely.

'The Lim family had been the guardians of the Moonbeam Diamond for generations: my father and my grandfather protected it before me. Legend has it that it was a gift to one of our ancestors from the Lady of the Moon herself. He was a noble warrior who had righted a terrible injustice: as a reward, she gave him the diamond, which was magically endowed with the power to protect him and his descendants from harm. Being a wise and good man, the warrior did not keep the diamond for himself, but bestowed it upon the monks so that all might share its good fortune. He remained with them in their temple to watch over it, and so he and his descendants prospered.

'But it was also said that an ancient curse was laid upon the diamond. If ever it were stolen, any who possessed it would be destined to ill fortune. Their crops would fail, their

11

families would fall ill, and every foul misfortune imaginable would visit them unless the diamond were returned. Stories were told about those who had foolishly tried to take it, who had come to the most fearful ends –'

'Mei! Are you still half asleep? Run along now, and remember your brother's boots from the cobbler's.'

Mei took the basket a little reluctantly, still half-thinking about Granddad's story. She didn't really like going to the cobbler's, which was some way off, down towards the river and the docks, beyond the familiar streets of China Town. She had always been a little shy – *scaredy-cat*, Song had said when they were both younger – and she found crowded places daunting. But Mum was looking at her expectantly, her arms folded, and for all she was jolly, Mum was not to be trifled with.

Outside, the streets were full of morning life. People were bustling in and out of the Eating House; carts and bicycles were clattering by on the road; and busy activity was going on behind the dusty windows of the sailmaker's and the wheelwright's.

She called at the baker's first, and found the shop full of people: old women with baskets; younger ones gossiping while they waited for their turn; serious-faced little girls on errands; and two small, dirty ragamuffins, pressing their noses up against the counter and looking longingly at the hot currant buns coming out of the oven. As Mei entered, she noticed the woman who was being served turn and look at her, then nudge her companion and whisper something. The two women cast covert glances at her as they left the shop. Mei stared after them, disconcerted. She was used to nudging and pointing and even rude words, but not here, on the fringes of China Town, where faces like hers were hardly out of the ordinary.

She turned her attention to the baker's wife, Mrs O'Leary, who greeted her pleasantly. She was always kind to Mei, and especially to her little brothers, and today even more so, insisting on tucking a paper bag with some broken biscuits into Mei's basket alongside the two new loaves. Mei tried to protest, but Mrs O'Leary wouldn't have it. 'Take them, my dear,' she insisted, pressing her hand, telling her to keep her pecker up and wishing her a good day with more than her usual warmth.

Mei wondered if Mrs O'Leary had overheard whatever the woman had said, and had felt sorry for her because of it. Thinking that made her feel uncomfortable, so as she went back out into the street, she turned her mind back to Granddad's tale.

'When your father was no more than the age that you are now, everything changed for our family,' he would continue, an ominous note creeping into his voice. 'A party of men came to our village. They told us they wished to learn about our lands, and mark it upon their maps.

'Their leader was a young Englishman: a gentleman and a fine swordsman. We called him *Waiguo Ren*, which means "foreigner". We welcomed Waiguo Ren and his men into our village, believing that they did us honour. They were taken to the temple, and shown the Moonbeam Diamond. Waiguo Ren himself had long talks with the monks, telling them he wished to learn what they could teach him.

'But what we did not know was that Waiguo Ren was deceitful. He was in league with the Emperor, who was jealous of our temple and its wealth and prosperity. Waiguo Ren lied to the Emperor, telling him that the monks were secretly working against the Qing dynasty, plotting with foreign powers to rise up against them. Angry, the Qing sent many men, and with their help, Waiguo Ren and his men attacked us in the night when we were sleeping. They seized the riches of the temple and burned our village. Whilst we fought to save our homes and families, Waiguo Ren himself seized the Moonbeam Diamond and took it for his own.

'It was a dark and terrible time. Many people were killed, and our village was destroyed. I knew that I had failed in my duty to watch over the Moonbeam Diamond, but Waiguo Ren had disappeared, and there was nothing to be done. Not long afterwards, your father, your uncle and I departed.

The Emperor had ruined us: our home was gone, but we knew there was work to be found on the steamships. The long voyage across the sea was hard and full of danger, but at last we came to rest here, safe on these shores.'

At this point, Granddad had a way of opening his hands, as if he were releasing the story into the air, like a bird taking flight. 'And the rest of this tale, you know for yourself,' he always concluded.

'And what happened to the diamond?' Mei would ask eagerly, when she was small.

Granddad would smile, yet his eyes were cloudy with sadness. 'That I do not know. But what I do know is that the Moonbeam Diamond has its own destiny.'

Then his expression would change into a beaming grin, and he would sweep her into a hug and say: 'You and your brothers are more precious to me than any diamond, my dear one. You are the only jewels that an old man like me could ever need.'

But all the same, Mei knew that Granddad had often thought of the Moonbeam Diamond. Sometimes, after he had told her the story, he would sigh and say: 'You know, often in my dreams, I see our temple. How I would love to see the diamond sparkling there again, where it belongs.'

Mei had heard Dad and Uncle Huan saying that Granddad lived too much in the past. They were young men when they arrived in London, and had made lives for themselves here. Father had Lim's shop, and Mum, and the children, whilst Uncle Huan had taken a liking to a sailor's life and now worked as First Mate on one of the great steamships that came in and out of West India Dock. He came home every few months, his pockets stuffed with packets of cinnamon or curious ornaments carved from ivory, or long ostrich feathers that he used to tickle Mei's cheeks. Whenever he returned, there would be a family celebration, and he would take up his old room in the attic opposite Granddad's for a few happy weeks. But this time, when Uncle Huan came back, Granddad would not be there.

Mei's stomach felt hollow. She still missed him every day.

She had almost reached the river now. The air here had its own peculiar tang: a part-sour, part-spicy odour of smoke and turpentine, flavoured with rum from the West India Docks, and always the distinctive smell of the water. Everything started with the river: it was here that Granddad and Dad and Uncle Huan had first arrived in London, all those years ago. Mei could see the dark lines of its myriad cranes and masts sketched against the sky, as she picked her way carefully down towards it.

The streets were busier here: she had to weave her way between horses pulling carts stacked high with wooden crates; a boy selling papers for a ha'penny; clerks on their way to the Customs Office; a gaggle of barefoot children, chasing through the crowds; and men unloading cargo: sacks of grain, great coils of rope and lengths of timber. Everyone was far too busy to pay the least attention to a girl alone with a basket, and Mei began to relax and enjoy the spectacle of the docks at work. The river was usually grey, but today the June sunlight caught it and made it sparkle – here silver, there blue or green. Seagulls were calling above her head; smoke was curling from chimneys on the other side of the river; and boats were jostling their way across the water: steamboats and sailing ships, barges and coasters. She was almost disappointed when she came to the cobbler's shop and had to turn away from the river to go inside.

The cobbler was a jolly red-faced man, who spent much of his free time in the Star Inn. 'Boots for your brother, Miss Mei? Here you are. Good as new,' he said heartily, handing them over to her. But just as he was about to put them into her hands, he suddenly pulled them back. Mei gazed up at him, confused.

'Will you give your father a message for me,' he said, in a much lower voice, a grave look on his usually cheerful face.

'Course,' said Mei, surprised.

'Only for your father, mind. Keep mum: not a word to anyone else. Not even those rascal little brothers of yours.'

Mei nodded, increasingly puzzled.

17

For a moment, the cobbler hesitated. Then, even more quietly, he said: 'Tell him he's in the soup.'

'What?'

'Up to his neck in it. He'll know what I mean. Now run along, my dear, and *mind how you go.*'

He said the last words with a particular emphasis. It was not an ordinary run-of-the-mill farewell – he was warning her about something. She had not the faintest idea what the warning might mean, but in spite of the warm day, a sudden chill crept over her as she left the shop.

The docks that had seemed so lively felt different now. Sailors and stevedores jostled past as she hurried back towards China Town. One man, already drunk, staggered out of an inn doorway into her path then dropped his bottle on the ground and began cursing angrily. She dodged away, but then a little gaggle of children crowded around her, the smallest pulling at her frock to distract her while another's dirty hands snaked inside her basket. But Mei had not lived her whole life in the East End for nothing. She knew what to do: she pushed the thieving one away, scowled at them all and thundered, 'Leave off! Or I'll set the constable after you!' in her loudest voice, until they scattered into the crowd.

Her heart bumping now, she walked as fast as she could back to China Town. She did not run. She knew that to run would be to appear frightened and to appear frightened was to be weak, but with every step, the words of the cobbler's warning were ringing in her ears as loud as the bells of Bow Church. *He's up in his neck in it. In the soup. Mind how you go.*

She plunged through the shop door, making the bell clamour loudly, but then stopped dead in her tracks.

The shop was ruined. Furniture was overturned and the shelves had been ransacked: bottles and jars were scattered in all directions, and tins of tea and coffee had been pushed to the floor, spilling their contents. For a moment, the chaos was all she saw: then she realised that in the centre of it all was a single crumpled figure, lying like a broken puppet in the middle of the floor.

'*Dad!*' Mei screamed.

CHAPTER TWO

All the way across the smoky city of spires and slums, in the heart of the West End, was a shop of a very different kind. London's most fashionable department store was crowded with people: the London Season was now in full swing, and anyone who was anyone simply *had* to be seen at Sinclair's.

Outside, it was a glorious June morning, and the skies above Piccadilly Circus were a perfect blue. Inside, all eight storeys of Sinclair's department store were astir with activity. Elegant ladies were perusing gloves and parasols, whilst dapper gentlemen examined flannels and straw boaters. Giddy groups of young people were gathering around the ice-cream counter – Mr Edward Sinclair's latest American innovation, fast becoming a favourite with London's fashionable set. At the top of the store, stylish couples were strolling through the roof gardens, which, since Mr Frederick Whitman had chosen them as the setting for his marriage proposal to West End star Miss Kitty Shaw, were considered to be quite the most romantic place in the city. All the while, porters in smart uniforms hurried by with boxes, and the Head Doorman, Sid Parker, swung open the doors to admit more customers to the tune of a merry waltz drifting down from the gallery, where a pianist played a gleaming white grand piano.

Out in the stable-yard, there was just as much going on. A procession of vans was streaming into the yard, each piled high with crates and boxes. Many of them had come directly from the docks of the East End, loaded with cargo from all over the world. There were crates of China tea, bolts of Indian silk, and the finest goods from every corner of the British Empire. It was here that everything arrived, and it was from here too that all the deliveries went out to the grand houses of West London. Even now, another group of porters were busily preparing the next batch, each item carefully wrapped and placed inside a Sinclair's box. The boxes were loaded into the motor vans and delivery carts, and then they flowed out again in a long cavalcade into London's streets.

Meanwhile, above them in the store, the elevators swept up and down; the tables in the Marble Court restaurant were laid for luncheon; and in the Millinery Department, several groups of customers had gathered to admire exquisite displays of the latest summer hats – gorgeous creations all fluffy with ostrich feathers or wreathed in flowers. A stylish lady swept by, fanning herself and holding forth to her companion:

'I do think that white is the *only* suitable colour for a debutante. Perhaps ivory or *écru*, or I could tolerate a pale mauve, but to wear anything else would be in very poor taste – don't you agree?'

The girl walking with them was clearly a debutante herself – a young lady making her first appearances in society. She was gazing around open-mouthed, as if she could hardly believe her eyes. But her amazement was not really so very unusual; after all, Sinclair's was the most extraordinary store in London, with its lofty ceilings painted with clouds and cherubs, the fountains in its magnificent marble entrance hall, its beautiful golden clock. But it wasn't just the celebrated decor of Sinclair's that made it so special. Nor was it the magnificent entertainments that Mr Sinclair always seemed to be staging – one week an elegant *thé dansant*, the next an exhibition of some remarkable new invention. There was quite simply something magical about the place, from the way that the very air seemed always to be scented with rose and violet and caramel and melting chocolate, to the famous blue-and-gold Sinclair's boxes, inside which any kind of delightful dreams might be discovered nestling amongst snowy folds of tissue paper and tied with a satin bow.

Even Sophie Taylor, who had been working as a salesgirl at Sinclair's ever since the store first opened, still sometimes found herself gazing around the store, enchanted by the beauty of her surroundings. Not, of course, that there was a great deal of time for standing around on such a busy morning as this one.

'Deliveries for the Millinery Department, Miss Taylor!' called a porter, whizzing by with a trolley stacked high with hat-boxes.

'To the storeroom please, Alf,' she replied, as she deftly whisked a hat decorated with bluebirds from the very top of an elaborate display and placed it into the eager hands of a waiting customer.

It was strange to think that today was her fifteenth birthday. A year ago, she would never have believed she would be spending it working as a salesgirl at Sinclair's department store. As she hurried into the storeroom to fetch more hats for a group of debutantes, she found herself marvelling at how much her life had changed since her last birthday. Papa had been home on leave, she remembered, full of tales about the recent adventures of his regiment. There had been a trip to the theatre and a special tea on the lawn at Orchard House. Cook had made a birthday cake decorated with strawberries, and they had drunk her health in ginger beer. Papa's present had been a lovely new frock – her first grown-up evening dress – and her dear old governess, Miss Pennyfeather, had given her a pretty silk sash to match. She remembered Papa smiling at her as they had all sung 'For She's a Jolly Good Fellow' around the tea table . . .

For a dangerous moment her eyes began to feel hot and prickly, but she shook the sensation away at once. This was not the time for blubbing – she was a professional young woman now. Being a shop girl was hard work, and sometimes rather boring – each day the same round of taking deliveries, tidying the storeroom, recording sales in the ledgers – but she did it well, and she was proud of it. As she swept back out of the storeroom with the stack of hat-boxes, she held her head high. Papa might be gone now, but it was a comfort to know that he would have been proud of her too.

Just a few months ago, the idea of working for a living had been daunting. Life as a shop girl had seemed so difficult – and she had felt so awfully alone. But then she had fallen headlong into a peculiar adventure, and together with three new friends, had saved Sinclair's department store from disaster. She still felt a little shy of putting it that way, even to herself – after all, 'saving Sinclair's' sounded rather grand and conceited. But it was the truth, just the same. Together, the four of them had prevented Sinclair's from being destroyed by an infernal machine – an explosive device planted by the mysterious and sinister criminal who called himself 'the Baron'. In the process they had also helped to recover Mr Sinclair's priceless clockwork sparrow, which had been stolen from the store.

It had been a strange and rather frightening experience – but there was no doubt that it had changed her life for the better. She had been able to use some of the reward money that they had been given for finding Mr Sinclair's stolen jewels to move out of her horrid old lodgings and into a far nicer room. Mrs Milton in the Millinery Department had been delighted to have her back to work at the store, and the other shop girls, who had not always been especially agreeable to her in the past, had become much more pleasant. Indeed, the youngest girls had become rather awestruck in her presence, treating her quite as if she were a heroine from a story in a twopenny paper. Even Edith, her old adversary, was carefully courteous; and as for the great Mr Sinclair himself, he always had a smile or a nod for her on the occasions he passed through the Millinery Department.

Best of all, though, she no longer felt so lonely. Papa and Orchard House were gone forever, but now she at least had her friends: Lil, Billy and Joe. Like Sophie herself, they all worked at Sinclair's. Lil was one of the glamorous 'Captain's Girls' – mannequins, whose job it was to display the latest gowns, hats and shoes to the most important customers in the daily dress shows. She combined being a mannequin with performing as a chorus girl at the Fortune Theatre, and always seemed to be rushing between dress parades and rehearsals and performances.

Meanwhile, Billy had been promoted from his old position as an apprentice porter to that of office boy in Mr Sinclair's own office. Far from loitering around as he used to do, Sophie now regularly saw him hurrying busily through the shop on urgent business for Mr Sinclair's private secretary, Miss Atwood. He always grinned at Sophie when he saw her, but rarely seemed to have time to stop and speak. He had grown taller since the spring, and stood much straighter now: already he seemed quite different from the nervous boy who had always been getting himself into scrapes and who had needed Sophie's help.

Joe worked in the stable-yard. Sophie saw him most mornings on her way into the store, brushing down one of the horses with his sleeves rolled up, cheerfully whistling a music-hall tune. Joe had once been part of a gang working for the Baron, and when Sophie had first met him he had been injured and penniless, begging outside Sinclair's. He looked quite different now – well-fed and happy. She knew that having a proper job and a place to live meant a very great deal to him. She could understand how he felt: she too had known what it was like to be alone, without any way to support herself. She knew they both felt very fortunate now.

But, she acknowledged, not everything about their adventure had changed things for the better. For one thing, it had brought a new sense of danger into her life. She could not forget that she alone had caught a glimpse of the Baron. He was renowned for the prodigious care he took to keep his identity a secret: no one but his closest associates knew what he looked like, but Sophie had seen him, and because of that, she knew she was in jeopardy. Indeed, in the first few weeks after their adventure, Mr McDermott – the private detective who worked for Mr Sinclair – had instructed a policeman to escort her to and from the store, to ensure her safety. Even once that had ceased, Mr McDermott himself had called in several times to check that all was well. She had welcomed his visits: in those first days she had found herself jumping at unexpected noises, starting at the sound of footfall behind her, and lying awake at night, staring into the dark, unable to help picturing the Baron's face looming at her out of the shadows.

But as spring had stretched into summer, there had been not even the smallest sign of the Baron, nor the Baron's Boys – the gang of East End ruffians who worked for him.

'Do you suppose that perhaps he didn't realise I had seen him, after all?' Sophie had found herself asking Mr McDermott.

Mr McDermott had frowned. 'Who can say?' he said,

shaking his head. 'The Baron is a hard man to second-guess.'
Then he gave Sophie a rare smile. 'Either way, Miss Taylor, it
looks as though he has forgotten about you – and I must say
that I'm very relieved about that.'

Well, the Baron might have forgotten her, but she doubted
she would ever forget about him. Perhaps, she thought now,
as she unwrapped the hats, it was simply that he believed a
mere shop girl could not possibly pose a threat to him. And
in a way, he was right – he was one of the most powerful men
in London, with the whole of the East End in his thrall, and
she was here, spending her fifteenth birthday selling hats.

'Here is the style with the rosettes you asked for, madam,'
she explained politely, showing the first of the hats to the
three young ladies waiting by the counter. 'And this one has
a cluster of rosebuds, while this pink one is a brand new Paris
model,' she went on, with careful courtesy. At Sinclair's, it
was drummed into all staff that they must provide the very
best service to customers at all times.

The smallest of the young ladies, who was dressed in an
elaborately flounced gown, seized on the Paris hat at once.
'I'll try this one,' she announced in a very self-confident tone,
positioning herself in front of the mirror. 'Lord Beaucastle
says I look awfully pretty in pink, you know,' she added to
her companions.

The girl next to her – slender, dark-haired and rather

more simply dressed than her companion – rolled her eyes, but said nothing. She picked up the hat with the rosettes and turned it over in her hands. Sophie thought she saw her eyes flick very quickly to the price, which was marked discreetly on a small ticket inside the hat-box.

'Cynthia has one just like this,' she said disdainfully, dropping the hat back into its box. 'Goodness knows, I wouldn't want anyone to think I was copying *her* taste.'

'What do you think of this one?' the third of the debutantes, who had dimples and yellow curls, asked anxiously as she tried the hat with the rosebuds. 'It would be rather lovely for a tea party, don't you think, Emily? With my lace tea-gown?'

'Well, get it if you like it, Phyllis, by all means,' said Emily, the dark girl. 'Though I must say it's not to my taste.'

'I suppose *you* would prefer this one,' said the first young lady sharply, as she appraised the Paris hat in the mirror.

'Oh *no*, I don't think so,' said Emily dismissively. 'I don't care for pink. I'd rather that blue with the spotted veil,' she said, nodding at a hat on display on another of the glass-topped counters. 'It's more stylish.'

Phyllis's face looked shocked under the wide brim of the hat she was trying. 'But you couldn't possibly wear something like that!' she exclaimed. 'It's so bold! We're only just out, after all – we mustn't look *fast*!'

'Oh, Phyllis, don't be such a prig,' said Emily with a little laugh.

'Why don't you try it on then, if you're so daring?' suggested the first young lady, still not taking her eyes off her own perfect reflection in the mirror. Sophie thought it sounded like a challenge.

Emily yawned daintily behind a gloved hand, as if the whole situation was boring her. 'No, I don't think I will,' she said coolly. 'Really, it's a little vulgar to buy from a department store, don't you think? Why, imagine if someone else turned up to a party wearing the same hat as you? It would be just humiliating!'

'Not so humiliating as wearing the same evening gown to three different parties in a row,' muttered the first young lady. Emily ignored her, but Sophie noticed a flush of crimson appearing on her cheeks.

An uncomfortable silence fell, until at last the first young lady removed the hat and cast it carelessly down on the counter. 'I'll leave this one, thank you,' she said airily to Sophie. Then she turned to Phyllis. 'Do make your mind up. Are you going to buy that, or not? We'll be late for luncheon if you don't hurry.'

Phyllis hurriedly removed the hat and handed it back with an apologetic smile, and the whole party set out for luncheon in the Marble Court Restaurant, rather to Sophie's relief. She might be grateful to have her job at Sinclair's, but she could think of better ways to spend her birthday than dealing with bickering debutantes, she thought ruefully, as she tidied the hats away.

'Letter for you, Miss Taylor!'

A porter approached the counter, giving her a cheeky wink as he handed her not one, but two envelopes.

'Young gentleman friend, eh? Sending you a few sweet nothings?' he teased, grinning as he went on his way.

Sophie ignored him and glanced down at the envelopes. The sight of the familiar, rather untidy handwriting at once made her spirits lift. She slipped behind the counter, and tore the envelope open, revealing a card with a birthday greeting on the front, surrounded by a pretty wreath of poppies and daisies and some swooping swallows. Inside was scribbled a cryptic message:

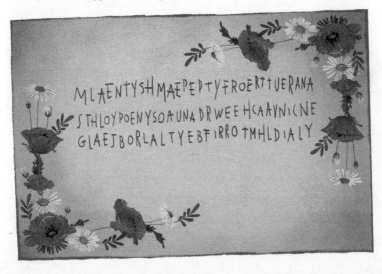

Sophie grinned to herself. She knew exactly who the birthday card was from. During their adventure, Sophie and her friends had had to decipher some mysterious coded messages, and ever since then, Lil had thought it was great fun to write the others notes in code. Sophie frowned and picked up a pencil, trying to work out this one, determined not to let Lil get the better of her. After a few unsuccessful tries, she cracked it: the secret was to read every other letter, starting with the first – and when she came to the end, to start again with the letters she had missed.

MLAENTYSH MAEPEPTYFROERTTUERANA
STHLOYPOENYSOAUNADRWEEHCAAVNICNE
GLAEJBORLALTYEBFIRROTMHLDIALY

MANY HAPPY RETURNS HOPE YOU ARE HAVING A JOLLY BIRTHDAY
LET'S MEET FOR TEA AT LYONS AND WE CAN CELEBRATE FROM LIL

A birthday tea! The day that had stretched ahead of her just like any other suddenly seemed bright and festive. She felt altogether more cheerful as she glanced down at the second envelope – perhaps Billy had sent her a birthday greeting too?

But the second envelope did not look in the least like something Billy might have sent. The envelope was thick ivory paper, the address written in violet ink in an elegant but unfamiliar hand:

Miss Sophie Taylor &

Miss Lilian Rose

Sinclair's Department Store

Piccadilly

London W1

How curious! It was addressed to both her *and* Lil. She frowned for a moment, trying to think who on earth could possibly be writing a note to both of them. But there was no time to wonder – another customer was hurrying towards her. Hastily, she stuffed both envelopes into the pocket of her frock. 'May I help you, madam?' she asked.

CHAPTER THREE

Several hours later, Sophie pushed open the door of Lyons Corner House, breathing in the lovely aroma of hot buttered toast and coffee. It had been a very long day, and now her feet ached and her back hurt, but she was certainly not too tired to relish the prospect of a birthday celebration. Going out to tea was a rare treat; she and Lil would occasionally come here when they had a shilling or two to spare. It was one of the few places in London that welcomed young girls like themselves, alone, and it always gave her a satisfying feeling of freedom and independence.

She caught sight of Lil at once, sitting at their usual table in the corner. Lil was conspicuous whenever she went, being both unusually tall and unusually beautiful. Even dressed as she was this afternoon, in a simple summer frock and a straw hat with a ribbon round it, her glorious mass of rich dark hair, chocolate brown eyes and magnificent figure made her look more like a goddess than an ordinary girl. Sophie had long since got used to Lil's remarkable appearance – but what did immediately take her by surprise was that Lil was not alone. Sitting beside her, both looking rather as though they had been starched and ironed especially for the occasion, were Joe and Billy.

'Hullo Sophie!' said Billy as she approached. 'Happy birthday!'

Lil was almost bouncing out of her seat with excitement. 'I say, isn't this jolly? Are you surprised? Do sit down – we've already ordered some iced buns. I hope you don't mind – I do think there's something awfully birthday-ish about iced buns, don't you?'

Even Joe was grinning at her, in spite of looking a little self-conscious to have found himself in a tea shop. Billy and Joe had each brought her a birthday card, and Lil had a present for her too – a handkerchief with embroidered corners. By the time the tea had been poured and the iced buns and sandwiches arrived, she felt quite a different person from the weary shop girl who had walked through the door.

It was the first time in two weeks that they had all been together, and they had lots to say for themselves. Billy was eager to tell them the latest about working in Mr Sinclair's office.

'Of course, I'm only the office boy, so I'm jolly unimportant really,' he explained, as he shovelled a third spoon of sugar into his tea. 'But there's no danger of being bored, I can tell you! There's always something going on – you should see some of the people who come to see the Captain!'

'Lots of ladies, I bet,' said Joe, with a grin.

'Yes and not just any ladies, either – actresses, opera singers, dancers,' Billy said, his eyes wide. 'If they're someone important, he has them sign a window pane in his office. He has a special long stick with a *diamond* at the end of it, so they can write their names on the glass!' he explained, clearly most impressed by this. 'It's fearfully busy, but I'm learning a lot. Miss Atwood is showing me all the ropes. Then I have to take evening classes three times a week – typing and shorthand and bookkeeping.'

'You must hear all sorts of interesting things,' said Lil, her eyes sparkling, much more intrigued by Mr Sinclair's glamorous visitors than she was in typing or bookkeeping. 'All the gossip and scandal! Mr Sinclair's deep, dark secrets.'

Billy grinned. 'Well, I don't know about that,' he said. 'I think he keeps his secrets to himself. But I'll tell you what – I do know all about the plans for the summer fête.'

The Sinclair's summer fête was a great source of

excitement amongst the staff at present. Mr Sinclair was renowned for taking good care of his workers, and he had determined that just as London's high society had their summer entertainments – their trips to Ascot and Cowes and the Henley Regatta – so too should his staff. He had charged the new store manager, Mr Betteredge, with planning a day of festivities for them, to reward them for their hard work during the year so far. Mr Betteredge was a cheerful gentleman, who was about as different from the previous store manager, the duplicitous Mr Cooper, as it was possible to be. Mr Cooper, of course, had turned out to be secretly in league with the Baron: he was the one who had stolen the clockwork sparrow, and might have done far worse had they not discovered what he was up to. But even disregarding all that, Sophie could not imagine that he would ever have jumped at the chance to plan a jolly day out for the Sinclair's staff.

They were all looking forward to the following Sunday, when they were being taken for an afternoon of tea and boating by the river. There would even be a boat race for staff teams, which the young salesmen, grooms and porters were taking very seriously indeed. Sophie knew that Billy's uncle, Sid Parker, who was the Head Doorman, would be captaining one of the boats, and Joe would be rowing as one of his crew, whilst Billy himself was immensely proud to have been chosen as the cox, whose job it was to shout out instructions to the rowers. There was already much competition developing over which team was going to win.

'Uncle Sid bet Monsieur Pascal five shillings that our team is going to take first prize,' related Billy now, managing to stuff in a potted-meat sandwich at the same time.

'Well I'm glad he's feeling so confident,' said Joe, 'because I can tell you now, I'm not. It's blooming hard work, this rowing lark.'

'I just think it's a fearful shame that girls aren't allowed to take part in the boat race,' said Lil. 'Why should the men have all the glory? I can row just as well as anyone. What are we supposed to do, just stand about and *watch*? Where's the fun in that?'

Billy opened his mouth to share his views on girls taking part in boat races. 'Er – what else will be happening at the fête, apart from the boating, I mean?' Sophie interjected quickly.

'There's a super tea,' Billy went on, taking obvious pleasure in being the one with all the inside information. 'I saw the menu on Miss Atwood's desk. Cold chicken. Salmon mayonnaise. Strawberries and cream, ices, ginger beer. And afterwards, there's going to be a band and dancing.'

'I heard about the dancing. The girls in Millinery and Ladies' Fashions are awfully excited about it. Most of them are getting new frocks specially.'

'I wish *I* could have a new frock. I'm jolly short of cash,' said Lil, with a heavy sigh. She turned to Sophie: 'I've had some rather rotten news. They've just announced that the show is going to end its run this week, so I'll be out of a job.'

'But why? It's been a tremendous success, hasn't it?'

'Yes, it did ever so well – but silly old Kitty Shaw is leaving the stage to be married, and they've decided that the show can't go on without her. It's really an awful bother.'

'Don't worry,' said Joe, loyally. 'You'll get another part in two shakes.'

'That's the bright spot,' went on Lil, sounding more like her usual self. 'I've found out that Mr Lloyd and Mr Mountville are going to be putting on a new show at the Grosvenor Theatre. It's called *The Inheritance* and it's all about high society. It sounds terribly elegant, and I'm determined to get a part – a *real* part, not just the chorus line. But the auditions aren't until next month, so I'm going to be rather broke until then.'

'Well, at least you've got Sinclair's and the dress shows,' said Sophie.

Lil made a face. 'Ugh! Parading around in absurd gowns

for all those stuck-up old ladies! But you're right; it is better than nothing. At least it pays for my lodgings. But this is going to be my last tea out for a while. It's plain bread and butter for me from now on,' she said grimly, before hurriedly helping herself to another iced bun, as if she thought they might be about to vanish from the plate at any moment.

'Haven't you got any of your reward money left?' asked Billy curiously.

Lil shrugged. 'Not exactly. I mean, I have a little, but it won't go far. I spent some of it on singing lessons, and dancing classes, and I thought I ought to get a new outfit for auditions, and then one of the other chorus girls was in rather a fix, so I said I'd lend her two pounds – and, well, it's perfectly dreadful how easy it is to spend money when you have it,' she finished up.

'Couldn't your mum and dad help you out till you get another part?' asked Joe, wondering how anyone could possibly spend such a vast sum as twenty-five pounds in just a few short months. He knew that although they were not as grand as some of the rich society ladies and gentlemen who came into Sinclair's department store, Lil's family were still well-to-do.

'I won't ask them,' said Lil, a very stubborn expression on her face. 'I'm determined to prove that I can stand on my own two feet. If I give them half a chance, Mother will have me back at home embroidering idiotic fire-screens, and entertaining eligible young men to tea.'

Lil's tone made this sound like such a ghastly proposition that Sophie couldn't help laughing, although the truth was that sometimes she felt a little envious of her friend's family. She wondered what it would be like to have a mother worrying about you: she could scarcely even remember her own Mama, who had died when she was very small.

'Oh, I almost forgot!' she exclaimed, all at once remembering the unopened envelope in her pocket. She produced it now and handed it to Lil. 'Look at this. It came earlier.'

'I say, how strange! Could it be something for your birthday?'

'That's what I thought at first, but it has both our names on it,' said Sophie, pointing.

Lil looked intrigued. 'Let's find out,' she said, tearing it open at once.

But once she had taken out the letter and put it on the table in front of them between the teacups and the sandwiches, they were as perplexed as ever. On what was clearly expensive writing paper, there were a few short lines:

Dear Miss Taylor and Miss Rose,

I write to present my compliments to you, and to respectfully request the pleasure of your company tomorrow afternoon, for I have an urgent matter of business that I wish to discuss with you. I understand that you were responsible for finding Mr Sinclair's missing jewels when they were stolen earlier this year, and I have a new commission to offer you.

For reasons that I will explain when we meet, this is a matter of some discretion. You will, of course, be well compensated for your assistance.

I will expect you to wait upon me in the Ladies' Lounge at Sinclair's department store at four o'clock.

Yours sincerely,

Veronica Whiteley (Miss)

'Well, what does it say?' asked Joe, looking at the others expectantly. Growing up on the streets of the East End, he had never learned to read.

'She wants to hire us!' exclaimed Lil excitedly. 'As *detectives*!'

Billy reached across the table and took hold of the note for a closer look. 'But why would she want to do that?' he demanded, frowning.

'It says right there, in black and white,' said Lil. 'She heard about how we found the clockwork sparrow!'

'Well I'll be blowed,' said Joe. 'That's a turn-up for the books!'

'But why just you and Sophie?' asked Billy. 'I mean, you're –' and here he broke off suddenly, his cheeks turning rather pink.

'*Girls?*' demanded Lil, at once. 'Girls can be detectives just as well as boys can,' she burst out indignantly. 'Girls are just as brave and clever as boys, you know! I realise they aren't in those silly detective stories of yours – all the girls in those are perfect idiots who do nothing but swoon all over the place – but that's a lot of old rot.'

Billy looked rather indignant, and opened his mouth as if he was about to argue, but Joe was frowning. 'It's a bit of a rum do, though, isn't it? I mean, why not go to a professional – a private detective? Or the coppers, come to that?'

Sophie frowned. After what had happened in the spring, the last thing she wanted to do was get in any more trouble with the police. 'Do you think there's something fishy about it? Perhaps we oughtn't to meet her?'

'Of *course* we should meet her,' exclaimed Lil. 'Goodness, don't be such a lot of stick-in-the-muds. Here I am, at a loose end and desperate to earn a bit of money – and then along comes this letter! It's absolutely perfect.'

'But we have no idea what she wants us to do,' said Sophie. 'And we aren't really detectives. How do we know we'll even be able to help?'

'We managed to find Mr Sinclair's missing jewels, didn't we?' replied Lil at once. 'Have you forgotten what Mr McDermott said to us?'

Sophie had not forgotten. The truth was that she had thought of his words very often during the duller moments in the Millinery Department. '*You have first-rate instincts, Miss Taylor – and with Miss Rose here to help you act on them, I suspect you would make rather a formidable team. If you ever find yourselves tired of Sinclair's, come and find me. I think there could be quite a different sort of career out there for a couple of young ladies like you.*' Remembering them now gave her a sudden prickle of pride.

'Anyway, the absolute worst that could happen is that we go along and aren't too keen on what she has to say. Then we can just say no to this job – or what does she call it? –

commission,' went on Lil stoutly.

'Well . . . I suppose there couldn't be any harm in at least going to talk to her,' said Sophie. In spite of her caution, she felt a pleasing buzz of excitement.

Across the table, Billy's face was screwed into a peculiar mixture of eagerness and indignation. Sophie realised that he was just as enthusiastic as Lil, but still rather resentful that he had not been included in the invitation. Joe was watching with a look of quiet amusement on his face, and now he grinned at Sophie as if he knew exactly what she was thinking.

'Of course, we'll need both of you to help too,' said Sophie.

A look of relief crossed Billy's face. 'Well, it's a bit busy at the moment,' he said in a deliberately casual tone. 'You know, working for the Captain and the evening classes, and practising for the boat race and everything. But I expect I'll probably be able to help out.'

Lil looked eagerly at Joe. 'Course I'll help, if I can,' he said, with a smile and a shrug.

'Hurrah!' said Lil. 'That's settled then!'

'Lil and I will go and see this Miss Whiteley tomorrow,' said Sophie with a decisive nod. 'Then let's meet again after the store closes, and we can tell you all about it.'

CHAPTER FOUR

Song was angry. 'What on earth were you thinking?' he demanded.

'That's no way to talk to your father!' snapped out Mum. 'I'll thank you to take a more civil tone!'

'But they might have killed you!'

Dad gave a little snort. 'It would take more than that gang of brainless thugs to finish me off,' he muttered.

Mei stared at him anxiously across the table. She hated to see him so white and tired-looking. The bruises on his face were a constant reminder of the moment she had found him, crumpled on the ground – she had been quite sure that he was dead.

Song looked at their father for a long moment, then sighed and sat back in his chair, his hands bunched into fists in front of him. 'All I'm saying is that you can't just *refuse to pay* the Baron's Boys,' he said in his usual quiet voice. 'That isn't how things work.'

'It's a matter of principle,' said Mum, rather stiffly. 'People round here look to us to set an example, Song, you know that. We all work hard. We've all got precious little as it is. We can't let them turn up here and demand our money. It's nothing more than bullying. If we all stand up to them, maybe we can put a stop to it.'

Song made a noise of frustration in the back of his throat. 'But you can't *stand up to them*, Mum. That would be like . . . one mouse against a hundred cats! Besides, no one else is going to put themselves in danger, especially when they see what happened to Dad. People are *afraid*.'

There was a long pause. Then Dad spoke. 'Song is right . . .' he said slowly. His voice was heavy. 'We can't stand against the Baron, Lou. He runs the East End. Everyone knows that. We should be grateful it's taken him this long to reach into China Town.'

Mei felt a slow chill creep over her. She knew about the Baron, of course: everyone in Limehouse did. He was the villain of every whispered tale – the monster who was 'coming to get you' in all the children's games. No one had ever seen him, but almost everyone claimed to know someone who'd caught a glimpse, just once, and come to a bad end. To see the Baron himself would be the worst of all bad omens – worse than a black cat crossing your path, worse than breaking a looking glass. There were dozens of stories about him. Some people said that he was a bloodthirsty murderer who had left a trail of horribly dismembered victims all across the East End. Others said he had once been an ordinary man, until he had sold his soul to the devil. Either way, everyone was afraid of him. To Mei, he was the dark shadows underneath the bed, the creaking floorboards, the distant shriek in the night.

But the Baron was much more than just a fairy tale, a bogeyman from a child's nightmare. He was the top man in the East End and everyone knew it. His net stretched from Spitalfields to Bow. The Port of London Authority might think that it ran the docks, but the folk of the East End knew better. They knew that the Baron had eyes on every load that came in or out of every ship that docked. They knew that he did his own business there too, and they carefully looked the other way when ships slipped in and out under the Baron's protection. No one would dare to cross him.

As for the Baron's Boys, they were almost as feared as the Baron himself. They were the ever-growing gang of toughs who did the Baron's business – legitimate or otherwise. They collected his rents – the protection money he demanded from most of the East End – and dealt with those who got in their way. People hurried in the opposite direction if they saw them standing on a street corner. Conversation fell away when a group of them swaggered up to the bar of the

Star Inn, demanding the landlord's best beer, or when one or two came striding into the fish shop for their penny bit and ha'p'orth of chips. And now they had been here, to Lim's shop.

Mei felt sick. The back room had always seemed like the safest place in the world when the family were sitting around the table, in the warmth of the range. But suddenly it was just a room, any room, small and cold. All the laughter had gone out of it. The green parrot in the corner was silent, and even the twins sat still and quiet, their eyes round as saucers.

As if it was their silence that had suddenly reminded her that they were there, Mum glanced over at the twins. 'Boys, go outside,' she said curtly. 'Run along now, chop-chop.'

Dad shook his head weakly. 'No, Lou. I don't want them out there. It's too dangerous,' he said.

'Upstairs then,' said Mum firmly.

'But, Dad – we've got to go out.' Jian spoke up, looking alarmed and astonished. 'We're s'posed to meet Spud and Ginger for a kick-about after tea. They'll be waiting for us!'

'Well they'll be waiting a long time, then, won't they?' snapped Mum. 'You heard your father. You're not to go out. So upstairs you go. And Mei, you can get started on clearing things up in the shop.'

They wanted them out of the way so they could talk, Mei knew. There was no sense in arguing. She got up, and obediently shepherded the boys out of the back room and up the crooked stairs towards the bedroom. The twins had forgotten about the Baron's Boys already. They were babbling away in the funny mixture of playground slang and their own peculiar twin language that they used when they were speaking to each other. Now, they seemed to be jabbering something about a game of cowboys and Indians.

'Come and play with us, Mei,' said Jian. 'We'll let you be the squaw.'

'We'll make Song's bed into our fort,' said Shen with a grin.

But Mei shook her head. Normally she'd have been happy to have the excuse to join in with one of the twins' make-believe games, but today, she couldn't think about anything beyond Dad's bruised face and the Baron's Boys.

Instead, as they bounded up the stairs, she went slowly through into the deserted shop as Mum had told her. It looked quite sad and unlike its usual self. The door was locked and bolted, and Song had nailed boards over the broken windows so that only one or two beams of light broke through. Dust motes danced in the shafts of light.

She decided to light a lamp to try and break through the gloom, but the glow it cast out seemed somehow feeble. She looked around her, feeling despondent. There was so much to do that she hardly knew where to begin. Listlessly, she took up the broom and began to sweep the floor, making a little mound of spilt tea and tobacco and broken glass.

She could hear more voices now, in the back room. It sounded like Ah Wei, Song's boss at the Eating House, and Mr and Mrs O'Leary from the baker's, and Mrs Wu from the Magic Lantern Show. Their voices sounded solemn and grave. Traces of their conversation reached her as she swept: '. . . *can't go on like this*', '. . . *that sort of money*', '. . . *making an example*', '. . . *far too dangerous*'.

She didn't want to hear them. To block them out, she began to tell one of Granddad's stories to herself, an old tale about a talking fox, but she could not concentrate. She was getting it all wrong. The story of the fox kept getting mixed up with the cobbler's warning, with Dad lying crumpled on the floor, and then with Granddad himself. Thinking of Granddad made her want to cry, and that would not do – Song would say she was being a cry baby. He said she needed to grow up now she had left school: she was too old to be a feather-brain; she shouldn't spend so much time playing with the twins; she oughtn't to always have her nose buried in a book.

Once, she and Song had been the best of friends. They had done everything together; told each other all their secrets; but things had changed. He seemed so much older, all of a sudden. She could hear him now in the back room, his voice forceful and authoritative, although she couldn't make out what he was saying. When had he become one of the grown-ups?

Then someone in the back room made an unhappy gasping sort of sound – a strangled sob. It wasn't Mum or Dad or Song, but all the same it pulled her up short. She even stopped pretending to sweep. Instead, she sat down on the stool behind the counter, and wedged her hands over her ears. There was a copy of yesterday's newspaper lying nearby, and she pulled it towards her and opened it, hoping for a new episode of the serial story to distract herself with. She turned the pages rapidly over a report of a murder in Whitechapel, and a robbery in Shoreditch, but there was no story today, so instead she fixed her attention upon the society pages. She liked to look at them, sometimes, intrigued by the pictures of young ladies in white dresses with elegant-sounding names like *Lady Cynthia Delaney* or *Miss Louisa Hampton-Lacey*. The fancy descriptions of grand balls and elegant gowns could have so easily come from one of her favourite fairy tales.

Now, she read them with grim determination, taking in every word of an account of a charity fashion show at a West End store; a report on the upcoming marriage of a glamorous actress; and an article about a lavish society ball. The voices rose and fell in the back room, but Mei read on, filling her mind with words like *opera* and *bazaar* and *waltz*.

Then she stopped short. Two words jumped out at her from the page, and all at once, it was as if the sounds in the next room had vanished into abrupt and ominous silence. She saw and heard nothing: all that was left were those two words, printed in smudgy black ink, in the middle of a paragraph: *Moonbeam Diamond.*

The loveliest of the Season's debutantes were out in force at a grand ball at Hill Lodge, Kensington, hosted by Lady Fitzmaurice.

Pictured: Miss Emily Montague, Miss Mary Chesterfield, the Honourable Phyllis Woodhouse, and Miss Veronica Whiteley. Miss Whiteley is shown wearing an exquisite gift presented to her to mark her debut: the prized Moonbeam Diamond, set into a specially commissioned brooch by London's jeweller à la mode, Thackeray's. Also in attendance, Count and Countess of

CHAPTER FIVE

The Ladies' Lounge at Sinclair's was a most elegant place. Arrayed like a fashionable drawing room, it was decorated entirely in white and gold, with bowls of flowers set here and there, and plenty of soft chairs and comfortable sofas. It was no wonder it had become a favourite destination for London's society ladies to meet after a busy day of shopping. That afternoon, the room was full of them: ladies drinking iced lemonade in tall glasses served to them by maids in frilled white aprons; ladies talking vigorously in lively groups; ladies sitting alone, studiously reading the newspaper. There was a low buzz of civilised conversation in the air, and the delicate chink of china and silverware. As Sophie and Lil entered the room, they could not help feeling a little awkward, unsure of exactly who they were looking for, or what they ought to do.

But almost at once, one of the maids came up to them, and directed them to a corner over by the window. Glancing at each other apprehensively, they hurried over. Sophie was not quite sure who she had expected to find, but it certainly was not the young lady who sat waiting, small but very upright, in a large velvet armchair, coolly drinking a cup of tea.

'You are Miss Taylor and Miss Rose, I suppose,' she said in a high, rather petulant voice, looking them up and down critically.

'Yes, I'm Sophie Taylor. How do you do?' said Sophie, holding out a hand. The young lady looked at it uncertainly for a moment, then gingerly took it in her own lace-gloved fingers.

'And I'm Lilian Rose,' said Lil, seizing the young lady's hand in her turn and giving it such a hearty shake that she looked alarmed and pulled her hand hurriedly away.

'My name is Veronica Whiteley. I am pleased to meet you,' said the young lady, with a haughty nod. Sophie looked at her in surprise. The tone of her letter had conjured up a vision of an elderly spinster, but this girl was young – really, she couldn't have been much older than Lil – and she was dressed very beautifully in a much ruffled, lace-trimmed ivory gown. She must be one of this season's debutantes, and a particularly wealthy one at that. What was more, Sophie realised that she knew her. She was one of the three young ladies who had been in the Millinery Department the previous day – the one who had tried on the Paris hat.

But Miss Whiteley gave no indication that she recognised Sophie. 'Do sit down,' she said, giving a queenly waft of her hand towards the two hard chairs placed opposite her. As they took their seats, Sophie watched the young lady with interest. Although her clothes were expensive and beautifully made, Sophie couldn't help thinking that they didn't suit her very well. She was pretty, with china-white skin, a small pink mouth and carefully waved red-gold hair. But all the frills and flounces made her look rather like one of the expensive porcelain dolls that were on sale in the store's Toy Department. Yet there was nothing at all doll-like about her expression: she was looking at them both with eyes like gimlets, a frown creasing up her white forehead as she sipped tea from a bone-china cup.

'How can we help you?' Sophie asked curiously.

'I have been told that you were responsible for finding Mr Sinclair's stolen jewels,' Miss Whiteley began, assuming a very formal manner. Lil opened her mouth to say something, but Miss Whiteley was evidently not expecting there to be any interruptions, and swept onwards. 'I contacted you because I wished to discuss a similar commission. It is of a highly confidential nature – I trust I can be assured of your complete discretion.'

They said she could, and she went on:

'I was recently given a gift by a gentleman. It's one of

a kind and extremely valuable – a jewelled brooch in the shape of a moth, made especially for me. Last week it went missing, and I would like you to undertake to find it.'

Veronica found that her hand was shaking slightly as she replaced her teacup in its saucer. She had borrowed her haughty manner from the Dowager Countess of Alconborough, always so imperious in her black velvet and jet beads, assuming complete control of any conversation. Today, she wanted to be no less impressive. It was imperative that these girls took her seriously: she would not be dismissed as just another idiotic debutante.

Although, looking at them again, her lips pursed. She had not expected them to be so very *young*. Why, the smaller one looked even younger than she was herself! She had expected them to be older: sophisticated and perhaps a little daring, women of the world, like the heroines of the rather scandalous novels she borrowed from Isabel, her stepmother, on the sly. These two looked more like a pair of schoolgirls than young lady detectives! But it was too late: she had already told them about the jewelled moth, and she would simply have to go on with it now.

It was quite a ridiculous position to find herself in, she thought crossly. If only she were an adult, she would have been able to hire a real detective to find the missing brooch for her. But being a debutante meant that every moment of the day was supervised, from the moment that her maid woke her in the morning, to the moment she went to bed at night after yet another ball or reception. Father and Isabel treated her as if she were a baby. She'd had far more freedom back in the schoolroom with her governess! Now, she was chaperoned every minute of the day, and there was no chance whatsoever that they would ever let her go off alone to a secret appointment with a private detective.

Thankfully Sinclair's department store was different. Here, Isabel didn't mind letting Veronica wander off on her own to look at the hats and gloves or the counters selling scent and powder, whilst she shopped and gossiped with her friends. It was here that Veronica had first had the idea of hiring someone to help her find the jewelled moth. She didn't read the newspapers much – all dreadfully dull stuff about the navy and taxes – but it had been impossible to miss the stories about the dramatic robbery at Sinclair's. Everyone in London had been talking about it, and she'd heard that Mr Sinclair's private detective had been helped by two fearfully clever young ladies who worked at the store and who had been the ones to find the jewels. The idea of hiring them to find the jewelled moth had seemed rather a stroke of genius. After all, no one could possibly make a fuss about her talking to two other young ladies in Sinclair's department store. She had felt as clever and daring as one of the characters in Isabel's novels.

But now she wondered if it had been quite such a brilliant idea after all. They were so very ordinary. The tall one, Miss Rose, was rather *unusual-looking*, she supposed, but otherwise they could have been any old shop girls in plain, cheap-looking frocks and no ornaments at all. They didn't look particularly clever either.

Well, she would simply have to hope they were brainier than they looked, she thought with a sigh. She had to get the moth back and would do anything to find it.

'I must have the jewelled moth in time for my debutante ball next week,' she said firmly, as she fixed the two girls with her most haughty, determined look. 'You'll be well rewarded, you may be assured – but you *must return it to me.*'

Half an hour later, Veronica was back with Isabel, up in the Marble Court restaurant, acting as if she had done nothing more that morning than look for a new fan. But she couldn't stop thinking about the jewelled moth. Telling those girls about what had happened had made her uncomfortable all over again, and she found herself simply toying with the fish course instead of eating it. She felt tense and irritable. This was supposed to be the most thrilling time of her life, and now it was quite spoiled, all because of the loss of the brooch.

Of course, she reminded herself, it wasn't as though everything about being a debutante was so very thrilling. There were the endless boring dress-fittings for new gowns, where she was stuck all over with pins as though she were a pincushion; the tedious dinner parties where she had to make polite conversation with fearful old bores; and the balls where she got lumbered with partners who trod all over her feet – but all the same, most of her first Season had been splendid. Now, all of a sudden it did not seem glittering and exciting; instead it was simply horrid.

She couldn't even concentrate on the conversation going on amongst her luncheon companions, who were ranged around a table covered in spotless damask and arrayed with gleaming silver. Instead, she eyed them from under her eyelashes. First of all there was Isabel – Veronica's very own not-so-wicked stepmother, her round blue eyes widening at something the Countess of Alconborough was saying. As usual, Isabel looked exactly like a fashion plate, with her crimped blonde hair, carefully rouged and powdered face, and outfit straight from the pages of *La Mode Illustrée*. Next, the Dowager Countess herself: tiny yet stately in her rustling black gown. Then, beside her, Lady Alice, the Countess's daughter: taller, plumper and infinitely more insipid, nodding in agreement after every word her mother said.

With them were Veronica's fellow debutantes: first of all Phyllis, Lady Alice's eldest daughter and the Countess's granddaughter. She had yellow hair and smiled a lot. Veronica thought contemptuously that she had probably never said two interesting words together in her life – though of course, Lady Alice and Isabel had decided between themselves that she and Phyllis were the very best and dearest of friends. Then there was Miss Emily Montague. Emily's family lived next door to Lady Alice's London residence, and Emily had been to finishing school with Phyllis, though the two of them were quite different. Where Phyllis was gentle and placid, Emily was quick and shrewd and sharp. At that very moment, Emily was staring around the restaurant, looking quite as bored by the conversation as Veronica was herself. She looked distracted and out of sorts, though Veronica suspected she was probably just sulking because she hadn't yet managed to attract the attentions of any eligible beau.

'So, my dears, how are you enjoying your first Season?' the Countess asked suddenly, smiling indulgently at the three young ladies.

Lady Alice answered for them. 'They're having a simply delightful time!' she bubbled. 'There have been so many lovely parties for them to enjoy.'

'Well of course, Lady Fitzmaurice's ball is always quite an occasion,' said the Countess, nodding in agreement. 'Dear Sylvia is such a wonderful hostess. And Beaucastle's garden party too – his grounds are quite spectacular.'

'Then there is the York House ball tonight,' went on Lady Alice. 'Phyllis has a divine new dress for it, don't you darling?'

Isabel had just noticed Veronica's plate. 'Veronica!' she exclaimed, sharply. 'You've hardly touched your luncheon!'

'Is there something wrong with it?' demanded the Countess, swivelling her flinty gaze back in Veronica's direction, and peering through her eyeglass suspiciously at the fish.

'No – nothing,' said Veronica. 'I'm not very hungry today, that's all.'

'She obviously has a modest appetite,' said the Countess, staring at Veronica. Her eyes were like dark grey pebbles. 'Well, a ladylike appetite *can* be an excellent thing, just as long as you keep your strength up. The Season can be *exhausting*, you know, especially for the more delicate young girls.' She turned to Isabel. 'Is she delicate? She looks rather . . . peaky.'

They all peered at her over the table: the Countess critical, Lady Alice concerned, Emily smirking with amusement and Isabel just annoyed. Veronica burned with indignation under their gaze, whilst beside her, Phyllis continued eating her stuffed grouse quite cheerfully, apparently not noticing that anything was wrong.

'She's probably just excited about the dance tonight,' said Lady Alice, kindly. 'I remember how excited I used to be before a ball. Why, I could never eat a thing at supper! Perhaps she'd be better off with something sweet – an ice, perhaps? You love your sweets, don't you Phyllis?'

'Yes, Mama,' lisped Phyllis happily.

The Countess glanced at Phyllis for a moment, her lips pursed, looking rather displeased, then turned back to pin her steely gaze upon Veronica. 'Well, from what I hear, she has rather good reasons for being excited,' she said archly, addressing Isabel and Lady Alice, although her eyes remained fixed on Veronica. 'I understand that Beaucastle has been paying her attentions,' she went on in a suspicious tone, rather as if she suspected Veronica of having somehow tricked him into it.

Isabel was positively delighted by this change of subject. She jumped in at once: 'Yes, Veronica is a dreadfully lucky girl. Lord Beaucastle has been so very attentive and kind.'

Veronica couldn't help feeling pleased to see that both the Countess and Lady Alice were looking rather peeved. She suspected that they were disappointed that Lord Beaucastle – who was, after all, one of London's most eligible bachelors – had chosen to pay attention to her over their dear little Phyllis.

'He gave her the most wonderful gift, you know, to mark her presentation at court,' Isabel was saying blithely.

'The jewelled moth – yes, I heard about it,' said the Countess, rather shortly. 'A *very* special piece, I understand. Not at all the sort of present one would give to a young girl. I would have thought a nice pearl string more suitable.'

'Papa gave me a pearl necklace for my debut, didn't he Mama?' said Phyllis, with a smile. Everyone ignored her.

'I must say, I was surprised that he would give away a treasure like that. I hope you're taking very good care of it, my dear,' the Countess snapped out to Veronica.

Her words were like a gush of cold water. Veronica reeled for a moment. Surely the Countess could not possibly know the truth about what had happened to the jewelled moth? The Countess was still talking, and Veronica realised gradually that her comment had no special significance. But the ice-cold feeling still lingered and there was a rushing in her ears that seemed to drown out everything else being said.

The truth was that Veronica had disliked the moth brooch on sight. It was so big and heavy: it had quite spoilt the look of her white satin court dress, and had torn an ugly hole in the beautiful rose-coloured gown she had worn to Lady Fitzmaurice's ball. She knew the brooch was expensive and fashionable, and had been made especially for her by the most elegant London jewellers, and that was all very well – but she did think there was something a bit creepy about it.

Of course, she had been terribly proud when Lord Beaucastle had given it to her. It meant he wanted to marry her, and it went without saying that she was pleased about that. After all, he was rich, titled and a society favourite – everyone knew him and liked him. It was a tremendous compliment to have been singled out by a man like him! None of the other girls in her 'set' was even close to a proposal, and here she was, with one of society's most eligible gentlemen showering her with attention. She knew that the others were all terribly envious of her. Why even now she could see Emily watching her with the oddest expression; and the other girls were forever making snide remarks that smacked of jealousy.

And yet . . . it had all happened so quickly. She had barely been out in society for a month! One minute Lord Beaucastle had been just a friend of her father's – rather old, though awfully nice, of course – and the next he had been sending her bouquets of hothouse flowers, taking her into supper at balls, and then presenting her with this extravagant gift. Although she had dreamed about finding a husband during her first Season – that was what all the girls hoped for; no one wanted to be left on the shelf until next year – she had imagined it happening so differently: meeting a handsome young man in a ballroom, drinking champagne on a moonlit balcony, falling head over heels in love and then having a triumphant wedding, all ivory lace and orange blossom, and living happily ever after. Lord Beaucastle was perfectly pleasant, and certainly very generous – but she was not *in love* with him. The thought of it made her squirm.

Perhaps that was why she hadn't wanted to wear the brooch at Lord Beaucastle's garden party. Isabel had been nagging her about taking care of it, but instead of doing what she was told, she had left it inside the house, pinned to her silk shawl. Now, she cursed herself for being so reckless. For when she had come back in from the garden, the shawl was lying exactly where she had left it – but the jewelled moth had vanished.

She dared not tell anyone what had happened. She couldn't tell Isabel – she would be simply furious if she knew that Veronica had left Lord Beaucastle's valuable gift so carelessly unattended – and the other girls would be sure to crow over her if they knew. She could all too clearly imagine the cutting little jibes that Emily would make. She had known that she must find a way to get the brooch back – and quickly. If she lost the gift that Lord Beaucastle had given her, he might be so offended that she would lose her chance at an offer of marriage from him. He would probably never speak to her again! Everyone would know about it, and she would be utterly shamed.

Her coming-out ball was due to take place in less than a fortnight. Lord Beaucastle had offered to host it at his own splendid mansion, and everyone was whispering that he was going to propose. They would all expect to see her wearing the jewelled moth. She simply had to get it back!

'But I've always said, Beaucastle knows his own mind,' the Countess was saying, her voice suddenly loud again in Veronica's ears. 'We all thought he was quite set on bachelor life, but evidently that is not the case. I must say, though, I'm surprised to see him paying his addresses to a debutante. Why, he must be twice her age!'

'Well, those matches can work, you know,' said Isabel, hastily, turning rather pink.

Veronica's father was almost twice *Isabel's* age, come to that, Veronica thought.

The Countess waved her hand, as if swatting Isabel's words away. 'Oh, I quite understand. There could scarcely be a finer suitor. Why, the man has everything: a title, a fine income, that beautiful estate. And such a distinguished military record! He joined the army when he was a very young man, you know,' she added in a conspiratorial tone. 'He never did see eye to eye with his father – a nasty, cantankerous old fellow, if you ask me.' She paused for a moment, as if daring the others to disagree with her, but of course, no one did.

'Was he really?' fluttered Lady Alice.

'He was indeed,' confirmed the Countess. 'But the army was the making of Beaucastle –'

Isabel interrupted suddenly, changing the subject. 'Look – over there! Isn't that Edward Sinclair?'

They all turned to look, even the Countess. The owner of Sinclair's department store was something of a celebrity, even amongst London's society set. Beautifully dressed, with his signature orchid in his buttonhole, he bowed to a distinguished customer, and then went to talk to the Head Waiter.

'He's rather handsome, isn't he?' said Isabel, looking over at him with interest.

'Hmmm,' said the Countess, peering through her eyeglass. 'Too showy, if you ask me. These Americans always are. And he's new money of course.'

Veronica saw that Isabel's cheeks were going pink again. No one could be more 'new money' than Charles Whiteley, Isabel's husband and Veronica's father. He might now live in Mayfair and dine with the city's most eminent families, but London society would never quite forget that he was not an aristocrat. He was an industrialist: the wealthy owner of several very lucrative mines in South Africa. Isabel, on the other hand, was from real society stock, which was exactly why Veronica's father had married her, after Veronica's mother died. That, and because he liked having a beautiful, expensively dressed young wife on his arm. And Isabel had married him for his wealth, and for as much shopping at Sinclair's as even she could ever desire, thought Veronica with a shudder.

'They say he's quite the ladies' man,' Lady Alice was commenting, still watching Mr Sinclair. 'Why, Mrs Balfour told me . . .' She leaned forwards, and began murmuring something under her breath, whilst Phyllis craned around curiously, and even Emily looked over at Sinclair with interest. But Veronica didn't even bother to glance in his direction. What did she care for some ridiculous American shopkeeper? She was simply grateful for the distraction, which allowed the waiter to take her plate away without anyone noticing that she hadn't taken a single bite more.

PART II
Excursions and Amusements

There is no more pleasant entertainment than an excursion out of town. The absence of all ceremony and formality is certain to be conducive to a delightful gaiety of spirit. Yet whilst relishing the novelty and freedom of an excursion, a young lady in society must at all times guard against rowdiness and unseemly behaviour, just as she might in the confines of the most fashionable drawing room.

Lady Diana DeVere's *Etiquette for Debutantes: a Guide to the Manners, Mores and Morals of Good Society*, Chapter 17: Excursions & Amusements – On Picnics – On Field Sports – Boating – Cycling – On the Conveyance of Guests and of Provisions – Things Not to be Forgotten – Tea

CHAPTER SIX

'**A** jewelled *moth*?' said Billy in surprise. 'That's a bit odd, isn't it?'

'Actually, it's jolly fashionable,' Lil informed him. 'It's quite the thing these days to have a brooch in the shape of a beetle, or a necklace in the shape of a dragonfly, or something like that. Heaps of the ladies who come to Sinclair's have them.'

Billy screwed up his face, as if to convey that the peculiarities of fashion were quite beyond him.

It was the end of another long day at Sinclair's, and the four of them had strolled down to the river, where they stood enjoying the evening sunshine.

Joe was a little apart from the others, leaning against the railing, watching the boats surging up and down the river: colourful strings of pleasure boats, a big sailing ship cruising slowly between them and little dinghies bobbing in its wake. It was hard to believe that this was the same river that flowed through the East End. There was perhaps something of the same smell of tar and salt and smoke, but otherwise, it was a different creature altogether, peaceable and pleasant. Here, a man in a striped jacket passed by with two Dalmatians on leads, and a young couple strolled by, arm-in-arm, eating ices. Not far away from them, a lady was sitting on a folding stool, painting the view across the river in watercolours; and beyond her, a Punch and Judy man had set up a striped tent, and was performing a show for a circle of enraptured young spectators. There was a festive mood in the air. Joe could smell warm caramel, and hear a trickle of music blown across on the breeze from one of the passing pleasure boats.

This was his London now. The East End had fallen off his map of the city, as remote to him as Timbuktu. He would never go back there – Whitechapel Road and Spitalfields Market, Shadwell and Limehouse, the East India Docks – they could have simply vanished into thin air. He grinned to himself, only half-listening to Sophie and Lil as they talked over all the interesting details of their meeting with Miss Veronica Whiteley, quietly marvelling at the fact that a fellow like him could have such luck.

Billy, on the other hand, was taking the whole matter very seriously indeed, in spite of what he had said about being too busy to help them much with their investigations. He had brought an exercise book and a pencil with him, and was scribbling notes busily as Sophie and Lil talked. Miss Atwood always said it was jolly important to write everything down, he had informed them all, in an earnest voice.

'Besides, if we're doing this properly, then we'll need real case notes, like proper detectives,' he explained gravely. Billy considered himself to be quite the authority on what real detectives did. He had, after all, read practically every story about schoolboy detective Montgomery Baxter that had ever been written.

'We *are* proper detectives,' said Lil, who had grown bored of all the note-taking, and had stepped up on to the bottom rung of the railing to look out over the water, shading her eyes with her hand in the manner of a ship's lookout. 'We've been hired to solve a case – I think that makes us as proper as anyone.'

Billy looked doubtful, but went on scribbling. 'Tell me more about the brooch,' he said to Sophie. 'What does it actually look like?'

'It's decorated with emeralds and sapphires and chips of opal on the wings. The moth's body is made of a single large diamond. Miss Whiteley called it the Moonbeam Diamond – apparently it's a famous jewel,' Sophie explained. 'The brooch was made especially for Miss Whiteley by Thackeray's, the jewellers. I think it must be worth an awful lot of money.'

'Right,' said Billy, writing all this down at a rate of knots.

'So – the brooch was given to Miss Whiteley by a gentleman named Lord Beaucastle. It was stolen at a garden party at Lord Beaucastle's house last week. She left it pinned on a shawl inside the house when she went out into the garden, and when she came back it had gone,' he summarised quickly, glancing down at his notes. 'She didn't tell the police because she wants us to get it back for her without anyone knowing that it was taken in the first place. If they find out, she thinks she'll be blamed for being careless.'

'She thinks it will put this Lord Beaucastle off her, more like,' added Lil, with a snort.

'But here's a thought – how does she know for sure that it was stolen?' suggested Billy. 'Maybe it just fell off the shawl and got lost.'

'I wondered that too,' said Sophie. 'But I don't think it's likely. Miss Whiteley said the clasp was stiff and strong – it was difficult to unfasten. And judging by what she told us, Lord Beaucastle lives in a very grand style. He has a beautiful manor house out by the river. He's probably got dozens of servants: if it had simply fallen off her shawl, it's more than likely that one of them would have found it by now.'

'So chances are someone nicked it,' suggested Joe, finding himself increasingly drawn in by the conversation. 'Probably they just saw an opportunity and grabbed it for the chance of making a few bob.'

'There weren't many people who had that chance,' Sophie went on. 'From what she says, there were only half a dozen other people who went in and out of the room where the shawl was left during the party.'

'Who were they?' asked Billy eagerly, poised to write them down.

'Apart from Miss Whiteley herself, some of the other debutantes,' Lil explained. She frowned as she tried to remember them. 'Mary Chesterfield, Emily Montague, and the Honourable Phyllis thingummy-bob.'

'*Thingummy-bob?*' repeated Billy in exasperation.

Lil just shrugged.

'Then there was Lord Beaucastle's butler, and a lady's maid who had accompanied Miss Montague. Miss Whiteley wasn't sure of either of their names.'

'Well, surely it must be one of the servants then – the butler or the maid,' said Billy, slamming shut the notebook as if the case was already closed. 'After all, debutantes are rich, aren't they? So they wouldn't need to go stealing anything.'

'That isn't what Miss Whiteley thinks,' said Sophie. 'She believes that one of the other debutantes might have been envious of the attention that Lord Beaucastle had been paying her. She said they were all jealous, and that one of them might have taken the brooch to stir up trouble between her and Lord Beaucastle.'

Billy looked slightly disgusted. 'This is beginning to sound like something from an awful romance novel,' he said.

'Well, awful or not, we're going to work it out,' declared Lil. 'She said she would pay us ten pounds if we get the brooch back for her.'

'By gum!' said Joe. 'This detective lark's all right, isn't it?'

'If we could earn that – even split between us – I'd have something to keep me going until I get another part,' said Lil, happily. 'And a new frock too, perhaps!'

'Did you believe her – Miss Whiteley?' Joe found himself asking them both suddenly.

'What do you mean?'

'Did you think she was telling you the truth? Not spinning you some tall tale?'

Sophie thought for a moment. 'She didn't give us any reason to doubt her.'

'I didn't like her very much,' added Lil, bluntly. 'She seemed stuck-up and spoilt. And she was rather rude. But I did believe her.'

Billy had opened his notebook again. 'Was there anyone else at all that could have taken the brooch?'

'Miss Whiteley didn't think anyone else could have gone into the room without being noticed,' said Sophie.

'Then it's the maid or the butler,' argued Billy again.

Joe shook his head slowly. 'You'd have to be off your

head to do that,' he said. 'Think about it. Working in a posh house, you're in clover. You aren't going to do anything to risk losing your place. All right, I suppose you might get the odd housemaid who'd risk filching a bit of silver, or a butler who'll half-inch a bottle or two from his master's cellars. But that ain't the same sort of thing at all. And even supposing you were in desperate need of a few quid, there's got to be a dozen things you could nick from such a grand place that would be far less noticeable than some fancy lady's brooch with a great big diamond in it.'

'That's true,' said Sophie, nodding.

'What's more,' said Joe, warming to his subject now, 'if you did nick it, you'd be in a pickle then, wouldn't you? Because it's recognisable, this brooch. It's not going to be easy just to pop along to any old jeweller's shop and sell it. They'd have too many questions. You'd have to know a good fence.'

'Whatever do you mean, a fence?' asked Lil, curiously.

'A middleman,' explained Joe. 'Someone who'd buy it off you and then sell it on, make it look legit. With something like this brooch, they might even take it to pieces and sell off the stones. I used to know a couple of fences, and that's what they did sometimes, if they came across something a bit flashy.'

'Well, if you know them, maybe we could go and talk

to them,' said Billy, excitedly. 'We could find out whether anyone's sold them the jewelled moth!'

'Not a chance,' said Joe. The words were out of his mouth even before he realised he had spoken. He was taken aback by how forceful he sounded. Trying to speak lightly, he went on: 'You can't just go and see a fence and ask them what they've been buying and who they bought it off. They'd have a fit!'

What he did not say was that there was nothing on earth that would persuade him to go back east. He knew he wouldn't last two minutes over there, not now he'd crossed the Baron's Boys. Besides, now he was someone else altogether – a respectable sort with a clean shirt and shined boots, who could stroll along the riverbank on a summer evening, perhaps even in the company of a girl like Lil. He shot her a quick glance, suddenly wishing he hadn't opened his mouth and started on about fences and nicking things.

But Lil was talking away, not seeming to have noticed that he had fallen silent. 'I think we should talk to the debutantes first,' she was saying.

'But how?' asked Sophie, furrowing her brow. 'What possible reason do we have to talk to a debutante? Unless, perhaps, any of them come to Sinclair's – we might speak to them there, I suppose.'

'Oh, I've got a better idea than that,' said Lil, looking

pleased with herself. 'Do you remember how I went undercover in the Marble Court Restaurant, when we were trying to find out about Sergeant Gregson and the Baron?'

Billy was heard to mumble something that sounded rather like, 'I wouldn't exactly call that *undercover*,' in a low voice.

Lil ignored this and went on. 'Perhaps that's what we should do this time?'

'Go to the Marble Court Restaurant?'

'No, silly! *Go undercover!*' Lil's eyes gleamed. 'Do you know,' she went on thoughtfully, 'I've always thought that I would make a rather excellent debutante.'

Miss Veronica Whiteley's Missing Jewel

Possible Suspects:
Mary Chesterfield
The Honourable Phyllis?
Emily Montague
Miss Montague's maid
Lord Beaucastle's butler

CHAPTER SEVEN

Safe in her bedroom, behind the screen of the curtain, Mei took out the piece of paper with trembling fingers. She had torn it from the newspaper and put it in her secret hiding place, under a broken floorboard beneath her bed, with her other treasures: a book of Chinese fairy-stories that Uncle Huan had brought her back from one of his trips; her collection of pebbles and smooth glass that she'd gathered along the river at low tide; a little carved jade ornament that had once been Granddad's; and a curved white shell. Shen and Jian had never found the hiding place; even Song did not know about it – it was hers alone. She did not know exactly why she had felt the need to hide the newspaper, but some instinct had made her feel that it was important, precious, full of the same kind of magic she felt when she held the jade ornament in the palm of her hand.

Now, she smoothed it out and looked at it again. She had already done this so many times that the paper was becoming thin and soft from handling, yet she could not stop re-reading it, gazing again at the blurry photograph, squinting at the little dark smudge at the neck of the young lady's gown.

There could not be two Moonbeam Diamonds – there simply could not. She gazed at the young lady's face. Who was Miss Veronica Whiteley? How had she come to be given the Moonbeam Diamond? However had it ended up in the society pages of the newspaper – part of this peculiar world of balls and tea parties and fashionable gowns? And what about the diamond's curse?

There were so many questions she almost did not know where to begin. The most important one of all was what she should do with the newspaper now. Her first thought had been to take it straight to Dad, but when she had gone down to him, for once, he had been in no mood to listen. He was distracted: since the meeting, he had been poring over the shop accounts book from morning until night. When she had tried to show him, he had simply said, 'Not now, Mei,' and paid no attention at all.

As for Mum, she was busier than ever. She dashed about like a whirlwind, working energetically on restoring the shop; but she was out of the house a great deal too, often slipping off to Mrs Wu's with a covered dish in her hand, or hurrying over to the Eating House to speak to Ah Wei. Left behind to look after the twins or cook the supper or wash the dishes, Mei knew that this was no time to try and talk to Mum about anything.

That only left Song. He worked long hours at the Eating House, but that evening he was at home. The twins were in bed, and Mum and Dad were working in the shop. Mei made up her mind, and a moment later she had started down the stairs, the cutting clasped tightly in her hand.

She found Song in the back room, making dumplings. He had always had a passion for food: he took his job in the Eating House very seriously, and cherished ambitions to become a fine cook one day. His dreams reached far beyond Ah Wei's and China Town. Once or twice, when he had been in a pensive mood, he had talked to Mei about the great hotels and restaurants of London's West End, and what it might be like to work there. He had made Granddad teach him everything he knew about Chinese dishes, and pestered Uncle Huan to bring him back unusual spices from foreign ports, or to describe the exotic dishes he had tasted on his voyages.

That was one of the things about Song, Mei thought now, as she sat at the table and watched him carefully shape the dumplings: he had always been so certain about things, whereas she never really felt certain at all.

She sat quietly, waiting until he had finished with the dumplings and had tidied everything away, knowing he would not be able to concentrate on anything else until he was done.

Then, at last, she handed him the cutting.

'What's all this?' asked Song, looking baffled.

'Look,' said Mei, trying to contain her excitement. 'Read it. See what it says here. *It's the Moonbeam Diamond*, Song.'

'What are you talking about?'

'The Moonbeam Diamond! The diamond from the temple in Granddad's village. The diamond that belonged to our ancestors, that protects our family. The diamond that Granddad watched over, until it was stolen by Waiguo Ren. It's here – here in London!'

Song laughed shortly. 'Mei, don't be silly,' he said. 'It's just got the same name, that's all. It's a coincidence.'

'But maybe it isn't. Remember Granddad always said that Waiguo Ren was an Englishman. It would make sense that he would bring the diamond here, to London, wouldn't it?' Mei's eyes widened, before she went on. 'It could be why Granddad first came here! What if he came to London to try and get the diamond back?'

Song stared at her for a moment, and then his face

softened. 'I know you miss Granddad,' he said quietly. 'We all do. But this – this is just make-believe.'

'No, it isn't,' said Mei stubbornly. 'What are the chances of another stone – as rare and special as this – having exactly the same name? It's the same diamond, I know it is. *And we could get it back!*'

Song pushed the article aside impatiently. 'And how would you do that, exactly?' he demanded. 'Are you planning to go waltzing up to this young lady, and just say: "Excuse me, miss, but please can we have our diamond back?" Don't be ridiculous. Even if it is the Moonbeam Diamond, it doesn't belong to our family any more. It's gone. It was taken years ago, before you or I were even born. This young lady is hardly going to care about some old story, is she? It's her diamond now.'

'But . . . it was stolen!' protested Mei. 'It was taken from a temple – a holy place. That isn't right. Besides, there's a curse on it. She most likely doesn't know about that. It says here she was given it as a gift – what if something terrible happens to her? She ought to know.'

'And you're going to be the one to tell her?' Song snorted. 'Mei, you can hardly work up the courage to step outside China Town! How on earth are you going to manage to find some rich young lady you've never met before and convince her to give you a priceless diamond?

You'd never have the pluck.'

'I thought maybe you could help me . . .' said Mei in a small voice.

'And even if I did, what then? She wouldn't listen to anything we have to say. Look at her, Mei. She'd laugh in our faces!'

'But what if she didn't? Don't we at least have to try? What about Granddad – and – and honouring our ancestors? Granddad said that protecting the diamond was our family's duty – our destiny. It's important,' Mei went on, blinking back tears now.

'Don't you understand?' Song's voice was exasperated. 'None of that matters. Look, if Mum and Dad don't find a way to pay the Baron's Boys what they're demanding from us, we're finished. The others are in the same boat too. Didn't you hear what happened to Mrs Wu's son? They broke his arm in three places. They aren't sure he'll ever be able to work again. This is really *serious*.'

'But the diamond is supposed to bring us luck, isn't it?' said Mei, her voice wavering but determined. 'It's supposed to protect us. Granddad always said so. If we could get it back, it might protect us against the Baron's Boys!'

'Grow up, Mei,' said Song, shortly. 'It's time you stopped believing in fairy tales. Granddad is gone now and you need to wake up.'

As if to put an end to their conversation, Song crumpled the article in his hand, and threw it on to the fire before Mei could stop him, turning the last remnant of Granddad's story to ash.

CHAPTER EIGHT

'**A**re you *certain* that this is a good idea?' asked Sophie, for at least the dozenth time.

Lil smiled beatifically at her reflection in the looking glass, as she tilted her hat to a better angle. 'Of course I am. It will be fun – rather like acting and, after all, I *am* an actress. I shall simply be playing the role of the perfect debutante.'

The two girls were in the deserted mannequins' dressing room at Sinclair's department store. The dress shows were over for the day, and the other mannequins had left, but Lil had stayed behind to dress for a different performance altogether – going undercover as a debutante at a tea party at Miss Whiteley's house.

Sophie stepped back to survey her friend as she stood in front of the looking glass. There was no doubt at all that Lil *looked* like the perfect debutante. Her hair, which had already been carefully coiffured by Monsieur Pascal, the hairdresser at Sinclair's, for that afternoon's dress show, was a heap of beautiful glossy curls, and the delicate lace frock she wore was immaculately white. It had been borrowed from a rack of gowns in the mannequins' dressing room. Sophie had been rather doubtful about this, but Lil had been adamant that no one would notice. 'Look around – there must be hundreds of frocks in here. I promise you that no one will ever miss *one*, especially just for an afternoon.' With the final addition of a hat wreathed in flowers and a pair of white gloves, Lil looked every inch a lovely young debutante.

The only problem, Sophie thought, was that Lil was simply too excitable to be convincing as a proper society lady. After the disappointment of learning that the show at the Fortune Theatre would be ending, Lil had thrown herself into this new challenge with even more energy than usual, and was fizzing around the mannequins' dressing room.

'You'll have to try and blend into the background,' Sophie warned her. 'Don't draw too much attention to yourself. Be . . . inconspicuous.'

'I'm not going to start a riot at this tea party, you know,' said Lil. 'Remember, I've seen hundreds of debs at the dress shows. I know exactly how they behave, and I'll be as prim as the best of them.' She paused to practise a demure smile in the looking glass.

'Just make sure you find out as much as you can about

the other debutantes from Lord Beaucastle's garden party. Even if none of them took the jewel, they might have seen something suspicious,' Sophie went on.

'Of course I will,' said Lil promptly. 'That's what I'm there for, isn't it? I shall be an *undercover detective*. I say, isn't it thrilling?'

Yet as she approached the front steps of Miss Whiteley's town house later that afternoon, Lil had to admit to herself that she was, after all, feeling just the tiniest bit nervous. The house alone seemed designed to intimidate: a great white wedding-cake of a town house on Belgrave Square, one of London's most fashionable addresses. It seemed to grow larger and larger, looming over her as she approached.

She cleared her throat, straightened her hat, and willed herself forwards, going briskly up the steps that led to the large, black, forbidding-looking front door. She rang the bell with decision: a few moments later, a smart maid came to answer it.

'Yeeeeees?' she demanded, haughtily.

'Er . . . good afternoon,' said Lil, suddenly realising that she was not at all sure how a debutante would typically address a housemaid. 'I'm Miss Rose. I'm here for Miss Whiteley's tea party.'

The housemaid nodded. 'Please come in, miss,' she said,

holding open the door. As she did so, she glanced over Lil's shoulder, as though she expected someone else to be there. Lil followed her gaze, but of course, she was quite alone on the threshold.

'Is your chaperone with you, miss?' asked the housemaid.

'My . . . chaperone?' repeated Lil, confused. Then she realised: debutantes were not allowed to go anywhere alone! She had seen them at the dress shows at Sinclair's, perpetually accompanied by a mother or an aunt or a married older sister or at least a lady's maid – and here she was, turning up to a tea party completely unescorted. She felt her face turning pink.

'Oh – I'm afraid she's feeling unwell so she sent me on alone. Such a shame she couldn't come too,' she said hurriedly, fixing the housemaid with her best demure smile.

'I'm sorry to hear that, miss.'

Warming to her story now, Lil went on: 'Yes it's simply terrible, she came down with the mumps, the poor thing. Awfully sudden.'

'The mumps, miss?' repeated the housemaid, looking alarmed.

Lil remembered too late that mumps were dreadfully catching. 'Of course, it may not be the mumps. It may be something else. And as it happens I was away visiting my

91

grandmama, so I'm not in the slightest bit infectious. Shall I go through?'

She flashed her smile again at the confused housemaid, and stepped purposefully forwards into a showy hallway with a parquet floor, a large chandelier and several paintings in elaborate gilt frames. Still looking bemused, the maid directed Lil towards the drawing room, where Miss Whiteley's tea party was taking place.

As she stepped through the doorway, Lil saw that gathered together at one end of the large, sunny room were some twenty girls of about her own age, all dressed in dainty pale frocks and strings of pearls. At the other end were a group of ladies wearing more luxuriant costumes – richly coloured gowns trimmed with brocade, and a great deal of expensive-looking jewellery. But in spite of their differences in appearance, both groups – the debutantes and their chaperones – were behaving exactly alike, standing in polite circles, or sitting in confidential groups, sipping tea from gold-rimmed teacups.

Lil sensed a little murmur of interest run around the room as she entered, and several pairs of eyes swivelled in her direction. Realising that most of these girls – and certainly their mamas – had likely seen her in dress shows at Sinclair's dozens of times, she felt suddenly self-conscious. But there was nothing for it now but to plunge in. She could see Miss Whiteley standing across the room, at the centre of one of the little groups of young ladies.

Miss Whiteley did not look exactly overjoyed to see her coming. She had agreed to the undercover plan with obvious reluctance. Lil suspected that she was not at all keen on the idea of entertaining a mere shop girl to an intimate tea party in her own home, whether disguised as a debutante or not. Well, she would jolly well have to get over such idiotic affected nonsense if she wanted them to find the jewelled moth, thought Lil emphatically, as she strode decisively towards her.

As she did so, she passed a long table covered with a snowy-white cloth and laid with silver stands of cakes and sandwiches, and she forgot all about Miss Whiteley and the jewelled moth for a moment. There were prettily decorated *petits fours*, luscious strawberry tarts, delicate pastel-coloured *macarons*, and sandwiches sliced into tiny, perfect triangles. It felt like a very long time since the midday meal in the Sinclair's refectory, and Lil's mouth began to water. Just in time, she remembered that she was supposed to be a polite debutante, and glanced away from the glorious spread, hoping that no one had noticed the very unladylike growl her stomach had made.

'How do you do, Miss Whiteley?' she said in her most genteel voice as she approached the hostess. Sophie would have been proud of her, she thought, as she smiled. She simply couldn't have been any more ladylike.

Miss Whiteley, on the other hand, was not much of an actress. She looked distinctly uncomfortable, but nevertheless did as she had promised.

'Please do call me Veronica,' she said to Lil stiffly, through tight lips. 'I'm glad to see you here,' she added, though she sounded anything but. Then, to the two girls standing immediately beside her, she went on: 'Phyllis, Mary, this is Miss Rose. Miss Rose, these are Miss Woodhouse and Miss Chesterfield.'

The other two girls eyed Lil curiously as she smiled and bowed, all the while taking them both in. Phyllis was a plump, placidly smiling girl with round pink cheeks. Mary was small and lively-looking. She was dressed like all the other debutantes, but there was something about her that was different – perhaps the way her curly brown hair seemed to be trying to escape from the myriad of pins and combs holding it into place, or the sprinkling of freckles across her nose, or simply the rather jolly-looking twinkle in her eye.

Veronica murmured a polite excuse and moved away.

'So you're a friend of Veronica's?' asked Mary at once.

'Oh, just an acquaintance really,' said Lil, breezily. 'It was very kind of her to invite me today.'

'Is this your first Season too?' asked Phyllis.

'That's right,' said Lil, still smiling.

'I don't believe I've seen you at any balls,' said Mary curiously.

'Perhaps you just haven't noticed me,' said Lil, with a little laugh. The demure smile was beginning to feel rather forced now. Mary was looking at her with a penetrating expression: Lil tried to make her own face as bland and innocent as possible, but all the same, felt thoroughly relieved when a maid appeared offering cakes. Lil accepted at once, glad of the distraction as well as awfully hungry. It was only when she had taken a bite of chocolate eclair - simply divine - that she noticed that the other two were not eating anything.

'Didn't you want one?' she asked in surprise, her mouth full of chocolate and cream.

Phyllis was watching her wistfully. 'It looks awfully delicious,' she said longingly. 'They've brought in all the cakes from the *pâtisserie* at Sinclair's, you know. Heavenly!'

'Shall I call the maid back?' asked Lil, looking around for her.

'Oh no!' said Phyllis quickly. 'That is, I couldn't possibly. Mama wouldn't like it.'

'Why?' asked Lil, baffled, forgetting for a moment that she was supposed to be being ladylike as she licked the cream off her fingers.

'I've already had three cucumber sandwiches. *And* a

macaron,' explained Phyllis, her words heavy with meaning.

'But that's hardly anything!' exclaimed Lil. 'Those sandwiches are the size of a postage stamp.'

'I know, but Mama says that a young lady ought to have a dainty appetite – which I definitely *don't*,' sighed Phyllis. She turned to Mary, 'When we went to luncheon with the Whiteleys on Wednesday, Veronica hardly ate *anything*. Grandmama said afterwards that I ought to take a leaf out of Veronica's book if I wanted any gentlemen to notice me.'

Mary rolled her eyes. 'Of course. Because now that she's managed to catch Lord Beaucastle's eye, we all have to be exactly like Veronica.'

Lil opened her mouth to try and say something more about Lord Beaucastle – maybe even to lead the conversation around to the garden party – but Mary was looking at her curiously and asked: 'Doesn't your mama ever nag you about that sort of thing?'

'Grandmama made me read the whole chapter on luncheon parties in Lady Diana DeVere's etiquette book when I got home,' added Phyllis sorrowfully.

Mary smiled ironically. She quoted:

'*A young maiden's appetite should be gracefully restrained at all times. There is no more unladylike quality in a debutante than that of intemperate gluttony.*'

'How fearful!' exclaimed Lil.

'I take it that you haven't read Lady Diana DeVere, then?' asked Mary, with a quirk of her eyebrows.

Lil decided that there was no sense in pretending. 'I'm afraid I haven't, but she sounds perfectly dreadful,' she said, directly. 'Look here, Phyllis – I say, you don't mind me calling you Phyllis, do you? – if you're worried about your mama catching you eating these glorious cakes, why don't we just slip around there, behind that screen? No one will be able to see us, and I can see there's a whole plate of eclairs on that table simply *begging* to be eaten.'

The other two followed her gaze. 'Do you know,' said Mary, slowly, 'I believe that's a rather good idea.'

'Could we really?' asked Phyllis, her eyes round as saucers.

'Yes,' said Mary, 'and do come quickly, while Lady Alice is looking the other way!'

As they slipped across the room, Mary whispered to Lil: 'I'm not quite sure what your game is, Miss Rose – but I rather think I like you.'

Two hours later, Miss Whiteley's tea party was drawing to a close. Ladies were beginning to depart, talking of dressing for dinner and preparing for yet another round of balls and suppers and concerts. Veronica could not help feeling relieved that the gathering was coming to an end. Knowing that Miss Rose was here had made her feel twitchy and out of sorts: it was certainly true that the girl looked the part, but she was not, after all, a *real* debutante, and there was no knowing what she might say or do. Suppose she asked too many silly questions and gave the game away about the jewelled moth being missing? Suppose she spoke to Isabel and said something idiotic? Really, Veronica felt quite vexed. She had spent so much of the afternoon fretting that she had not been able to enjoy showing off her new tea gown nearly as much as she had expected. Nor had she been able to take satisfaction in being complimented on the beautiful bouquet of roses that Lord Beaucastle had sent her that morning.

To make matters worse, she had got stuck in a long conversation with someone's tiresome maiden aunt who had really seemed to think she was *interested* in discussing her church's charity bazaar for hours at a time. Finally managing to extract herself, she had looked around for someone to talk to – Cynthia, or Dora, or Emily, or goodness knows even Phyllis would do – but they all seemed to have vanished into thin air.

At last, after pacing around the room twice, she found them grouped in a corner, concealed behind an ornamental screen and surrounded by cake plates littered in crumbs. Not only Cynthia, Dora and Phyllis, but Mary and Louisa too – and in the centre of their ring was Miss Rose, who was evidently in the midst of relating a very entertaining story.

The others were hanging on her every word.

'And *then* Miss Pinker said: "And that, Miss Rose, is why you shall never be a credit to the first lacrosse team!"'

The girls erupted into riotous laughter. Veronica stared at them all incredulously. She had never known them to be so rowdy. Whatever had Miss Rose done to them?

'Have any of you seen Emily?' she demanded abruptly, noticing that she alone was missing.

Dora goggled at her. 'Oh, Veronica! Don't say you haven't heard?'

'Heard what?'

'Why, the simply extraordinary things everyone is saying about Emily, of course,' said Cynthia, with a little giggle.

'What things?' demanded Veronica.

'She's *gone*! Vamoosed!'

'Whatever do you mean, she's gone?' she snapped.

'It's true,' said Dora. 'Tell her, Phyllis.'

Phyllis dropped her voice to a low, conspiratorial whisper. 'Yesterday there was a dreadful uproar next door,' she said. 'Then this morning, Mrs Montague came to call upon Mama. She said that no one had seen Emily. She ran away on Wednesday night – *eloped*, with one of the family footmen! Can you believe it?'

Veronica's mouth fell open. 'What – *Emily*?' she said in amazement.

'Isn't it shocking?' exclaimed Cynthia, sounding as though she was enjoying it immensely. 'It must be so dreadful for her family.'

'Her mama is terribly upset of course, but *I* think it's romantic,' Phyllis went on. 'He must have been divinely handsome, and they fell in love, and eloping was the only way they could be together. It's like something from a novel!'

Veronica could hardly believe her ears. Could this be what had made Emily so distracted at luncheon on Wednesday? Had she been sitting there planning her elopement? What an idiotic thing to do, running off to marry a penniless footman only a few short weeks into her first Season! Veronica had never liked Emily all that much, but she had thought she had more sense.

She snorted. 'How preposterous!'

'I never would have pictured *Emily* as the romantic type,' said Mary, shaking her head so vigorously that her curls bounced.

'It's such a scandal!' exclaimed Dora.

The girls all looked around at Lil, evidently very interested to hear what she would have to say about the this new piece of gossip, but she had taken advantage of their conversation to tuck into the last of the cakes. 'Oh, mmm, yes, dreadfully shocking, frightfully scandalous,' she said hurriedly, through a mouthful of meringue. Veronica stared at her, baffled. How had Miss Rose suddenly become the centre of attention?

'*Everyone* is going to be talking about it at Mrs Balfour's ball tonight,' said Cynthia gleefully.

'Oh, Miss Rose, do say you're coming,' said Mary, turning to Lil again. 'We'll have heaps more fun if you're there.'

Lil swallowed the last bite of meringue, and looked up into Veronica's flinty gaze. 'Well . . . er, I'm not at all sure about that, I'm afraid,' she said quickly. 'It all depends on my chaperone. You know, with the mumps and all.'

'Yes, the poor thing. Don't you think you really ought to be going now? So that you can see how she is getting on?' said Veronica in a dangerous voice.

Lil put down her cup. 'Oh yes, I suppose I really should.' She grinned at the girls. 'It was awfully jolly to meet you all. I hope you have a splendid time tonight.'

But Veronica was marching her through the room and out into the hallway almost before she had the chance to finish saying goodbye.

'What do you think you're doing?' Veronica hissed, as she marshalled Lil towards the door. 'You were supposed to be finding out information about my missing brooch – not gossiping and . . . and . . . making intimate friends!'

'But I *was* finding out information,' said Lil in surprise. 'I –'

But the rest of her sentence was not destined to be heard.

Before she had got out another word, she found herself standing on Miss Whiteley's doorstep, with the black shiny front door closed unceremoniously in her face.

CHAPTER NINE

Mei tiptoed up the stairs to the attic, quiet as a mouse in her bare feet. It was very late, and she was not supposed to be out of bed. Mum and Dad had long since blown out their candles; Shen and Jian were buried fathoms deep in dreams; and beside them, Song tossed and turned and muttered to himself, as he often did while he was sleeping. But Mei had been lying awake for what seemed like hours, staring up at the familiar map of cracks in the ceiling, her thoughts flittering as busily as the moth that made dizzy circles around the candle flame. At last, unable to lie there a moment longer, she had clambered out of bed, heading to Uncle Huan's room.

In the last day or two, Uncle Huan's empty attic had become a refuge for her. She wasn't sure exactly why she was drawn to it - perhaps because it wasn't bare and sad, like Granddad's old room, or maybe just because she and Song had loved to play up here when they were small. She put her stub of a candle down on the little table that stood by the bed: the small yellow light flickered, chasing the shadows away from the corners.

True sailor that he was, Uncle Huan always left his room perfectly tidy when he was away at sea. A couple of blankets were folded at the foot of the bare mattress; his few books were piled in a neat stack beside the bed; and a cap and scarf hung on a nail behind the door – the whole room was as neat as a pin. Mei dragged a wooden stool over to the window set into the roof, and climbed on to it. She unlatched the window, opened it and leaned out into the smoky night air.

When they were small, she and Song had been delighted by this rooftop view. China Town looked so different from up here – a higgledy-piggledy landscape of grey rooftops and tall chimney pots and sky and sparrows. Once or twice, they had even dared to clamber out of the window and had gone a little way along the roofs of the houses – at first tentatively, and then scampering along the flat strip that ran along their centre as if it was a pathway, delighting in exploring this strange new territory. That was until Mum had got wind of what they were doing, and had expressly forbidden them to go out there, threatening to nail shut Uncle Huan's window if they ever even thought of doing it again.

But Mei had never before seen the rooftops at night. It was quite dark outside. There was only a sprinkling of stars in the sky above her, and the moon, round as a silver shilling, cast out a cool, pale light. It fell across the rooftops, catching tiles and skylights, making them gleam pearl-white in the dark.

She found herself thinking about how the Moonbeam Diamond had been a gift from the Lady of the Moon to their long-ago ancestor. On a night like this, Mei thought, it was quite easy to imagine the moon as a person; or rather, as a single glowing eye, looking down upon her. She gazed up into the silent sky, and heaved a great deep breath of the cool night air, trying to make sense of her tangled thoughts.

She had felt miserable ever since her conversation with Song in the back room. She heard over again his scornful voice. *Don't be silly. Grow up. You'd never have the pluck.* After what he had said, she hadn't dared mention the diamond to Mum or Dad, especially now that she no longer had the piece of newspaper to show them. Besides, Song had been right about one thing: Mum and Dad already had more than enough to think about. It was rumoured that the Baron had taken charge of the Star Inn. Mr and Mrs Perks were still there, but they'd been told that one of the Baron's men would be running the show from now on. The Baron's grip on China Town was tightening. Outside, on the streets, people looked afraid. There had been more gatherings in the Lims' back room, but fewer of their neighbours joined them now, and those who did seemed jumpy and fearful.

The shop was beginning to look more like its usual self again, but Dad now had a permanently worried expression, and he was still spending most of his time frowning over the accounts. He and Mum had whispered conversations about bills and payments that made Mei feel queasy. Mrs Wu had visited them again, and Mei had seen her crying into her apron as Mum tried to comfort her.

The whole house felt strange. No one was playing the fool now, no one was ragging or laughing – even Shen and Jian were unusually quiet.

In the sudden silence that had fallen over the usually noisy house, Mei had found that she had a lot of time to spend with her own thoughts. She had been thinking as she swept and dusted in the shop, as she carefully refilled jars with tea and toffees, as she arranged tins on the shelves. She had been thinking as she fed Tibby and the green parrot; and she had been thinking as she had lain in bed, wakeful and alone. She was not dreaming any longer, nor telling herself Granddad's stories. She was thinking about what Song had said to her about trying to get back the diamond – and as she thought, the idea crept up on her that maybe, just maybe, he was wrong.

Of course, there was the chance that it was not the same Moonbeam Diamond. And of course, even if it was the same, it might be that there was no way for her to get it back. Speaking to the young lady who owned it would be difficult, if not impossible. And yet somehow, the thought of the diamond would not leave her alone. If only she could get it back, she was convinced that it would help to protect them.

For a wild moment, Mei imagined herself as a cat burglar, creeping into a strange house by night, and *stealing* the diamond from the young lady's jewel cabinet. She would almost be within her rights to do it – she would only be taking back what belonged to her family. But that was ridiculous – perhaps she really had been reading too many stories. She knew that stealing from anyone was wrong, no matter what the circumstances – Mum had taught them that when they were very small, slapping their little hands sharply when they reached towards the jars of sweets in the shop. Besides, Mei added with a small smile to herself, it was just plain silly to imagine herself as a master jewel-thief. Song always said he could hear the clatter of her boots coming a mile off.

But all the same, as she looked out over the rooftops at the moon, she felt suddenly ablaze with the desire to do *something*. She thought of Mum in the back room, and how she had talked about sticking up for themselves; and then of Dad's tired face; and of Mrs Wu weeping; and of the way that the Baron's Boys were trying to take what did not belong to them, just as the Moonbeam Diamond had been taken from the temple where it belonged, all those years ago.

Imagine what they'd say if she could manage, all alone, to reclaim the diamond!

The first step was to find out where the young lady lived, she decided. If she knew how to find her, then she would be able to tell her about the diamond and the curse. Mei had taken to scouring the newspaper each day, sneaking it away after Dad had finished with it, and searching the society pages for any mention of Miss Whiteley. Perhaps then she could write to her – there would be nothing wrong in that.

Song might think she was a timid scaredy-cat, but she wasn't. Perhaps she was not as naturally brave as he was, but that did not mean that she couldn't be brave in her own way. Wasn't she the descendant of the noble warrior who had righted a terrible wrong? And she also believed in standing up for what was right. This was her chance to prove that she too could be brave, she too could be plucky, she too could be certain.

She who dares, wins. It was something that Song himself had said to her once, trying to get up her courage for some playground ordeal. 'If you don't even dare to try, then you won't get anywhere, will you?' he had said. She gazed out over the night-time rooftops, and his words hummed to her now, like a refrain, like the moon herself was singing them to her. *She who dares, wins.*

CHAPTER TEN

'Well, I'll tell you one thing I'm quite sure of,' said Lil, tucking into a thick slice of meat pie with enthusiasm. 'Mary and Phyllis don't care for Miss Whiteley very much.'

Sophie and Lil were sitting in the Sinclair's refectory, eating their midday meal. Around them were a host of Sinclair's staff – waitresses and salesgirls, doormen and delivery drivers – most of them talking excitedly about the summer fête, which was taking place the very next day. Snippets of conversation drifted around them about boat races and best hats and whether they might get up a lawn tennis tournament. But Sophie and Lil were not talking about the fête. Instead, Lil was relating to Sophie everything that had happened at Miss Whiteley's tea party the day before.

Sophie pondered this for a moment as she buttered a slice of bread. 'So do you think there's anything in her theory that whoever has the brooch has taken it simply out of spite – or jealousy perhaps? To stir up trouble between

Veronica and Lord Beaucastle, or even prevent them becoming engaged?'

Lil screwed up her nose. 'I suppose it's *possible*,' she said slowly. 'But I really don't think they mind about it as much as all that. I don't think Mary and Phyllis give a fig about whether Veronica and Lord Beaucastle become engaged, although he's obviously quite the catch. They're all just rather browned off about the way Veronica's been behaving since she got his attention. As a matter of fact, none of them even mentioned Lord Beaucastle to speak of – they were a jolly sight more interested in talking about frocks and hairstyles and so on. Not that there's anything wrong with talking about frocks,' she added, reflectively. 'I mean, I like a nice frock just as much as the next person. But they were mainly just talking about things like that – and gossiping about the latest society scandal, of course.'

'And what's that?'

'Oh, one of the other debutantes has apparently eloped with one of her family's footmen. She was one of the names on our list, actually – Emily Montague. By all accounts they disappeared on Friday, leaving everything behind them, and haven't been seen since. They're supposed to have gone abroad together.'

'Well, there's something,' said Sophie, promptly.

'What do you mean?'

'If they were about to run away together, they would need money, wouldn't they?'

'Oh I say – so she could be the one who stole the jewelled moth?' Lil's dark eyes widened in sudden excitement. 'That's a jolly good thought.'

'Well, it's one theory,' said Sophie. 'We need to talk to the butler and the lady's maid, too, and see what else we can find out.'

'It's going to be a good deal more difficult to find a chance to talk to the two of them, though, isn't it?' said Lil. 'Gosh, don't you think it must be reams easier for Mr McDermott than it is for us? All he has to do is waltz up to the kitchen door, knock and explain he's a private investigator and wants to ask the servants some questions. No one would take us seriously if we did that.'

'And I doubt Veronica would thank us if we did,' said Sophie, with a laugh. 'After all, the whole point is that she doesn't want Lord Beaucastle – or anyone else for that matter – to know that the brooch is missing. But there is a way we could just go up to the kitchen door, you know,' she added, after a pause.

'Do you want me to impersonate a housemaid?' asked Lil, her eyes gleaming.

'No, you donkey,' said Sophie with a giggle. 'I don't think you'd be very convincing! I was thinking about something much more straightforward. Think of the other sorts of people who might go to a kitchen door, and talk to servants . . . Such as a *delivery boy*, for example?'

Lil seized her meaning at once, and as soon as they had finished their luncheon, the two went in search of Billy. They tracked him down at last in the Toy Department, where he'd been delivering a message. He was keen to hear about everything Lil had discovered at the tea party, and made several more enthusiastic scribbles in his notebook. But when they suggested their new idea to him, they found that he was not at all keen on reverting to his previous role – even if it was to help solve a mystery.

'I work for Mr Sinclair himself now, you know,' he said, rather grandly, as they followed him between a magnificent display of dolls' houses and a train set that was chugging its way through a painted landscape of woods and fields. 'I can't just start taking out deliveries, willy-nilly. Miss Atwood wouldn't like it.'

'Oh bother Miss Atwood,' muttered Lil.

'Well, look here, couldn't you at least find out if there is anything that's due to be delivered to Lord Beaucastle's house in the next day or two?' Sophie asked.

'Yes, and then Joe could take it,' said Lil, promptly. 'Perhaps *he* isn't too busy to help,' she added, under her breath.

Billy ignored her. 'I should be able to find out. But I have to go now. I'm afraid I've got rather a lot to do before the summer fête tomorrow.'

And so saying he swept away towards the elevators, leaving the two girls to look at each other and burst out laughing.

Miss Veronica Whiteley's Missing Jewel

Possible Suspects:
Mary Chesterfield – dislikes VW
The Honourable Phyllis ? Woodhouse – dislikes VW
Emily Montague – may have needed money for forthcoming elopement
Miss Montague's maid
Lord Beaucastle's butler

CHAPTER ELEVEN

The day of the first annual Sinclair's Staff Summer Fête had finally arrived. There had been much speculation in the store about whether the day would be fine. Mrs Milton had said sagely that such beautiful weather as they had been having could not possibly be expected to last, and Mr White from the Book Department had gone so far as forecasting a storm, so there was relief all round when the day dawned bright and fair, with a cloudless blue sky.

The journey out to Putney had gone without incident, and now here they all were, enjoying an afternoon's amusements along the river. It was quite a lark to see them all like this, Joe thought, from where he was standing with Titch and Paddy and one or two of the other stable fellows, enjoying the spectacle. The shop girls were quite as fine as the ladies they served on the shop floor, all rigged out in their Sunday best, with their parasols and gloves and flowered hats. The salesmen too were immaculately turned out for the occasion in crisp white flannels and blazers. But it was the porters and doormen who looked the most unlike their usual selves, dressed in ordinary clothes instead of their uniforms.

The riverbank where they would be spending the day had been decked out for a celebration too. Iced lemonade and strawberries were being served from a striped tent adorned with strings of gaily-coloured bunting. There were games to play on the lawn – Joe could see Minnie, Dot and Edith from the Millinery Department attempting a round of croquet with Jim and a couple of the fellows from Sporting Goods. Billy's Uncle Sid, smart as paint for the occasion, came strolling through the crowd with Mr Betteredge, pausing to laugh at a joke or clap a young porter on the shoulder. Monsieur Pascal was solicitously delivering a glass of lemonade to Claudine, the window-dresser, who was sitting in a striped deckchair, frowning rather suspiciously at the bright sunlight from under the shade of her parasol. Mr Sinclair himself was nowhere to be seen, but that hardly mattered, Joe thought. Had he been here, the staff might have felt they had to be on their best behaviour – as it was, they were all simply enjoying the day out.

It was really something to work for a place that treated its staff like this, Joe thought, as he savoured another mouthful of his strawberries and cream. This time last year he'd never even tasted a strawberry, and now look at him. Today more than ever, he felt as though he'd stepped through a sort of magic door, leaving the darkness of his old life behind him. He smiled at himself and his fanciful notions. That sounded much more like something Billy might have come up with than anything he might think himself.

Across the lawn, he could see Billy talking earnestly to Lil and Sophie. They were probably discussing some development in the case, but he felt no need to rush over and hear it. They'd tell him in good time. Instead, he stood enjoying the sensation of the sun on his back and wondering whether he might pluck up the courage to ask Lil for a dance later on.

Sid Parker came striding over, jacket off and shirtsleeves already rolled up in preparation for the boat race. 'Right then, lads,' he announced. 'Almost time to start. Let's show those fellows from Sporting Goods what we're made of!'

Down by the river's edge, Sophie, Lil and Billy had not yet noticed that the boat race was about to begin.

'I've checked the records, just like you asked, but there isn't anything due to be delivered to Lord Beaucastle's address. So I'm afraid that's that,' Billy was saying.

'Well, not necessarily,' said Lil, promptly. She turned to Sophie. 'Maybe we don't even need a *real* delivery. We could deliver something to Lord Beaucastle's house *by mistake*. That would offer the perfect opportunity for a conversation with the butler!'

Billy looked thoroughly alarmed at this idea, and launched into a long discourse about the importance of protecting Sinclair's hard-won reputation for efficiency – which Miss Atwood said was of paramount importance – and the painstaking care that must be taken with each and every delivery. Sophie and Lil couldn't help feeling rather relieved when Sid Parker called Billy over to him.

'Oh look, it's starting,' said Lil. 'You'd better hurry.'

Billy grinned, excited. 'Wish us luck!' he said, and rushed away.

Lil sighed after him. 'I don't know why he's being such a goody-goody at the moment. I thought he wanted to be a proper detective! I'll bet that Montgomery Baxter that he's always reading about wouldn't let all these idiotic rules stand in his way.'

'It's the new job, that's all,' said Sophie, with a grin. 'He wants to prove himself. He'll calm down soon enough.'

She spoke rather absently. They were walking slowly after Billy, towards the wooden jetty where the rowers were clambering into their boats. Mr Betteredge was directing operations, looking very enthusiastic and rather hot, and the rest of the staff who were not taking part in the race had gathered to watch the fun. It was gloriously cool by the river – a light breeze rippled the surface of the water, and a family of swans sailed past. Suddenly Sophie felt tired of Miss Whiteley and the jewelled moth, and even of being detectives. She would be quite happy to forget about it all, and simply enjoy being here, on the riverbank, for a little while.

The boats were lining up for the start now. From where they stood, Sophie could see Uncle Sid's boat, with Joe just about visible amongst the rowers, and Billy's fair head at the back. Lil waved her handkerchief excitedly. 'Good luck!' she cried, although there was not much chance that Joe and Billy would have been able to hear anything above the music from the band and the noise of the other staff cheering and clapping.

'Oh look! They're ready!' squealed Minnie, from somewhere a little behind Lil and Sophie.

All at once, Mr Betteredge fired the starting pistol, and then the boats were off. Uncle Sid's boat pulled out in front to a roar of cheers, but then another boat, captained by Jim from Sporting Goods, began to gain on them.

'Come on! Hoe in! Go to it!' shrieked Lil, hopping from one foot to another, very much excited, having apparently forgotten how annoyed she had been to have to merely stand by and spectate.

'Go for it, Jim!' came another voice from behind them.

'Show 'em how it's done, Sid!' called someone else.

The two boats were neck and neck now: the rowers' arms moved like pistons, and on the riverbank, the spectators grew more and more excited.

'Go on, Alf!' shrieked someone.

'He's going to take the lead!'

'I say, whatever's happening?' exclaimed Lil, suddenly.

Out on the river, Jim's boat was racing ahead, everyone rowing as hard as they could, focused on reaching the finish line. But behind them, Sophie saw to her astonishment, Uncle Sid's boat had come to a standstill.

'What's happened, Sid? Lost your bottle?' yelled someone rudely from behind them, but Uncle Sid was paying no attention. He was pointing and shouting something they could not hear. Sophie saw that Billy had his hand clapped over his mouth, whilst two of the rowers seemed to be struggling with something in the water that was caught up in their oars. As Sophie watched, the next boat drew up behind them to help instead of racing ahead towards the finish line. The watchers on the riverbank quietened, murmuring, confused, as together, the rowers began to wrestle something out of the water.

'Oh goodness,' said Lil in a shocked voice. 'It's a . . . *body!*'

Sophie said nothing: she couldn't speak. By now, the

rowers had managed to haul the object aboard the boat, and it was quite plain to see that it was the body of a girl dressed in white, her fall of long hair dark with water. Sid bent over the figure, but even from where they were standing on the riverbank, it was obvious that she was dead.

The first boat had crossed the finish line, but no one was clapping or cheering now – the riverbank was full of whispers and startled exclamations. Sid was waving his hands and saying something to the rowers, and a moment later, they began moving again, coming straight towards the jetty with its bright strings of bunting, towards where Sophie and Lil were standing.

As they reached the riverbank, Sid took charge. The rowers climbed out of the boat, silent and pale. Joe and two others were instructed to carry the body on to the shore. The watchers on the riverbank pressed closer, intrigued and horrified, but Sid was having none of that.

'Here, you – Titch, isn't it? Run for the constable and look sharp about it,' he barked, pointing at the smallest stable boy. 'You two,' he instructed Joe and Billy, 'you stand guard here. The rest of you stop gawping. The race is over now. Go straight through to the tent and get your tea. Where the devil is Betteredge?'

He charged off, leaving Joe and Billy standing awkwardly in front of the body. With many curious glances at the shape beyond them on the ground, the staff of Sinclair's department store peeled away towards the tea tent: Sid Parker was not a man to be defied.

As they went, they muttered to each other in low, shocked voices.

'What a thing to happen!'

'It's a tragedy, that's what.'

'Poor thing!'

'Only a young lady, too.'

'What could have happened to her? You don't think she could have –?'

Lil and Sophie stayed where they were as the others drifted away.

'How ghastly,' said Lil at last. 'How perfectly ghastly. I say, are you all right?' she added, looking anxiously at Billy, who was very green and looked as if he was going to be sick.

Billy shook his head as if he didn't really trust himself to say anything yet.

Joe didn't speak either. He was still breathless and sweating from the race. His heart was pounding. He'd seen dead bodies before – more than he had ever wanted to, back on the streets of the East End. But he'd never expected to see one here, not like this. He looked away, feeling all over again the sodden weight of her as they had lifted her out of the boat. The sour river smell of decay seemed to have crept over him, obliterating all the scents of summer and strawberries. As Joe wiped the clammy perspiration from his forehead, his dream of being an ordinary, respectable fellow suddenly seemed a mere fantasy. He would never be able to escape what he had been.

Sophie looked down at the body on the grass. She was just a girl, not much older than herself. She wore no hat, but was dressed in what at first appeared to be a smart, stylish costume. But as Sophie studied her further, she saw that the girl's frock was not so new and expensive as she had first thought. The lace trimming on her skirt had been neatly mended – there was a discreet darn on one elbow – and the heels of her dainty little boots looked worn. Who was she, and why was she floating in the river? Was she the victim of some terrible accident – or had something more sinister happened to her? The very thought made Sophie's skin prickle.

'We should cover her up,' she found herself saying, in a voice that didn't sound like her own.

Lil took a cloth off one of the tables that had been set out on the grass. Together, she and Sophie knelt down beside the girl, and rather awkwardly spread it over her body.

Whether it was better or worse when she was covered, Sophie wasn't sure. Now she looked simply ghoulish, a blank white shape on the ground. She found herself tucking the cloth more carefully around the girl's form, as if she were trying to make her more comfortable somehow – a silly sort of thing to do, but she couldn't help it – and then something made her stop.

'I think I'm going to be sick –' said Billy suddenly.

But Sophie wasn't listening. She had seen something gleaming on the ground: bending down, she realised that the girl was holding a small silk purse, the drawstrings wrapped several times around her wrist, as though she had taken special care to secure them. The drawstring had come open, and something glittering had slipped a little way out. Sophie bent down to pick it up: it was almost as big as her own hand, a strange, spiky shape that felt very cold against her skin.

Behind her, she could hear Billy making horrid retching sounds, and Lil trying to say comforting things to him, but still she did not move. She was staring down at the object in her palm: a lacework of silver and enamel, dotted with rows of tiny emeralds and sapphires and chips of gleaming opals. At its centre was a single large stone: as the light played over it, it gleamed cold, silver-white as the moon, even in the bright sunshine. She had never seen anything so odd and beautiful in her life.

'We've found it . . .' she whispered, half to herself.

'It can't be!' said Joe hoarsely from behind her.

She whirled round to face him and held it out. 'Look!' she said, her voice quaking with astonishment. 'It's the jewelled moth.'

PART III
The Proper Paying of Calls

Young ladies making their first appearances in society must understand the importance of visiting. The ceremony of paying calls remains the basis upon which that great structure, society, rests. Following the proper etiquette is of paramount importance, whether one is paying calls congratulatory, calls of condolence, or calls of courtesy. The hours for calling are between three and six o'clock p.m., and on no account should a call be paid before luncheon, unless calling on a very particular friend.

Lady Diana DeVere's *Etiquette for Debutantes: a Guide to the Manners, Mores and Morals of Good Society*, Chapter 4: The Proper Paying of Calls – Occasions when Calls should be Paid – The Card Case and its Contents – Lengths of Visits – The Proper Conduct when Staying in a Friend's House – A Brief Word on Servants

CHAPTER TWELVE

Billy felt ill at ease as he sat in the office on Monday morning, trying hard to concentrate on the letters that Miss Atwood had given him to type. All around him was the usual bustling activity of Mr Sinclair's office – telephones ringing, typewriter keys clacking, clerks hurrying to and fro – but after the events of the day before, he found himself feeling peculiarly detached from everything around him. It was most likely because he was tired, he told himself stoutly, frowning at the letters. After all, he had slept very badly the night before, troubled in the early hours of the morning by horrible dreams.

In the dreams – or rather, the nightmares – the drowned body of the girl from the river had come to life, her limbs swollen, her hair dark and tangled and her skin glowing, eerily pale. Her eyelids flickered open; water ran off her in long streams. She had moved, swaying, towards him, her arms outstretched. Her mouth opened as if she was trying to say something, but her voice was only a hoarse, unintelligible croak – as if the river had stolen away her ability to speak.

He shook his head, trying to shake away the horrible memory. It still felt so very real, even here in the office, with the bright morning light streaming through the window. Of course, it didn't help that right behind him, two clerks were talking in low voices, sharing all manner of lurid speculations about what might have happened to the girl. There was a great deal of wild gossip buzzing around the store about the incident that had so dramatically disrupted the staff excursion, but Billy did not want to hear any of it. He leaned over his desk, trying to fix his attention on the typewriter keys.

But just at that moment, the office door opened. 'This way, please, constable,' came Miss Atwood's crisp tones from behind him, matching the brisk clip of her boots. 'Mr Sinclair is occupied at present. I'll show you into Mr Betteredge's office. He is the store manager here, and will be able to help you with anything you need. '

Billy looked up curiously to see a tall, uniformed policeman accompanying Miss Atwood.

'What d'you suppose that's all about?' whispered one of the clerks behind him. 'Reckon it's to do with what happened yesterday?'

'Search me,' muttered his chum, craning his neck to see

what was happening, even as the door of Mr Betteredge's office closed behind the policeman.

Miss Atwood saw them all looking and pursed her lips in disapproval. 'Back to work, please,' she instructed. 'Parker, fetch some tea for Mr Betteredge.'

Billy got up at once, and hurried for a tea tray – he had long ago learned that Miss Atwood did not like to be kept waiting. As he returned, balancing the tea tray carefully, he heard voices coming from the other side of Mr Betteredge's door.

'A terrible business, really, most distressing.' Betteredge sounded grave.

'It was indeed, sir. We were grateful for the prompt actions of your staff. I only hope the ladies were not too upset by the incident.'

'And have you been able to identify the body of the poor young woman?'

In spite of himself, Billy found himself listening with interest.

'We have, sir, this very morning. It's an extraordinary thing. I'm sure you'll understand that it's not so uncommon to come upon a body in the river, most of 'em poor unfortunates that have come to a bad end. It's an easy way to dispose of a corpse, you know, sir, if you'll pardon my being blunt. But a lady of quality, well that's quite another matter.

That's not something that happens every day, I can tell you.'

'Do hurry up please, Parker. That tea will be stone cold if you will insist on dawdling,' rapped out Miss Atwood from her desk across the room.

Billy hurriedly slipped through the door and into the office with the tea tray, just as Mr Betteredge said: 'A lady of quality, you say? Why, who was she, constable?'

What the policeman said next almost made Billy drop the tray – teapot, sugar bowl and all. 'A young lady from a fine society family, sir,' he said. 'Her name was Emily Montague.'

Sophie and Lil hurried up the steps of the Whiteleys' town house.

'Do you think we ought to have written first?' asked Sophie anxiously as they rang the bell. 'Or sent a telegram, perhaps?'

She was feeling peculiarly apprehensive. Like Billy, she had slept badly the night before, jerking awake from confused dreams in the darkness of the lodging-house bedroom, her heart racing, very aware that the jewelled moth lay only a few feet away on her chest of drawers.

It had been a split-second decision to take it. She had only had a few moments before the police arrived: if they saw it, she knew that they would claim it, and it would be gone for good. All right, she had reasoned, it would make its way back to Miss Whiteley in time, for it was bound to be recognised – but then its loss would not remain a secret, and all kinds of questions would be asked. More pragmatically, Joe had pointed out that if the police took it, they would certainly lose their chance of earning Miss Whiteley's fee.

But the real reason that Sophie had taken the moth had nothing to do with Miss Whiteley or with money. She had been struck by a sudden and not entirely rational feeling that she must protect the drowned girl – even if she was the thief. It had been so dreadful to see her waterlogged body dragged from the river. Somehow, Sophie felt that she could not let her be condemned as a criminal too. Better, perhaps, to return the moth in secret to Veronica Whiteley, and let the girl rest in peace. She had made her mind up and slipped the moth into the pocket of her frock just moments before several policemen had taken control of the scene.

Ever since, she had been wondering if she had made a terrible mistake. After all, the moth brooch was evidence – and taking evidence was bound to be some sort of a crime. Suppose by taking it she had stopped the police finding out what had happened to the girl, and had prevented justice from being done? Billy's discovery that morning that the drowned girl was none other than one of Veronica's fellow debutantes had made her feel even more confused. How had a wealthy debutante ended up dead, floating in the river? Sophie felt certain that something terrible had happened to Emily Montague – and the jewelled moth had played a part.

Now, outside the house in Belgrave Square, the haughty maid answered their ring. She did not appear to recognise Lil dressed in her ordinary clothes rather than her debutante finery, and looked surprised and more than a little affronted when they asked to see Miss Whiteley. Nonetheless, she showed them in. Instead of taking them to the drawing room where the tea party had been held, she led them along a passageway into a little sitting room furnished with draped curtains, overstuffed armchairs and many little cushions decorated with tassels. Veronica was alone, sprawled on a chaise longue reading a novel. Seeing her visitors, she sat up hurriedly, and shoved the book under a cushion.

'What are you doing here?' she asked them abruptly, as the maid left to fetch tea. 'You oughtn't to just *turn up* like this, you know. If Isabel had been here, she would think it was dreadfully odd. Or what if someone else had been here paying a call? I mean, who would I say you were? And we're expecting Lord Beaucastle to tea in half an hour!'

'I'm sorry we didn't let you know we were coming,' said Sophie, 'but we thought we should come at once.'

'Oh! Have you found something out about the brooch?' said Veronica eagerly, realisation dawning.

In response, Sophie simply held out her hand. Lying in her gloved palm was the jewelled moth.

Veronica seized it in delight. Her face lit up, and for the first time, she actually smiled at them. 'I don't believe it!' she exclaimed. 'Oh, thank *heavens!*'

Lil looked rather as though she was about to say that Veronica really ought to be thanking *them* and not the heavens, but Sophie gave her a warning poke with her elbow. Veronica had flopped down on the chaise longue again, clutching the brooch as if she was afraid to let it go. Sophie and Lil sat down rather awkwardly on the edge of a very soft sofa as the maid came back in, bringing tea in a silver pot and a plate of thin slices of sponge cake.

Veronica waited until she had closed the door behind her again, and then burst out: 'Where did you find it? Who took it?'

Sophie and Lil looked at each other uneasily. 'I'm afraid that we found it under rather unpleasant circumstances,' Sophie began.

'The body of a young lady was pulled out of the river yesterday afternoon,' Lil went on, looking unusually grave. 'The brooch was in her possession.'

'I'm sorry to say we believe she was someone you know,' Sophie continued. 'Her name was Emily Montague.'

'*What?*' exclaimed Veronica, baffled and utterly

disbelieving. '*Emily?* But that's impossible!'

Lil quickly explained what Billy had overheard in Mr Betteredge's office that morning. 'Apparently the story that Emily had eloped with a footman was quite wrong,' she said soberly. 'In fact, the footman had simply been called home suddenly as his mother had been taken ill. The note he left behind for the butler was misplaced, and everyone jumped to the wrong conclusion. Emily hadn't run away to be married – she was dead.'

'But – but – she can't *possibly* be dead,' said Veronica incredulously. 'Why – everyone would know – they would all be talking about it!'

'She has only just been identified,' said Sophie. 'I am sure it won't take long for the news to spread.'

'But *how* – why? What happened to her? Why did she have the moth?' burst out Veronica. Her face was quite white.

'We can only suppose that she was the one who stole it at the garden party,' said Sophie. 'When she was found, the brooch was in her bag. We ought to have handed it over to the police, but we thought you would want us to return it to you,' she added, rather pointedly, still not feeling sure about that particular decision.

Veronica did not say anything in response to this, nor did she ask them about how they had anything to do with the bodies of dead debutantes being pulled out of the river.

Instead, she was gazing down at the moth as if it possessed some sort of malevolent power. After a pause, she blurted out: 'I didn't care for this much to begin with, but now . . . You don't think – you don't think it had anything to do with what happened to Emily, do you?'

'What do you mean?' asked Lil.

Veronica muttered. 'There's a story about it. Something to do with a curse.'

'A *curse?*'

Veronica sighed. 'The Moonbeam Diamond is famous,' she explained reluctantly. 'When Lord Beaucastle presented it to me, he told everyone at dinner the story of how he found it. He's renowned for being a traveller, you know – exploring new places, bringing back treasures. He's supposed to be terribly brave. He used to be in the army, and he won all sorts of medals. Anyway, he told us a story about how he got hold of it during some sort of dreadful uprising in China. It was in a monastery that was burned to the ground by the rebels, and he saved it. There was a story that the diamond had magical powers – and that there was a curse upon it.'

'Lord Beaucastle gave you a *cursed diamond?*' repeated Sophie in astonishment.

'He said it was just superstitious nonsense!' said Veronica defensively. 'He didn't *believe* in the curse! He laughed about it. Everyone did. He said he wanted to give it to me because it was beautiful, and special . . . and that I was too . . .'

'Well, I'm quite sure he's right,' said Lil, in a matter-of-fact tone. 'There's no such thing as curses. After all, nothing awful happened to Lord Beaucastle when he had the diamond, did it? Or to you?'

'But if Emily took it . . . and then she died,' Veronica said faintly. 'What happened to her? How did she die?'

Sophie and Lil looked at each other awkwardly. The Sinclair's staff had been told in no uncertain terms that the young lady who had been found in the river had met with a tragic accident, but from what Billy had overheard in Mr Betteredge's office, the police suspected there had been foul play involved. 'We don't know,' said Sophie at last. 'All we're sure of is that the police think she died a few days before her body was found. They believe she died on Wednesday evening, or perhaps early on Thursday.'

'Wednesday?' Veronica's eyes widened even more. 'But – but we'd been shopping at Sinclair's on Wednesday! We had luncheon! Everything was completely normal –'

Her voice faded away, and she stared down at the jewelled moth lying in her lap, her eyes wide.

'Listen, whatever happened to Emily – it can't really have had anything to do with any sort of curse,' said Lil, directly. 'Even if she was killed – and we don't know for certain that she was – it's quite obvious that the murderer didn't know

137

anything about the jewelled moth. It's terribly valuable after all, and if they had known that she had it, surely they would have taken it for themselves.'

'But why *did* Emily have it?' asked Veronica, shaking her head. 'Why would she take it?'

'We wondered at first whether she might have taken it because she was planning to elope,' explained Lil. 'We thought she might need money to go abroad. But that theory doesn't make sense any longer.'

Sophie remembered the careful way that Emily's dress had been mended. 'Did Emily's family have any money troubles, do you know?' she asked suddenly.

Veronica looked bewildered. 'Money troubles?' she asked uncertainly, as if she had never even heard of such a thing. 'I don't think so. I mean, I suppose I do remember something about her brother losing money at cards, but . . .' She broke off, as her eyes flickered to the clock, and her manner changed abruptly. 'You have to leave now. Isabel will be down any moment. We're expecting Lord Beaucastle.' She got up, and went over to the small bureau in the corner, and took out a few notes from a drawer. 'Here is your fee,' she said rather formally, handing it to Sophie. 'The maid will see you out.'

'Phew! Well, Veronica has the jewelled moth back now, so I suppose that's that,' said Lil, as the maid shut the door behind them and they went together back down the steps to the street. 'Case closed.'

'But it isn't,' said Sophie at once. 'We've just been left with another mystery – what happened to Emily Montague?'

'Do you mean . . . you think we should try and find out what happened to her?' Lil's eyes widened.

Sophie shrugged. It seemed so strange that the very thief they had been looking for should turn up dead, with the jewelled moth in her pocket. She couldn't help feeling that they ought to try to find out why. But looking for a lost brooch was one thing – investigating what might well be a murder was something quite different. They would not be simply playing at being detectives any longer, trifling with a society girl's missing jewellery. This was something far more serious.

'We still have no real idea why Emily stole the moth,' she said at last. 'And if she was killed, then by whom – and why? Who would want to murder a debutante?'

Lil nudged her with her elbow. 'Look,' she said. While they had been talking, an impressively shiny motor had pulled up outside, driven by a uniformed chauffeur. A smart gentleman in a silk top-hat was getting out. 'That must be him – Lord Beaucastle himself.'

Sophie glanced up, only half-interested.

And then it happened. As Sophie and Lil stepped on

to the pavement, the gentleman passed them to go up the steps. He gave them a polite but cursory nod, and in that moment, his eyes met Sophie's. A split-second glance, under the brim of her hat – and it was as if a tempest rushed over her. In that single instant, everything whirled upside down; and then it was over, he had passed them. The maid was opening the door, and saying, in quite a different voice from that she had used for Lil and Sophie, 'Good afternoon, Lord Beaucastle, sir,' and he was going inside.

'I must say, I don't see what's so special about him,' Lil said under her breath. 'He's a bit on the old side, isn't he?'

The world had righted itself again, but Sophie's heart was pounding. Quickly, she grabbed Lil's arm and dragged her around the corner, away from Belgrave Square.

'Whatever is the matter?' Lil demanded, looking completely astonished.

Sophie could barely get out the words. 'That man – Lord Beaucastle,' she gasped. '*He's the Baron.*'

CHAPTER THIRTEEN

Mr McDermott's house looked quite different in the bright June sunshine. Sophie had last visited it in the middle of the night, so she hadn't noticed the red geraniums in the window box, nor the shiny brass knocker on the front door. Now, Lil rapped it sharply and they stood nervously on the front steps, awaiting an answer.

'We're here to see Mr McDermott,' said Lil, her words falling over each other in her hurry when the maid finally answered.

'I'm afraid he's away at present.'

The girls exchanged glances. 'When he is expected back?' asked Sophie.

'Not for two weeks, miss.'

Sophie's heart fell. McDermott wasn't here – he wouldn't be home for a whole fortnight. They wouldn't be able to tell him what they knew.

'Where is he staying?' Lil was asking. 'Is there an address

where we could reach him? It's important that we speak to him at once.'

'He's away on the Continent, on business,' said the maid importantly. 'But he did leave an address where he might be reached – just a moment, if you please.'

She came back with a sheet of paper. On it was written a *poste restante* address for a post office in Paris. Sophie took it, her heart sinking right down to her boots.

Lil thanked the housemaid politely, and they walked away down the street again, not knowing what else to do.

'This address is no good to us at all,' said Sophie, frustrated. 'If he's simply collecting his letters from a post office, it could be days and days before they reach him.'

'We should write anyway,' said Lil hopefully. 'He might receive it sooner than we think.'

Sophie nodded. 'But what should we do until then?' she wondered.

The question tormented Sophie all that night. She tossed and turned in her narrow bed in the lodging house, wrestling with her thoughts. Lord Beaucastle was the Baron. The respectable aristocrat who had given Veronica the jewelled moth was none other than London's most notorious criminal.

Whenever she closed her eyes, she fell into a strange half-dream, half-memory of when she had first crossed paths with the Baron. She was back in the stuffy darkness of the box at the Fortune Theatre, trapped behind the velvet curtains. Then she was waking up, locked in the Baron's study, lined with eerie ticking clocks; then scrambling through the shadowy cellars of an empty house, desperately trying to find a way out, alone and afraid in the dark.

Again and again, she saw the Baron's face before her, smiling his mocking smile. It was an expression that seemed to hint that he could read her thoughts, that he would always know her better than she would know herself. She saw him so clearly: the smart gentleman in the silk top-hat at the theatre, his face cast half into shadow. The man at the grand opening party for Sinclair's department store: glimpsed for a second amongst the blur of the crowd. Then standing on the steps of Miss Whiteley's town house that afternoon: that infinitesimal moment when their eyes had met. The thought of that exchange of glances made her feel cold as ice, even in the warm summer night.

Had he recognised her? His glance had been casual enough, and McDermott had said he had forgotten her – but somehow she felt certain that the Baron was not the sort of man who would easily forget anyone. After all, she had thwarted him. She and the others had prevented him delivering secret naval documents into enemy hands; they had stopped him destroying Sinclair's department store; they had restored the clockwork sparrow to its rightful owner. She thought of some of Joe's stories of how the Baron's Boys had taken revenge upon the Baron's enemies. If he had even an inkling that she knew his identity – his most closely guarded secret – she could not imagine what he might do.

And then her thoughts led her back to the jewelled moth and to Emily Montague. There had to be some connection, she thought. The Baron had given Veronica the jewelled moth – Emily had stolen it from Veronica – and Emily had ended up dead with the moth in her pocket. Had Emily been murdered – and could the Baron have been responsible? The questions went round and round in her head.

She knew that she must act on what she had discovered, but how? She had written a brief letter to Mr McDermott and managed to catch the evening post, but she knew they could not rely on his help immediately. They would have to act alone – and quickly. Plans rushed through her mind all through the long night, until at last a pink dawn broke over the rooftops.

At Sinclair's that day, she could not think clearly. She felt as though she were walking a tightrope and an unexpected movement might send her plummeting. She could barely concentrate on serving the customers, and made so many mistakes in the sales ledger that Edith began to sneer at her in her old way. As the day drew on, she became more and more weary, but there was no respite, and by closing time Mrs Milton was worried enough to express concern.

'You look pale, dear. You aren't your usual self. I do hope you aren't sickening for something,' she said, as the other girls prepared to head for home.

Sophie murmured something about not having slept well.

'Goodness, I do hope you're not worrying over that poor young lady,' said Mrs Milton sympathetically. 'Heaven knows, it's given me a nightmare or two since the weekend. So dreadful for you girls to see. What a thing to happen when Mr Betteredge had planned such a lovely day out for us all!'

But Mrs Milton found that she was speaking to empty air. Sophie had gone.

Finding a place to talk in private at Sinclair's was always difficult, but Joe had discovered an empty hayloft above the stable buildings, which made a perfect place to meet in secret. The four of them were sitting in a circle, perched on bales of hay, talking in low anxious voices.

'Are you certain – absolutely *certain*, that it was him?' Billy was saying.

'Of course I am,' said Sophie. 'There's no doubt about it – Lord Beaucastle is the Baron. I'd know him anywhere. He's the man I saw in the box at the theatre, with Fitz and

Cooper. He's the man I saw at the party at Sinclair's.'

'Do you realise what this means?' asked Lil, sounding rather awed. 'We've discovered his true identity – who the Baron really is!' She turned to Sophie. 'Don't you remember how Mr McDermott told us that they believed that the Baron had another identity in polite circles? Even Scotland Yard haven't managed to discover it – and now *you* have!'

'But I don't get it,' said Joe, looking troubled. 'If the Baron is really this toff, then how come no one has ever put two and two together? From what you say, Lord Beaucastle is top brass – the sort of fellow people know about. So how has he managed to keep his secret all this time?'

'That's what makes it so clever,' said Sophie. 'On the one hand, he's an immensely respectable aristocratic gentleman. He has a title, a grand house, important society friends. On the other hand, there's the Baron – a mysterious East End criminal whom hardly anyone has ever seen. There's no connection between the two. The people of the East End wouldn't have anything to do with society people. And the aristocrats in Lord Beaucastle's world, well they've probably never even *heard* of the Baron. Why would they? He has taken advantage of operating in completely separate worlds.'

'But what should we do now?' asked Billy, who had been running his hands through his hair anxiously until it was all standing on end. His important office-boy persona had vanished. Sophie knew that he too remembered just how alarming their previous brush with the Baron's Boys had been.

'I don't know. But we have to do something,' said Sophie. Her stomach twisted. 'We can't be sure whether he recognised me, and whether he realised that we know who he really is. But I don't want to risk waiting to find out.'

'Ought we to go to the police, then?' asked Lil earnestly.

Sophie looked uncertain. Their last encounter with the police had not been an encouraging one. The policeman responsible for finding Mr Sinclair's stolen jewels turned out to have been in the pay of the Baron himself, and to have aided him in his crimes. According to what both Joe and Mr McDermott had told them, this was not at all unusual. It was for this reason that simply walking into a police station to tell them what they had discovered was out of the question. They had no way of knowing who could be trusted. 'I wish we knew who Mr McDermott had been working with at Scotland Yard, so we could get in contact with them,' she said at last.

'Maybe we could find out,' said Joe, hopefully. He'd never set much store by the police, but he liked McDermott. Anyone McDermott trusted would be a good egg, he felt sure.

'And do you really think that the Baron had something to do with what happened to Emily Montague?' asked Billy, his face growing even more anxious.

Sophie shook her head, unsure. 'It just all seems like such an extraordinary coincidence.'

'It certainly wouldn't be the first time the Baron's Boys had got rid of a body that way,' added Joe, darkly.

'What I don't understand is where Veronica Whiteley comes into all this,' said Lil. 'It seems fearfully unlikely that the Baron would be courting a debutante. Do you think he really is planning to marry her?'

Sophie gazed at her for a long moment. In all her anxiety about the Baron, and Emily Montague and the jewelled moth, she had forgotten all about Veronica.

'Oh my goodness – *Veronica!*' she exclaimed. 'We can't possibly let her go ahead and marry the Baron. We must let her know the truth!'

'The girls at the tea party told me that they were all expecting him to propose to her at her debutante ball,' said Lil. 'That's taking place later this week, isn't it? That's why she was in such a terrific hurry to get the brooch back.'

'We'd better go and tell her at once,' said Sophie. She got to her feet. Lil jumped up too.

'Half a jiffy,' said Joe. 'We're coming with you.'

'To see Miss Whiteley? *Are* we?' asked Billy, looking rather taken aback at this announcement.

'Look, the way I see it is this,' said Joe patiently. 'We don't know if the Baron recognised you outside Miss Whiteley's place or not. But if he got even the slightest whiff that you were on to him, then you're in danger – both of you. And what's the first place he's going to expect you to go? Right back to Miss Whiteley of course – to tell her what you know.'

'You think he'll be waiting for us?' said Sophie.

Joe shook his head. 'Not him. He doesn't stick his neck out. But his Boys, maybe. There's no way you're going back there on your own.'

'We don't need looking after,' said Lil, a little haughtily. 'We can take care of ourselves.'

Joe laughed, breaking the tension. 'There's no doubt about that. But there's safety in numbers, I reckon.'

'Right,' agreed Billy loudly, as though he was attempting to sound more certain than he felt.

'Let's all go then, but let's hurry,' said Sophie impatiently. A minute later, all four were hastening down the hayloft ladder.

CHAPTER FOURTEEN

'This is starting to feel like a habit,' said Lil, as she once more rang the bell to Miss Whiteley's town house. For most of the walk to Belgrave Square, Joe had been casting glances all around them, as though he expected the Baron's Boys to pop out from behind a tree or a postbox at any moment.

'Is Miss Whiteley at home?' asked Sophie, as soon as the maid answered.

'She's dressing for dinner, miss,' said the maid, and made as if to close the door again.

'Well look here, do you mind asking if she will see us?' demanded Lil, stepping forwards before she could.

'The ladies don't receive visitors at this hour of the evening, miss,' said the maid, frowning. 'If you'd like to leave a calling card, you may do so.'

'You don't understand,' said Lil firmly. 'It's very important that we see her now. Tell her it's Miss Taylor and Miss Rose – and that it's urgent.'

The maid frowned, but to their relief, she nodded and went back inside, leaving the four of them still standing in an awkward clump on the steps. They were waiting there in silence for some time, but at last, the maid returned, looking flustered. She showed them through into the little sitting room, casting disapproving glances at Billy's untidy hair and hay-strewn trousers, and at Joe, who brought with him a distinct aroma of the stables.

The room was empty. Sophie and Lil sat down on the same low sofa they had occupied last time, whilst Billy perched himself on a spindly gilt chair. Apparently not quite daring to sit down in such a grand place, Joe began pacing about behind the sofa, swinging his arms restlessly, until he knocked over a fringed lamp that stood on a side table.

Lil was helping him right it again when Veronica swept in. It was obvious that she had indeed been dressing for the evening: she was wearing a stiff, rustling gown, but her hair was still hanging down her back. She looked very annoyed.

'Whatever do you want?' she began. 'I told you, you can't just turn up here. Why, these aren't even calling hours! You're just lucky that Sarah had the good sense to come straight to me rather than Isabel.'

'We need to speak to you,' began Sophie, unsure of how she was going to continue.

Veronica ignored her. 'Don't think I'm not grateful that

you got the moth back for me. And for telling me about what happened to Emily. But our . . . *business arrangement* is finished now. There's nothing else I need to speak to you about. And who are *these people?*' she demanded suddenly, taking in Billy and Joe.

The two boys gaped at her, unsure how to react to being referred to in such a manner by this imperious china doll. Lil, however, had no such hesitation.

'These are our friends,' she said indignantly. 'This is Joe and that's Billy. We've come here to help you!'

Veronica made a little sound of exasperation that made it quite clear that she didn't care in the least who they were. Sophie plunged on hurriedly.

'Please listen to us,' she said. 'We've got something enormously important to tell you.'

'Well for heaven's sake, hurry up then and *say it*,' said Veronica. 'At this rate I won't be half dressed before the carriage is ready.'

'It's about Lord Beaucastle,' Sophie went on swiftly. 'We saw him arriving yesterday. I recognised him. Miss Whiteley . . . Lord Beaucastle is the Baron.'

'The baron? Of *course* he's a baron. That's his title. Please don't say you came all the way here to tell me that!'

'Not *a* baron, *the* Baron,' said Lil crossly. 'He's a criminal! He and his gang, the Baron's Boys, are behind most of the crime in London. He was responsible for the theft of Mr Sinclair's jewels!'

Veronica gave a brusque laugh. 'That is nonsense!' she said.

'It isn't,' said Sophie. 'You have to listen to us. The Baron is a thief, and a murderer, and a spy. He had me drugged and kidnapped – and he tried to kill us all. He's always kept his identity carefully hidden, but I've seen him, and I'll never forget his face. When I saw him again yesterday, I realised who he was. *Lord Beaucastle is the Baron.*'

'I don't believe you,' said Veronica shortly.

'What's more,' Sophie plunged onwards, 'we suspect he might have had something to do with Emily Montague's death. He could be the one who had her murdered!'

Veronica was scarlet with anger. 'That's enough!' she spat out. 'How dare you insinuate that Lord Beaucastle could have had anything do with what happened to Emily! As if that wasn't awful enough without you coming here with your . . . your *horrid accusations*. Why, he's a very respectable man! He couldn't possibly have anything to do with any *criminals.*'

'Listen, whether you believe us or not, you mustn't marry him,' went on Sophie urgently. 'You have to do what you can to get out of the engagement – before it's too late.'

Veronica looked angrier than ever. 'I can't *get out of it,*' she spat out. 'That's not how it works. Don't you understand anything? Even if your ridiculous story were true, I couldn't just say: "I'm sorry, I won't marry you" to a man like him! Anyway, it's too late now,' she continued, her voice suddenly flat. 'Lord Beaucastle had an interview with Father yesterday when he came to tea. It's all been decided. Our betrothal is going to be announced at my debutante ball.'

Lil was gazing at her in horror. 'You mean, you don't even get to say yes for yourself? How perfectly beastly.' She looked suddenly as though she felt very sorry for Veronica, but the other girl only scowled back.

'You don't know the first thing about it,' she said in a low, furious voice. 'Look, I don't know what you think you're playing at. Maybe you think this is funny. Maybe you're trying to get more money out of me. But I'm not interested in games or silly tales or horrid attempts to slander Lord Beaucastle. You need to leave now, before Isabel comes down. And *don't come back again.*'

'Well, that's the second time this week I've had that door slammed in my face,' said Lil as the four of them made their way down the steps. 'I'm beginning to think that Veronica doesn't like me very much.'

Feeling that it would probably be best not to linger near Miss Whiteley's house, they crossed the road, and went through a gate into the pretty garden in the centre of the square, where they would be out of sight.

'Talk about ungrateful,' said Billy, disgustedly, flopping down on to a bench.

'We should have guessed she would never believe us,' said Sophie. 'Why would she?'

'It's like you said before,' said Lil. 'She's never even heard of the Baron. It doesn't mean anything to her.'

'So what do we do now?' asked Billy.

'*Hush up!*' said Joe suddenly. He had frozen still, his hand on Lil's arm.

'What's the matter?'

Joe's voice was low and hoarse. 'There's someone watching us,' he whispered.

CHAPTER FIFTEEN

She struggled as hard as she could, but the arms holding her were far too strong. Panic overwhelmed her as she was dragged out of her safe hiding place and into the sunlight.

'I say, do be gentle,' said a loud, clear voice. 'You're hurting her. Why, she's only a little girl!'

The grip slackened. Looking up, blinking in the light, Mei saw that she was standing in the middle of the square garden in front of two girls and a boy. The boy had untidy fair hair and looked about her own age, whilst the older of the two girls, who was tall and pretty and wore a straw hat with a pink ribbon round it, was probably the same age as Song. They were all gazing at her as though she was the strangest thing they had ever seen. She stuck out her chin and tried to stand straight, to seem bold and undaunted, just as Song had taught her.

'She's a little girl from China!' exclaimed the boy, in a surprised voice. 'Whatever is she doing here, hiding in the bushes?'

He spoke as if she wouldn't be able to understand a word he was saying, and all of a sudden, Mei stopped being frightened, and instead felt extremely annoyed. 'I'm not from China!' she burst out, crossly. 'I'm from *Limehouse*. And I'm *not* a little girl!'

To her surprise, she heard a laugh from her captor. Suspicious and indignant, she turned her head, and saw that the person holding her was a tall young fellow with curly hair. 'Never mind China. She's a cockney, from the East End, same as me,' he said. Unlike the others, he spoke like the people in Limehouse, though his voice was somewhat softer. 'You're China Town, ain't you?' he added, looking at Mei.

'Might be,' said Mei, defiantly. She didn't want to give anything away to these strangers, especially when the fellow was still holding on to her.

'From the *East End*?' exclaimed the other boy. There was some extra special meaning in his words that Mei didn't understand, and a look of alarm on his face. 'What are you doing?' he went on, in a quick, urgent voice. 'Were you sent here to spy on us?'

Mei frowned in confusion, but before she could say

157

anything else, the fellow who was holding her said in his low voice, 'Are you working for *him*?'

'For who?' asked Mei, even more perplexed now, and her fright renewed by the way they were all looking at her, watchful, like a circle of cats about to pounce.

'You know who. The top man. The *Baron*.'

Mei started in surprise. '*No!*' she exclaimed at once, without thinking. '*No!* I hate him!' But even as the words were out of her mouth, she realised what she had said, and she felt another rush of fear. They were all looking at each other again, a silent flash of communication passing between them.

'What do you know about the Baron?' demanded the other boy.

'I'm not daft!' she burst out. 'Everyone knows about the Baron. Leave off. I'm not doing any harm. I'm just minding my own business. *Let me go*,' she almost sobbed.

The dark-haired girl frowned. 'Joe, do let go of her. You're frightening her.' She turned to Mei. 'Listen, I'm sorry we grabbed you, but you must see that it's jolly strange to be skulking around in the shrubbery like this. All we want to know is what you're doing here; to be sure you aren't up to no good.

So why don't you just tell us – and then we'll let you go.'

Mei gulped in a breath, tried to calm herself. 'I just wanted to see the young lady.'

'The young lady?'

'Miss Veronica Whiteley.'

'You wanted to see *Veronica?*' repeated the girl, looking baffled. 'But why?'

'Because of the diamond,' said Mei, reluctantly. 'The Moonbeam Diamond.'

There was silence. The girl stared at her, agape. '*What* did you say?'

The other girl, the one with the fair hair, was looking at her sharply. 'Do you know something about the jewelled moth?' she asked.

Mei shook her head, confused by their reactions. 'I don't know anything about the moth brooch thing – it's the diamond that's in it. It's called the Moonbeam Diamond. I saw that Miss Whiteley – she's the girl that owns the brooch – lives here. It was in the society column, look.'

She held out a piece of newspaper in a trembling hand. The fair-haired girl took it and frowned as she looked over it:

Miss Emily Montague, one of this season's debutantes, was tragically drowned on Saturday, after an accident while she was walking beside the river. The family have announced that the funeral service shall be held next week at St George's Church.

Miss Kitty Shaw has chosen Tuesday next for her wedding to Mr Frederick Whitman. Miss Shaw will have two bridesmaids dressed in periwinkle blue, with wreaths of blue flowers; little Master Alan Shaw, aged seven, is to carry the bride's train.

Mrs Isabel Whiteley and Miss Veronica Whiteley hosted a tea party earlier this week at their elegant home on Belgrave Square. Amongst the ladies in attendance was Mrs Constance Balfour, who on the same day held a most delightful dinner, followed by a dance, at the Ritz Hotel, to celebrate the coming of age of her eldest son.

Messrs Lloyd and Mountville will inaugurate their tenure of the Grosvenor Theatre by presenting in September a play in three acts entitled 'The Inheritance', starring Mr Felix Freemantle

'I thought if I waited, I might catch sight of her and see which house she lives at,' Mei explained. 'If I knew that, I could talk to her, or write to her to explain. Tell her the truth about the diamond.'

'What do you mean by the truth?' asked the fair girl.

The young fellow who had been holding her had been casting anxious glances around them. Now, he swore quietly under his breath. Following his gaze, Mei saw that he was looking between the trees, through on to the street, where a couple of men dressed in chauffeurs' uniforms were standing, apparently quite aimlessly, smoking cigarettes.

'We should get out of here,' he said in an urgent voice.

The others followed his gaze. The younger boy's eyes widened.

'The Baron's Boys?' asked the dark girl, but it wasn't really a question. Mei's heart thumped faster.

The fair girl looked at Mei. 'You need to tell us more,' she said. 'We can help you – we can even take a message to Miss Whiteley if you like – but you have to tell us what you mean about telling her the truth. Will you come with us, somewhere we can talk safely?'

Mei glanced at the men on the street corner. They didn't look anything like the Baron's Boys as she had seen them on the streets of the East End – they were much too smart for that. But if they really were working for the Baron, the further away from them she was, the better.

She nodded.

'This way,' said the young fellow, and led them beneath the trees, across the garden, in the opposite direction to the two men. There was a gate on the other side. They slipped through it and out into the street, casting quick glances behind them. He'd taken hold of Mei's arm again, but his grip was gentler now. He led them swiftly into a patch of shadow, around a corner, and away.

Hyde Park felt wonderfully safe and ordinary to Joe. They walked across the grass until they found a spot where they could sit in the dappled shade of a tree, not far from where a group of children in sailor suits and straw boaters were playing with hoops, their nanny looking on indulgently.

The girl from the East End sat down amongst them, looking small and rather frightened. She was wearing a faded striped cotton frock and a pinafore, and her black hair hung in a long plait down her back. She looked shabby compared to the children that were playing just a few yards away from them, but Joe knew that she wasn't, not really. Why, some of the folks in the East End had not much more to wear than rags; this girl had clean clothes and a clean face, and her boots, though well-patched, looked decent enough. This was no street urchin. She might not be well off, but she was certainly well cared for.

Lil smiled at her. 'I'm Lil,' she explained. 'This is Sophie and that's Billy, and that's Joe.'

'My name's Mei,' said the girl in a small voice.

'Will you tell us what you know about the diamond?' asked Sophie earnestly.

Nodding, the girl began to tell her story. She told it rather timidly at first, her voice halting, but as she went on, she seemed to become more and more self-assured, until she was speaking fluently and confidently. The others sat quite still and listened, almost as if her voice was casting a spell over them. It was a queer old story she was telling, Joe thought – the tale of an old temple and a magic diamond and a moon goddess, which somehow seemed tangled up with Miss Veronica Whiteley and the jewelled moth.

'It all fits together,' said Sophie, when Mei brought her story to a close, having related how she had seen the Moonbeam Diamond in the newspaper and ventured across London to find Miss Whiteley. 'Remember?' Sophie went on, turning to Lil. 'Veronica mentioned that Lord Beaucastle had told her the story of how he came by the diamond. She said that it came from China and he saved it from an uprising at a monastery.'

'But it wasn't an uprising!' said Mei, fervently. 'Waiguo Ren started it himself. He betrayed the monks and attacked them, and stole all their treasures.'

'So that means that Waiguo Ren – the man who stole your diamond – must be Lord Beaucastle,' said Lil slowly, working it out. 'And Lord Beaucastle is also the Baron.'

Mei's face turned white. 'The Baron?' she whispered. 'I don't understand.'

Joe thought he knew how she felt. 'Don't worry,' he reassured her gruffly. 'You're safe with us here.'

Sophie tried to explain: 'We believe we've found the Baron's true identity – the identity he tries so hard to keep hidden. We've discovered that the Baron is really a wealthy society gentleman named Lord Beaucastle. By the sounds of it, he's the same man that you call Waiguo Ren – the Englishman who stole the Moonbeam Diamond.'

'So you mean that the *Baron* took the diamond?' said Mei, her face creased with concentration. 'Well, I s'pose that makes sense . . .' she said after a long pause. 'He's taken everything else.'

'What do you mean?' asked Billy, who had been busily scribbling in his notebook as Mei talked.

It had been Billy who asked the question, but it was Joe that Mei looked at as she answered. 'He's in China Town now,' she said sadly. 'He sent his Boys in, demanded everyone paid up. If you don't . . . well, my Dad didn't, not at first. Mum said we should stand up to them. But they came and . . .'

'They roughed him up – your old man?' asked Joe sympathetically.

Mei was blinking back tears. 'Yes, and they ruined our shop. Then they asked for even more money. Mum and Dad can hardly pay what they're asking, but it's much worse for the others. Mrs Wu – she runs the Magic Lantern Show – she couldn't scrape together what they wanted, so they broke her son's arm. They're taking over. They've got hold of the Star Inn, and they're running all sorts of rackets there, gambling and opium and . . .' her voice faded away.

'That's how he works,' said Joe, shaking his head. 'The Baron's like a leech. When he gets hold of you, he just about bleeds you dry. He'll move in somewhere and suck every penny out of a place, no matter what the consequences for the folks who live there. Anyone who stands up to him – well, you can guess.'

'But that's simply terrible!' exclaimed Lil. 'How can he get away with it? Why doesn't someone stop him?'

'No one cares,' said Joe, shrugging. 'You know, I was surprised at first that the Baron's some big toff, but I reckon it makes sense. You've got the grand folk out here, with their great big houses and money and fancy clothes and motors and anything else you like. Half of that's being paid for by the poor folk, isn't it? I mean, these people probably own factories where the workers aren't paid enough to feed their families. But folks are greedy. So long as they've got what they want, why should they care about anyone else?'

There was silence for a moment. Then Lil smiled at Mei. 'It was jolly brave of you to come all this way on your own,' she said. 'However did you persuade your parents to let you?'

Mei blushed: 'They don't exactly know I'm here,' she said.

Billy added a final vigorous scribble to the pages of his notebook. They were now a complex web of scribbled phrases and arrows and words like *BARON* and *BEAUCASTLE* and *MOONBEAM DIAMOND,* heavily underlined. 'What should we do now?' he asked, tucking his notebook and pencil back into his pocket.

Sophie looked at Mei. 'We'll make sure Miss Whiteley learns the truth about the diamond,' she said. 'Don't worry about that. But you should get home now. It's getting late, and your family will be worried.'

Mei nodded and got to her feet, but Lil stopped her. 'You can't go back alone,' she said. 'It's simply miles to the East End.'

'I can find my own way back,' insisted Mei, stoutly.

Sophie shook her head. 'Lil's right. We'll see you home safely.'

'Let's get a cab,' suggested Lil. 'That way we'll have chance to talk more on the way.'

A cab was an unusual luxury, but Sophie nodded at once. They had the ten pounds from Miss Whiteley, after all – and after their close encounter with the Baron's Boys on Belgrave Square, a cab would be safer than travelling on foot.

Billy was frowning. 'D'you think it's such a good idea for us to go to the East End?' he asked uncertainly. 'I mean – that's where the Baron's Boys *come from.*'

Billy looked at Joe as he spoke, but before he had the chance to reply, Lil spoke up again: 'We can't possibly let Mei go so far alone,' she said indignantly. 'Come on – we can get a cab at Hyde Park Corner.'

At first the cabman did not seem at all pleased at the prospect of taking five not particularly smart-looking young people all the way to Limehouse, but when Lil showed him five shillings, he suddenly became a great deal more accommodating, and they squeezed themselves inside.

No one said much as they rattled along Piccadilly and through Covent Garden. Billy found himself thinking about what Joe had said – was it really true that most people didn't care what happened to everyone else, as long as they had everything they wanted? Meanwhile, Sophie's mind was whirring. The legend of the Moonbeam Diamond was important, she thought to herself. It was another clue to the puzzle that was the Baron. She knew he was a collector, drawn to beautiful objects, and she knew too that he rarely did his dirty work himself, preferring to let others – in this case, the Emperor's men – take care of any unpleasant business. He had been in the army, and there was a military precision to everything he did, but there was something else too – a certain theatrical flair. The staging of the burglary at Sinclair's department store; the infernal machine in the clock rigged to explode at midnight; scheming to deceive the monks and betray them, taking their riches . . . She tried to imagine the Baron as a young man in China, masquerading as the brave hero of Empire, like one of the captains in Billy's story-papers. He had seized the diamond and transformed it from something sacred into a mere bauble, a trinket to be given away to a debutante and worn at a coming-out ball.

She was so busy thinking about it all that she hardly noticed them passing St Paul's, nor that in the corner, Joe was beginning to look restless. As they crossed the City, he became more nervous still.

'I – I can't,' he said suddenly.

The cab had stopped at a busy junction and without saying anything to the driver, Joe opened the door. 'I'm sorry,' he said over his shoulder. 'Be careful,' he warned, and then he jumped down into the street, where he was lost at once amongst the crowds.

CHAPTER SIXTEEN

The cab rattled on towards Limehouse.

'Oh dear,' said Lil, gazing out of the window in the direction that Joe had taken.

'Where did he go?' asked Mei, confused.

'He didn't want to go back to the East End,' explained Billy, soberly.

'I hope he's all right,' said Lil. 'I hadn't really thought about what it would mean to him to go back,' she added, guiltily.

'He told me once that he could never show his face there again,' said Billy. 'Once you leave the Baron's Boys, you're a marked man.'

'Did he really used to be one of the Baron's Boys?' asked Mei. She looked rather alarmed by this revelation.

'Yes, he was once, but he isn't any longer,' explained Lil. 'He wants to stop the Baron now – the same as the rest of us.'

By now they had left the City behind them and were

making their way through a labyrinth of narrow cobbled streets. To Sophie, the streets looked darker here, almost as if night was falling early. The buildings were crowded densely together on either side of the street – small, shabby houses, jostling up against shops and workshops.

'Where are we now?' she asked.

'Shadwell,' said Mei. 'It's poor round here. This is the Baron's territory, all this.'

Sophie stared out of the window. Here and there were a few signs of life: a ragged group of children, some without shoes, watching them pass by; a stray dog, nosing through rubbish. It was a gloomy place, and Sophie found her thoughts straying to fragments of stories she had heard about the horrors that happened in the East End – murders and mutilations.

They passed a queue of people, snaking all the way along a side street.

'What are they doing?' asked Lil, curiously.

'Queuing for their dinner,' Mei explained. She went on, rather shyly: 'If you've got kids and you can't afford anything to eat, the Board of Guardians'll give you tokens to get a bit of bread and milk. If we were coming along here later, we'd see all the old fellows queuing up for a bed in the Spike – I mean, the workhouse . . .'

Her voice drifted off. The others said nothing, but

silently gazed at the decaying buildings plastered with tattered advertisements; at a public house where two men were arguing over a bottle; at a woman crouched on a doorstep, feeding a baby. A rat skittered past her bare feet down a passageway and Sophie looked away, shocked. For some reason, she found herself thinking of Sinclair's: the tantalising glitter of the chandeliers; the hems of the ladies' dresses sweeping up the thickly carpeted stairway; the soft tinkling of the grand piano. It was hard to believe they were still in the same city. These dank streets felt like another country – even another world.

'It's better in China Town,' said Mei, seeming to sense her thoughts. 'It's not like this there. Not yet, anyway,' she added.

They were getting close to the docks now: the air smelled more strongly of the river. After a few minutes, they emerged on a street where a small market had been set up. There were people selling bits of fruit and vegetables from barrows and little stalls.

'Can we get out here and walk the last bit?' asked Mei, tentatively. 'It's awful kind of you to get me home, but Mum'll have forty fits if I turn up in a cab.'

They stopped the driver and hopped down. 'Why?' asked Lil curiously, as she paid the fare.

Mei snorted, her surprise making her less timid. 'How

often d'you think folk like us travel by cab? She'd probably think I'd got in trouble and was being brought home by the police!'

Sophie was looking around her; it felt much more cheerful here. The whole place was abuzz, the stallholders calling out constantly: 'A penny a pound for your apples.' 'Lovely taters, miss, fine as you'll see anywhere.'

Mei led them through the market, looking as at home here as she had been out of place in the leafy Belgravia square. A small boy came running up to Lil, holding out his hands to beg for pennies, but Mei sent him briskly on his way. She led the way boldly along a narrow street of shops and eating places. It was clear that they had reached China Town now, although the street looked much the same, the signs above the doorways of the shops were written in Chinese characters. There were new smells here: unfamiliar spicy aromas, and a rich, warm, savoury fragrance drifting from the door of a little eating place. A wall opposite was pasted with yellowing pages from Chinese newspapers, and Billy showed signs of wanting to stop to look at them, but Mei was already hurrying them onwards towards the shop on the corner, which had the words *L. LIM & SONS* painted in elaborate letters over the doorway.

As they opened the low door and stepped inside, a bell jangled above their heads.

'Mei!' exclaimed a loud, angry voice. 'Where on earth do you think you've been?'

Joe walked through the City with his hands in his pockets and his head down. He was not whistling now. It had turned into another beautiful summer evening, and yet he took no pleasure in it. Guilt hung over him like a raincloud. He couldn't believe he had been such a coward. As they'd left Sinclair's, he had felt fearless, ready to watch out for Lil and Sophie. He had been the one who led them safely away from the Baron's Boys without being seen. But then, at the first hint of crossing back over into the East End, he'd funked it – slunk away like the coward he was. Why, that kid from China Town had more backbone than he did!

Back when he'd been one of the Baron's Boys, Jem, their leader, had jeered at him for not having enough bottle. 'Nervous as a little girl, ain't you?' he remembered him saying through his yellowed, broken teeth. 'Well you'd better get yourself some guts, petal. You got to have a bit of pluck to get by in this line of work.'

Pluck was exactly what he did not have. Perhaps Jem had been right. Joe shook his head as he walked, feeling more and more despondent. Whatever would Lil and the others think of him now? He didn't want to be the sort of fellow who dodged away at the first sign of trouble. He wanted to be brave and decent – like they were. The sort of fellow you could count on. He thought again of Lil's surprised face as he had bolted from the carriage and felt sick at heart. If only he could be the sort of fellow she would admire – not someone who would only disappoint her.

He had tried so hard to leave the Baron behind, but somehow, he crept in everywhere: it didn't matter whether you were in the dark heart of London's East End or the bright lights of the West End. Wherever Joe went, the Baron would be there too.

But if that was true, then there was no sense in trying to hide any longer, he thought suddenly. It was no good trying to stick his head in the sand. The only thing for it was to do something – to use their new and dangerous knowledge to stop the Baron for good. All at once, he felt fired with a new resolve and determination – but what on earth could they possibly do against a man like the Baron without Mr McDermott's help? He buried himself deep in thought as he walked back home to Sinclair's department store.

'We were worried sick! Your father was sure that the Baron's Boys had got you! We even had to fetch your brother from work to go looking for you!' Mum's eyes were flashing. 'I couldn't believe it when I saw Jessie Bates's mother down at the market,' she went on. 'You told me she was sick in bed and that Jessie needed your help – but she's as right as rain. How dare you tell such dreadful untruths!'

'Now Lou,' said Dad. 'Calm down. We've got visitors.'

Mum paused suddenly, taking in the three newcomers standing behind Mei in the shop doorway.

But as it happened, neither Sophie, Billy nor Lil had really taken in much of Mrs Lim's outburst. They were too busy looking around the shop.

It was certainly quite different from Sinclair's department store, Sophie thought. The walls were lined from floor to ceiling with shelves, upon which stood everything from glass jars of humbugs to tins of sardines and balls of string. The air smelled richly of spices and tobacco and cocoa. Strings of scarlet Chinese lanterns stretched across the ceiling, and a white cat slept on a tea chest. Baskets laden with more goods were set out neatly on the floor, and they had to skirt around them as they approached the counter where Mei's parents were standing, staring at them in surprise.

Mr Lim was a small man with a strong resemblance to his daughter. His wife, who had red hair and freckles, overtopped him by a couple of inches. She looked especially astonished to see the visitors, and was looking at them indignantly, her hands on her hips.

'We're sorry for intruding,' said Sophie hurriedly.

'We just wanted to make sure Mei got home safely. We should go.'

'No – don't!' exclaimed Mei at once, reaching out to grab Billy, who was nearest to her. He looked a little alarmed, and she continued more quietly. 'Please stay. I need you to explain everything – about the diamond, and about the Baron.'

'The Baron?' demanded Mei's father, his face ashy pale. 'What do you mean?'

'Let's go into the back room,' said Mei. 'We can close the shop, can't we – just for a few minutes? Where's Song?' She looked anxiously at her parents. 'There's a lot I have to tell you,' she said.

CHAPTER SEVENTEEN

As she took her seat at the table in Lord Beaucastle's immense, dimly lit dining room, Veronica realised that she was nervous. She told herself she was being ridiculous, there was nothing to be anxious about. She'd been here a dozen times before, and what was more, this was a special dinner, given in her honour. Perhaps she was feeling so strange because of what had happened to Emily, she thought. Her death had cast a long shadow over the London Season.

Lord Beaucastle's dining room certainly seemed different tonight: gloomy and full of shadows. She had scarcely noticed it before, but now she saw just how different his house was from her own home in Belgrave Square. Isabel favoured dainty, decorative things – frivolous embroidered cushions, enamelled clocks and china figurines. Beaucastle's home was older, graver. In spite of all its gloss and polish, it felt like it had not changed for a very long time. The wood-panelled walls were hung with dark oil paintings, the ceilings embellished with strange carvings. The long table was set with glimmering silverware, trails of ivy and dishes heaped with grapes and peaches, all bathed in pools of light from tall white candles in heavy candelabras. Beyond, in the shadows, a host of silent footmen were ranged, ready to hand out dishes and pour out wine. Lord Beaucastle's butler slipped in and out of the darkness, as he directed operations in a low, almost inaudible undertone. It was so strange to think this would soon be her home. She couldn't imagine ever feeling truly comfortable here.

Guests stretched away from her along the expanse of table: gentlemen conversing in hushed, serious voices; ladies murmuring secrets to each other behind their fans. Some way down the table, she thought she glimpsed the Countess of Alconborough's ostrich plumes; and there were others too that she recognised: politicians, financiers, aristocrats. Surely that slim, elegant figure on the right was Sebastian Ambermere, the young Duke of Roehampton? And there on the left, in a cloud of tulle and rosebuds, was Lady Hamilton, whose portrait she had seen at the Royal Academy only a few days ago? There was no doubt about it: this was an august gathering. Lord Beaucastle regularly played host to some of the most eminent figures of the *beau monde*; and now here she was, sitting amongst them at his right hand, trying to look as if she belonged.

And then there was Beaucastle himself. He was the centre of it all, cordially speaking to first one guest then another, instructing the butler to bring more wine. Watching him, Veronica could not help thinking all over again of the unexpected visit from Miss Taylor and Miss Rose and their friends. Perhaps it was their visit, most of all, which had left her feeling unsettled. She thought again of all they had said about Lord Beaucastle – such nonsense about crime lords and spies and gangs! The very idea was insulting, she thought crossly. Why, she knew that he had been one of the first gentlemen to pay a call of condolence upon Mrs Montague, when the news about Emily came out.

She glanced under her eyelashes at him. He was so well-respected; a man who told anecdotes about shooting parties with His Majesty the King and lunches with the Prime Minister, who made amiable conversation with her father and who charmed Isabel. He was always kind and solicitous to Veronica herself, too, making sure her wine glass was full and that the soup was to her liking. He was so refined, she thought. He was the last person in the world to have a secret identity – especially not as some sort of East End criminal.

And yet, it was not as if she really *knew* him. The thought popped suddenly into her head, quite uninvited. She did not really know any of these people, she supposed, but now she was to be married to Lord Beaucastle, and all at once she felt sure that she knew him least of all.

The footmen began to serve the *hors d'oeuvres*, and as they did so, a young man came hurrying in to the dining room. He was tall with rumpled black hair and brown skin, and though he was elegantly dressed, his fingers were all over ink stains.

'You're late, Henry,' said Beaucastle, a rare note of disapproval creeping into his voice.

'I – I do apologise – I was rather preoccupied – lost track of time . . .'

Beaucastle looked along the table, but the only empty seat was on Veronica's other side. He introduced her to the newcomer genially. 'Miss Whiteley, may I present Henry Snow? He's a *protégé* of mine – a very talented young scientist – who is staying with me at present.'

Henry Snow gave her the most cursory of nods. As soon as he had taken his seat, he leaned across her to address Lord Beaucastle in a confidential tone. 'There have been some extraordinary developments that I'm most eager to share with you. The samples from South Ridge are exceptional, far better than the ones from Bethany.'

Veronica stiffened. South Ridge and Bethany were the names of two of her father's mines. Why on earth was this strange man talking about her father's mines?

'The structure of the mineral is such that –' he went on.

'My dear fellow, this is hardly the time or the place,' Beaucastle interrupted hastily. His voice was light, but Veronica had the sudden impression that he was watching her sharply. She tried her hardest to look innocent, as though she was absorbed only in eating. But she kept listening with all her might.

Henry Snow had followed Beaucastle's gaze. There was a pause, and she saw from the corner of her eye that he was shrugging, as if to indicate that Veronica was quite obviously not listening, and in any case would be quite incapable of understanding him. 'We must get access soon. I won't be able to continue without more materials,' he went on.

'I've already told you, that won't be a problem,' said Beaucastle shortly, sounding quite unlike himself for a moment before his usual affable manner returned as he added, 'We'll discuss it after dinner.'

Veronica couldn't help looking up at Beaucastle curiously. He caught her eye at once and she hurriedly smiled at him and manufactured an excuse. 'I was just admiring that pin you wear, sir,' she said, her voice coming out a little higher than usual. 'Does it have any special significance?'

Beaucastle glanced down at the little gold dragon that he wore pinned to his lapel. 'This one, my dear?' he said in his most indulgent, avuncular tone. 'Why it's the emblem of my club, Wyvern House. It's an old English gentleman's club. Wyvern is an ancient word for dragon.' He glanced across the table at Mr Whiteley and added in a rather louder voice, 'As a matter of fact, we're going to be considering new members soon, and I wondered if your father would object if I put his name forward.'

'My dear Beaucastle! Wyvern House! What an honour – what a tremendous honour indeed,' burbled Veronica's father.

'Very well,' said Beaucastle, looking pleased. 'It's settled. I shall put down your name for membership at Michaelmas.'

Everyone was quite delighted by this display of generosity. Along the table, Isabel was beaming. Even Veronica had heard of Wyvern House. It boasted a very selective, highly aristocratic membership, and was not the sort of place where a man like her father – however rich – would usually be admitted.

The evening drew on. More wine was served. *Hors d'oeuvres* were followed by fish, fillet of beef, and then by sorbet, and then by a dish for which Beaucastle's chef was apparently famous: roasted quails stuffed with pâté de foie gras. Then there was salad, and cheese, but before the dessert course, Lord Beaucastle tapped his silver fork against his glass just once, and the room fell silent.

'Ladies and gentlemen,' he said, lifting his glass. 'Thank you for joining me tonight. I wish to make a toast to the charming Miss Veronica Whiteley, who is making her debut this season. I have no doubt that she will shine just as brightly as the jewel I have given her to mark her coming out – the exquisite Moonbeam Diamond, which she wears so beautifully tonight. So I present to you now Miss Veronica Whiteley – London's brightest new star!'

He smiled at her: it was a warm, benevolent smile, but suddenly, she saw something wolfish in it that she had never seen there before. Only days earlier, she would have adored the chance to be singled out for such special attention; now, she felt uncomfortable and confused. She tried to smile back, hiding her unease. All down the table, as if drawn by invisible strings, hands raised their glasses, the ladies' bracelets gleaming in the light of the candle flames. 'To Miss Whiteley!'

CHAPTER EIGHTEEN

'The Moonbeam Diamond is here – in London? Why didn't you say something?' Dad asked Mei gently.

'I tried,' Mei faltered. 'I didn't want to bother you. I – I told Song, but he thought I was being silly.'

Across the kitchen table, Song shook his head. 'I'm sorry,' he said. 'I had no idea . . .' He looked genuinely ashamed, and Mei couldn't help gawping in surprise – Song never admitted he was wrong about anything.

'And the diamond really belongs to the Baron?' asked Dad, his voice sounding incredulous.

'Not any more,' explained Sophie, in her clear voice. 'It did belong to him, but he recently had it made into a brooch to give as a gift to the young lady he plans to marry – Miss Whiteley. She doesn't know him as the Baron of course, but by his real name – Lord Beaucastle.'

'Lord Beaucastle . . .' repeated Dad thoughtfully. 'I could swear that name sounds familiar. Lou, does it mean anything to you?'

Mum shook her head. Then suddenly she snapped her fingers. 'Yes – yes it does!' she exclaimed in an excited voice. 'Wait a minute.'

She bustled out of the room, but was back only a moment later, carrying a small wooden trunk, bound in brass.

'Granddad's trunk!' Mei exclaimed, recognising it at once.

Mum set the trunk down in the middle of the table, and opened it. Mei saw that it was crammed with papers: letters, envelopes and what looked like several old exercise books. Mum fished out a small black book, carefully tied with string.

'This is it,' she said. She turned to Dad. 'Remember? We didn't know what this was when we first went through Granddad's things – but now . . . look . . .'

She handed the notebook to Sophie, who untied the knots with careful fingers. Beside her, Mei felt breathless with anticipation, whilst Lil on her other side was twitching, evidently trying to repress the urge to grab the book and rip it open.

Sophie set the notebook on the table, and they all bent their heads over it. The pages were filled with a hotch-potch of yellowing newspaper cuttings, and photographs. They were surrounded by a latticework of notes in tiny handwriting, written in Chinese characters so faint that they were almost impossible to make out. But even without the notes, the newspaper clippings told them everything they needed to know. Every single cutting – whether a report of a society ball, or an article about a new bill being passed by the House of Lords – mentioned Lord Beaucastle. His name had been underlined in each and every one – sometimes neatly in pencil, other times with a wobbly line of red ink.

'He *knew*,' breathed Mei, her mind suddenly flooded with images: Granddad reading the newspaper from cover to cover each day; the careful notes he made; the candles he lit to their ancestors. He had never ceased in his duty, she realised in amazement. He had been the guardian of the Moonbeam Diamond all along. 'He knew that this man was Waiguo Ren! He must have been watching him all the time!'

'Waiguo Ren . . . Lord Beaucastle . . . *the Baron*,' said Dad, slowly. He wiped his forehead with his handkerchief. 'I never would have believed it.' He turned to Sophie, Billy and Lil, who were still gazing at the old scrapbook. 'It's hard to explain to you now,' he said in his soft voice. 'But what you have to understand is that being a guardian at the temple in the village where I grew up – well, it was the most important of responsibilities. It was not just a job: it was a sacred duty. My father – Mei's granddad – he was a sort of head man in the village. People respected him; they looked to him to

186

show them what was right. I know he often thought about what had happened: how they had been tricked by Waiguo Ren; how the temple had been destroyed; the loss of the diamond. He regretted it terribly. But even I had no idea that he was working to find the diamond all this time.'

'But if he knew all this – why didn't he tell us? Or do something about it?' asked Mei, wonderingly.

'Well the Baron is dangerous. What power would one old man have to stand against him?' Dad flicked through the notebook. 'Maybe he was trying to gather his evidence, biding his time . . .'

'Maybe he was trying to protect us,' said Mum softly. 'I just can't believe that Waiguo Ren was here – all along.'

'Except he wasn't,' said Song, suddenly.

The others looked at him in surprise.

'The Baron had never tried to move into China Town before, had he? Not until Granddad died. It was only then that he sent his Boys in and started threatening and making demands.'

'Do you think he *knew* about Granddad?' asked Mei incredulously. She turned to look at Dad. 'Could Granddad have been somehow – holding him back?'

Dad shook his head, mystified.

Song was leafing through Granddad's notebook. 'It's obvious that there's a lot going on here that we don't know about. It's so much to take in.' He looked curiously down the table at Sophie. 'What do you plan to do now?' he asked, directly.

Sophie looked around at the others, and then back at Song. 'We don't know for sure,' she admitted. 'We have a friend, a private detective, who we know is trustworthy, and who is working with Scotland Yard against the Baron. We want to tell him what we have discovered, but he's away at present.' She paused, and then went on, as though she was thinking as she was speaking: 'I suppose what we really need to do is to find some sort of proof that Lord Beaucastle is the Baron – some evidence that we can give to our friend Mr McDermott when he returns. If Scotland Yard had some firm evidence, then they could actually arrest the Baron and his men – and put a stop to them.'

Beside her, Lil nodded eagerly. 'Yes! And perhaps you could help. If the Baron is moving into China Town, you might be able to help us gather evidence we can use to prove who he is.'

Mei was conscious that Mum and Dad were exchanging glances. After a long moment, it was Dad who spoke.

'There is no doubt that you have found out something very important. We would like to help, and we wish you the very best of luck. But we can't risk more trouble with the Baron. We have talked long and hard about this with our friends here in China Town. The stakes are too high. The Baron could ruin us, take our homes and livelihoods and harm those we hold dear. We dare not stand against him. I hope you understand that.'

'But – but what about the diamond?' Mei burst out, unhappily. 'If we could get it back – it would help us. It could protect us against the Baron and the Baron's Boys!'

Dad shook his head slowly. 'If you would carry a message to this young lady, to tell her the truth about where the diamond came from, we would be in your debt,' he said, inclining his head to Sophie and the others. 'But I beg you, please do not mention our names. If she's to marry the Baron, she might tell him of our involvement.'

Lil opened her mouth as if to protest, but Sophie put a hand on her arm. 'We understand,' she said softly. 'Thank you, Mr Lim, Mrs Lim. We should go now – it's getting late.'

'D'you think we could borrow the notebook?' asked Billy, gently touching the pages.

'We'll translate the notes for you first,' said Song. 'It's the least we can do.'

A few minutes later, they had said their farewells and were walking towards the place where Mr Lim had told them they would be able to find another cab.

'We understand?' repeated Lil, rather crossly. 'Well, you

may understand, Sophie, but I certainly don't! They've just left us to sort everything out on our own.'

'It's different for them,' said Sophie, shaking her head. 'They want to protect their family. It's dangerous.'

'Well it's jolly dangerous for us too!' pointed out Lil, rather indignantly. 'Look at us now, wandering the streets of the East End at goodness knows what time of night. One of the Baron's Boys could quite easily jump out at us at any time!'

It was perhaps unfortunate that it was at that moment that Sophie felt a hand fall upon her arm. She jumped in alarm, but almost at once realised that it was only Mei's brother Song.

'Wait,' he panted breathlessly, still gripping her arm. 'Stop. I wanted to tell you – we'll help you, Mei and me.'

'What do you mean?' she asked, taken aback.

He fixed her with serious dark eyes. 'Never mind what Mum and Dad said. We've made up our own minds. We want to help with this. We want to finish Granddad's work and help you stop the Baron. Just tell us what you need us to do.'

CHAPTER NINETEEN

At last, the long meal drew to an end. At Beaucastle's discreet nod, the ladies rose, leaving the gentlemen to their port and cigars.

'We'll join you in the drawing room presently,' said Lord Beaucastle to Veronica.

'Excuse me, I must go to the powder room,' she whispered to Isabel, darting away from the group of ladies before her stepmother had chance to object.

An unsmiling footman directed Veronica down a long corridor. As soon as she had turned the corner, she let out a long, trembling breath of relief. She felt tense and agitated in ways she couldn't even explain. She couldn't stop thinking about the strange things that Henry Snow had been saying to Lord Beaucastle and the even stranger way that he had responded.

'May I help you, miss?'

It was Lord Beaucastle's butler. She hadn't heard him

coming, and now he had happened upon her, standing by herself in the middle of the corridor.

'I – I'm looking for the powder room,' she said awkwardly.

'Please, follow me.'

He escorted her silently down the corridor, and pointed to a door, bowing to her with exaggerated politeness. Veronica felt very glad to slip inside and close the door firmly behind her. She didn't much care for Lord Beaucastle's butler, with his cadaverous face, silly little moustache and obsequious manner.

Alone once more, she tried to order her thoughts, glancing at her reflection in the looking glass on the wall. Her imagination was running wild, she told herself; she was simply nervous about her betrothal. And that was natural enough, wasn't it? She carefully rearranged a hairpin, admiring the way that the lamplight gleamed on her red-gold hair. The moth brooch sparkled in the light, and she touched it with a fingertip. It seemed full of secrets: as if it possessed some mystical power that might at any time be released.

She ran her hands over its richly textured surface. It was so strange that the brooch was still here and yet Emily had gone. Could it really have had some part to play in her death?

Emily had certainly had secrets. She had stolen the jewelled moth, after all. She had been a criminal. She'd had another hidden life, which she kept secret from all around her.

Could it be that Lord Beaucastle had secrets too?

Veronica's thoughts kept sliding back to that strange conversation about the mines. Something about it was jarring, a wrong note struck on the piano in the middle of a melody. For the first time, she felt as though Lord Beaucastle might not be quite sincere. It was almost as though when he had made that toast, he had been acting the part of the amiable, generous gentleman, struck by the charms of a young lady.

If there really was something suspicious going on – if any part of Miss Taylor and Miss Rose's silly tale was true – then surely there would be signs of it, she told herself. There would have to be evidence here in Lord Beaucastle's home. She could find out for herself, she thought suddenly. She could seek out some proof of what they had told her – and if she found nothing, well, she would know that they were wrong. Then she could forget all about Miss Taylor and Miss Rose – yes, and Emily too, she thought guiltily. She didn't want to think about criminals and stolen jewels and dead bodies any longer – she just wanted to get on with enjoying her first Season, her coming-out ball, and the announcement of an engagement so impressive that surely everyone would be talking about it.

Feeling quite decisive now, she decided she would look in Lord Beaucastle's study while he was still in the dining room with the other gentleman. She knew that it was in this part of the house, adjoining the library. Lord Beaucastle had pointed it out to her when he had taken her into his library once to show her some rather dull old paintings and books that he had brought back from his travels and seemed to think fascinating. If there was anything at all untoward going on, she would surely find clear evidence of it there.

She had rather dreaded finding the butler still standing outside the powder room door, waiting to escort her back to the drawing room, but as she stepped out into the corridor, she saw to her relief that he had gone. She set out confidently in the direction of Lord Beaucastle's library.

It took her a little longer than she had expected to find it, but she saw no other servants on her way. When at last she stepped inside, the room was only dimly lit, and the hushed ticking of the grandfather clock seemed to echo her own heartbeat. She felt a most peculiar combination of fear and odd excitement as she quickly made her way through the shadowy room towards the study door. But on the threshold, she stopped – there was someone talking inside. She recognised Henry Snow's voice.

'The man is clearly an utter fool. He hasn't the slightest

idea of what those mines are really worth – or what's to be found there. We must get hold of them, and quickly. If you look at the results of the latest analysis, you'll see its potential for use in an incendiary – well, it's unprecedented. Ten times more powerful than anything we have seen before. It's extraordinary – if you come through and see my latest experiment –'

'Not now. I have guests to entertain,' Beaucastle's voice was brusque and unlike itself.

'Tomorrow then? In the morning perhaps?'

'I have business with my man in Shoreditch. But in the afternoon –'

The voice broke off abruptly. Lord Beaucastle had opened the door, stopping suddenly upon seeing Veronica standing there.

'Miss Whiteley!' he exclaimed. For a moment or two, a dark expression rushed across his face – but a second later it had disappeared, replaced by a look of bland confusion. His voice, when he spoke, was much more like the genial Beaucastle she knew. 'Whatever are you doing here, my dear?'

Veronica thought quickly. She gave a silly little laugh. 'Oh, I'm so terribly sorry,' she said, fluttering her lashes and trying to look contrite. 'But I confess, I lost my way coming back from the powder room – and then I was so fascinated by all the beautiful treasures you showed me last time that I just couldn't resist taking another peep at your marvellous library.'

'But this is Lord Beaucastle's study,' said Henry Snow rather crossly. He was standing behind Beaucastle, beside a desk that was littered with papers: Veronica glimpsed maps and documents, scrawled with numbers. He was frowning at her with a look of immense disapproval. 'The library is behind you,' he finished, pointing behind them from where they had come.

But Lord Beaucastle just laughed. 'Now, now, Henry,' he said, 'Miss Whiteley knows she is welcome anywhere in my home – and to look at my collections whenever she chooses. I'm only too delighted they please her,' he added, gallantly. 'Now I'm going to escort Miss Whiteley back to the drawing room and rejoin the party. If you insist on continuing your work, we will leave you in peace – and we can finish this conversation tomorrow.'

There was extra emphasis placed on his final word: Mr Snow did not argue.

Lord Beaucastle offered Veronica his arm. 'Come along, my dear.'

Veronica did her best to smile obediently, but her heart was racing as they left the room.

*

Veronica felt like an automaton for the rest of the evening, as she smiled and played cards and went through all the motions of having a wonderful time, until midnight came and at last it was time to go.

'What a delightful evening!' exclaimed Isabel, as they travelled home in the carriage.

'Beaucastle certainly is a fine host,' agreed Father, looking very well pleased with himself, as if anticipating many such evenings to come.

'You are a very lucky girl, Veronica,' said Isabel. 'My goodness. What a match. Just think how wonderful it will be when your engagement is announced!' She gave a complacent little laugh. 'The Countess will never forgive us. I'm sure she was quite determined that poor little Phyllis was going to be the first to find a husband.'

Veronica said nothing. She glanced over at her father, but he was smiling at Isabel's joke.

When they arrived home, Isabel hurried away to take off her gown, but Veronica lingered in the hallway. She felt awfully tired, and longed for nothing more than to escape to the peace of her room, where her maid would be waiting to help her undress and to take down her hair. But she had to say something, before it was too late:

'Father,' she began tentatively. 'May I speak with you?'

'Of course, my dear.'

He led her into his study and urged her to sit down on a leather chair, pouring himself a glass of port from the decanter.

'I want to talk to you about Lord Beaucastle,' she began awkwardly. 'Father, I know that you've granted permission for our engagement – I know that we're supposed to announce it at my coming-out ball.'

'At the stroke of midnight!' exclaimed her father jovially. 'Rather a romantic scheme of Beaucastle's, what!'

Veronica gripped the arm of the chair. 'But – but – I don't believe I can marry Lord Beaucastle.' Her father's face changed: he seemed about to speak, but she blundered on, 'I know he's rich and important, but I don't love him, and I don't believe he loves me. And that's not all –'

'Vee, my dear,' said her father, using the old baby name that he hadn't called her for years. He reached forwards and took her cold hands in his warm ones. 'You know that successful marriages aren't built on romantic fancies, but on compatibility. Lord Beaucastle is a fine match for you – you need a husband that can guide you. You're still so very young.'

'I know!' burst out Veronica. 'I'm not ready to be married yet, Father, I –'

'Remember that as I have no son, you are my heir,' Father explained. 'We have to think practically about your future. Lord Beaucastle is a wise man and a good one. I can trust him to take good care of you.'

Veronica pulled her hands impatiently away. 'But that's just it, Father! I don't believe he is! I – I'm beginning to believe that *he's not the man that he appears to be.*'

Her father laughed briskly. 'Nonsense,' he admonished her, taking a sip of port. 'Don't be silly, my dear. Why, I've known Beaucastle for years! There's no finer fellow in London.'

'But – I heard the evidence tonight for myself, at his house. You have to listen – I think he's plotting to get hold of the mines. There's something in them that he wants –'

Father set down his glass firmly. 'Enough,' he said. 'I know you're used to having your own way. God knows I've probably spoiled you more than I should. But this has got to stop, Veronica. I won't indulge you this time. Beaucastle has been a good friend to me, and he will be a fine husband to you. You will have everything you could ever want. I won't let you turn all that down for some sort of – of childish silliness. What do you know of mines and business? This is just a whim.'

'It isn't a whim –' Veronica began weakly, but Father shook his head.

'Let me be perfectly clear with you,' he said, leaning forwards. 'When Lord Beaucastle formally requests the pleasure of your hand at your coming-out ball this Friday, I *insist* that you say yes.'

CHAPTER TWENTY

'**B**eing a deb must be simply *ghastly*,' said Lil, tucking into her plate of toad-in-the-hole. It was midday, and she and Sophie were back in the Sinclair's refectory. Not far from where they were sitting, a group of the girls from Ladies' Fashions were gathered around the morning paper, admiring the ballgowns of the young ladies in the society pages. Lil screwed up her face.

'Imagine being told who to marry, and not having the tiniest bit of choice in the matter!' she went on. 'You know, I always thought it was terrifically unfair that my brother got to go off to university, just because he was a boy, while I was supposed to stick at home doing ladylike things – and then Mother and Father made such an awful fuss about me going on the stage. But compared to Veronica, I think that really I'm jolly lucky.'

Sophie nodded. 'And we're all of us lucky compared to Emily Montague.' She sighed and put down her fork. 'The more I think about it, the more I am sure that we *have* to find out what really happened to her,' she continued, her voice very determined.

'But how?' asked Lil. 'I suppose that the police will have information about how she died – but I don't know how we would be able to get hold of it.'

Sophie shook her head. 'I think maybe it's not her death, but Emily herself we need to know more about. Her friends, her family, who she was.' She took a sip of tea, and thought for a moment. 'You know, I think it might be time for Lil the debutante to make another appearance,' she said cautiously.

'Oh I say! What a good scheme!' exclaimed Lil, looking so immediately enthusiastic that Sophie couldn't help but laugh.

Several hours later, Sophie and Lil were standing on the pavement outside the residence of Miss Phyllis Woodhouse. Billy had looked up Phyllis's address in Sinclair's records, whilst the two of them had borrowed a copy of Lady Diana DeVere's etiquette book from the Book Department and scrutinised the chapter about paying calls.

Whilst Lil knocked and was ushered into Phyllis's house by the butler, Sophie turned her attention to the house next door, where Emily Montague had lived. She had made up her mind to see whether there was anything she might learn about Emily, or her family. But from where she lingered on the pavement, the house seemed completely still. In spite of the warm weather, the windows were tightly closed, the blinds drawn. Even the door knocker had been tied up with a strip of black crepe.

But after a few minutes had passed, a maid appeared out of the servants' entrance. She seemed to be in rather a hurry, and she was concealing something small under her apron. Sophie at once bent down, pretending to be fiddling with a button on one of her boots. To her surprise, the maid passed her and then slipped stealthily up the stairs of the next-door house. What could she be doing at the Woodhouses', Sophie wondered?

Inside, Phyllis had welcomed Lil with enthusiasm: 'Miss Rose! Why, how lovely to see you!'

'I do hope you don't mind me calling,' said Lil, perching herself sedately on a little chair in the spacious drawing room. She was heartily relieved to find Phyllis all alone. She was proud of her debutante performance, but she wasn't sure quite how well she would fare if she had to convince Phyllis's mama as well as Phyllis herself.

'Not in the least!' exclaimed Phyllis at once. 'Mama is out with Grandmama, and I'm fearfully bored. It's jolly to see you – but did you come all by yourself? Is your chaperone still unwell?'

Lil gave a nervous laugh. 'I'm afraid she is, rather,' she said, and then hurried on before Phyllis could start asking her difficult questions about the mumps. 'The thing is, I heard the awful news about Miss Montague. I didn't know her very well at all, but I know she was a friend of yours, so I thought I should call. I was so sorry to hear what happened to her.'

To Lil's alarm, Phyllis's large blue eyes at once filled up with tears. 'That's so awfully kind of you,' she said, in rather a trembling voice. 'Oh, Miss Rose – I do feel terrible about poor Emily.'

'It's tremendously sad. I'm so sorry – it must be dreadful to lose such a dear friend.'

'But that's just it!' said Phyllis, looking up at her unhappily. 'The honest truth is we weren't dear friends – in fact, we were barely friends at all. We ought to have been – we've been neighbours for years. We even went to finishing school together. But Emily could be so *beastly* sometimes! At school she was always ragging me about what a fearful dunce I was, and getting the other girls to rag me too. It's been the same since we came out – whatever I said, she always made me feel a perfect ninny.' She paused for a moment and dabbed her eyes with her handkerchief. 'But I know you oughtn't to speak ill of the dead – and now she's gone and it's all so ghastly. I can't help feeling that if only I had been better chums with her, maybe this would never have happened!'

'Oh, Phyllis – don't be silly,' said Lil, gently. 'That's stuff and nonsense. What happened to Emily wasn't your fault.'

'But perhaps if we'd *really* been friends, she would have been with us at the York House ball, not walking out along the river all by herself at night!' Phyllis wailed. 'And – and we all thought she had eloped – and we were all gossiping and laughing about it at Veronica's tea party!'

'There's no sense in feeling guilty about that now,' said Lil briskly. 'Look, perhaps you weren't always such a wonderful chum to Emily – but it doesn't sound like she was an awfully good friend to you either.'

'I suppose you're right,' said Phyllis, still sounding a little anxious.

'You really oughtn't blame yourself –' went on Lil, but before she could say any more, the maid came back into the room. 'If you please, Miss Phyllis, there's someone here to see you,' she said.

'Who is it, Elsie?'

'It's – it's Miss Montague's maid, miss. From next door. Susan, her name is. She says she's got something for you.' The maid pursed up her mouth as she said this. Lil thought that she looked as though she disapproved of Susan-from-next-door.

'Oh – how very strange. I wonder what she can mean? Do show her in, Elsie. You don't mind, do you, Miss Rose?'

Lil shook her head, even as the young woman came in to the drawing room. She was dressed like any other maid, but she looked boldly around the room as she bobbed a curtsey.

'Begging your pardon, miss,' she began at once. 'I don't mean to intrude. But I wanted to bring you something. My young mistress, Miss Emily, I know she was a friend of yours, and she'd want you to have something to remember her by. She always spoke well of you.'

She handed Phyllis a small green velvet box. Inside was a little paste brooch in the shape of a bow. Seeing it, Phyllis looked as though she was going to burst into tears all over again. 'Oh – I remember Emily wearing this!' she exclaimed. 'How thoughtful of you! But – but – does Mrs Montague know you've brought this for me?'

Susan looked quite insulted. 'Of course she does, miss. She said I could come. She was feeling too upset to come herself.' Then all at once, her expression changed. 'My poor young mistress!' she wailed. 'She was so good to me! And now she's gone, and I shall lose my place!'

Phyllis looked stricken. 'Oh heavens – you poor thing!' She fumbled for her purse, took out a pound note and pressed it into the maid's hands. 'Here – take this,' she said.

Susan stifled a sob, but Lil could have sworn that her eyes glinted as her fingers closed around the money.

'Oh thank you,' she breathed. 'She always said you were so kind, my poor mistress. Good day to you, miss,' she said, and scuttled out of the room.

Lil sensed an opportunity. 'Heavens, look at the time!' she exclaimed, leaping to her feet. 'I must go at once – my chaperone will be awfully worried. Chin up, Phyllis! Remember what I said – none of this is in the least bit your fault!'

'But – but – you've only just arrived –' stuttered Phyllis in confusion, as Lil rushed helter-skelter out of the room.

'I oughtn't to be talking to you.' Susan folded her arms defensively. She was eyeing Sophie and Lil across the table of the little tea room: it had taken five shillings to persuade her to accompany them. 'The mistress'd have my guts for garters.'

'Well, if you aren't going to tell us anything, we'll have our money back,' said Lil, promptly.

'We just want to find out what really happened to Miss Montague,' said Sophie. 'That's all.'

'You've worked out that it wasn't really an accident, then? Well that makes you smarter than the rest of them,' Susan gave a contemptuous snort. 'As if any respectable, well-brought-up young lady would suddenly decide to go strolling along the river at night, all alone!'

'So what was she really doing?' asked Sophie, leaning forwards across the table.

Susan sipped her tea, and said nothing.

'Go on,' said Lil impatiently. 'Five shillings, remember? And your tea. *And* we won't tell Miss Woodhouse what your little pantomime in her drawing room was all about. I suppose Mrs Montague didn't really know you'd taken that brooch?'

Susan shrugged. 'She won't notice, one way or the other. She doesn't have a clue. Besides, it was only a cheap thing – worth more to Miss Woodhouse than the pawnbroker, I reckon. Now Miss Emily's gone, I have to look out for myself.'

'So tell us what you know about what happened.'

Susan eyed a plate of sticky buns on the counter. 'I'm hungry,' she said plaintively. 'I can't talk when I'm hungry.'

Lil rolled her eyes. 'Fine. You can have a bun. But you have to talk.'

Susan heaved a sigh. 'Very well. I'll tell you. But keep it to yourselves. I've no mind to get myself in trouble.' She lowered her voice.

'The Montagues are flat broke,' she began. 'People don't know it yet, but they've barely a farthing left. Mr Montague had money troubles before he died – but after young Mr Raymond, Miss Emily's brother, inherited – *well!*'

'What happened?'

'Ran through everything that was left at the gaming tables, didn't he? The mistress was that ashamed. She wanted to keep up appearances just as always, and she pinned all her hopes on Miss Emily making a good marriage in her first Season. That way she could save the family fortunes. Only problem was, there was no money to pay for it – the Season's an expensive business. All those frocks and gloves and the like. But Miss Emily was smart – she had more brains than the rest of them put together. She came up with a way to pay.'

'She stole things – from the other debutantes,' said Sophie, realising what the maid was getting at.

'Too right she did,' said Susan, nodding sharply. 'And the silly fools were too feather-brained to notice. It was child's play for her to take a watch here, a brooch there. She had an eye for it. She'd take them and I'd pop them down to the pawnbroker's or the jeweller's shop, see what I could get. Oh I know it wasn't right and proper, but it kept me in wages – and it made sure she could keep up with the rest of the debutantes, more or less.'

'Didn't her mother know what she was doing?' asked Lil, all agog.

'Her? She didn't have a notion. She's the sort that can't even see the nose on their own face.'

'So *that's* why Emily took the jewelled moth at the garden party,' said Sophie.

The maid nodded. 'But that wasn't the only valuable thing she got hold of that day.'

'What do you mean?'

For the first time, the maid looked a little uncomfortable. 'The jewels and things – they weren't enough, not to settle all the bills. So she found another way of making money.'

'What way?'

Susan bit her lip. 'Miss Emily sometimes found out things that she wasn't supposed to know. *Secrets.* She was always the inquisitive sort – and she wasn't above listening at a few keyholes. It only happened a couple of times. A rich old geezer who was keeping a mistress on the side and didn't want his wife to know about it. A young fellow who got the boot from Cambridge and couldn't bear his family finding out.'

'So she *blackmailed* them?' asked Lil, shocked.

'I s'pose you'd call it that,' said the maid tersely. 'She asked 'em for a few quid to keep her mouth shut.'

'And that's what happened at the garden party?'

Susan nodded. 'I don't know what she found out, but when she came back she was full of herself. She didn't even seem to care about that brooch. She said that she'd overheard something – some secret – that was worth far more than any jewel.'

'What was it?' asked Lil at once.

Susan shrugged. 'Search me. She wouldn't tell. Said it wasn't for me to know. All I know is that it was something about Lord Beaucastle. She said it should make her enough to see her set up for the rest of the Season.'

'And then she disappeared,' said Sophie. Her mind was working furiously: she could see it all now.

'And they tried to say she'd gone off with young Robert, the footman!' scoffed Susan, indignantly. 'Idiots, the lot of them. She'd not give a young milksop like that a second look! She knew what side her bread was buttered, right enough. When she disappeared, I thought maybe she'd found some rich fellow and had run off with him. I cursed her for not taking me with her. I never thought they'd find her floating in the river . . .'

To their astonishment, Susan's eyes suddenly welled up with tears – and Lil could see they were real tears this time, not the false ones she had produced for Phyllis. 'I say, don't cry,' she found herself saying, rather awkwardly.

After Susan had left them, Sophie and Lil remained sitting at the table long after their tea had gone cold.

'What a story!' said Lil at last. 'I never expected she would say anything like that.'

'I suppose Emily Montague must have found out some secret about the Baron – something big,' Sophie mused. 'She tried to blackmail him, but he didn't take kindly to that – and so instead of paying her off . . .'

'He killed her off,' said Lil, her eyes round.

'Or his Boys did.'

'Gosh!' said Lil. 'Poor Emily. She might have been a thief – and a blackmailer – but she didn't deserve to *die*. She can't really have been any sort of real threat to the Baron, can she? Why, she was only a young girl!'

What she did not say, but what both she and Sophie were thinking, was that Emily Montague was not really so very different from themselves. They knew secrets about the Baron; were they too in terrible danger?

'No wonder Joe wasn't keen on going back to the East End,' Lil added, after a little while. When they had seen him next, he had been thoroughly shame-faced about having deserted them in the cab – but now, it was easy to understand why he had done it. It was only too clear that the Baron was not someone to be trifled with.

They were rather silent as they walked back towards Sinclair's department store.

*

It was evening now. The shadows lengthened, lights began to come on in the windows of the houses, and in Hyde Park, a little breeze stirred the leaves of the trees.

Night fell. Streetlights gleamed, and somewhere, a dog howled. In the East End, a lone policeman was striding along a gas-lit street, the beam of his lantern slicing through the shadows. An old woman slept in the small sanctuary of a church doorway, under the yellowing sheets of yesterday's newspaper. Big Ben chimed, first one, then two o'clock, until the last of London's revellers melted away into the night. In China Town, the Baron's Boys prowled along the street like ghosts in the shadows, whilst the Lim family stirred restlessly in their sleep.

Far across the city, Phyllis Woodhouse snored gently, whilst in next door's attic, Susan lay unhappily awake in the dark.

Not far away, in the sedate surroundings of Belgrave Square, Veronica was pacing around her bedroom, the lace-trimmed hem of her nightgown trailing along the floor. All the familiar things around her – the dressing table with its silver-backed brushes and the quaint jewel cabinet, the four-poster bed with the pretty curtains and soft coverlet – suddenly seemed as if they belonged to someone else. Her world had turned upside down. She felt sick to the pit of her stomach: there were just two days left until her coming-out ball, and Lord Beaucastle's proposal. Her thoughts were in turmoil, but through it all, there was one thing she knew for sure. Whatever else she did, she had to see Miss Taylor and Miss Rose as soon as possible. She had a feeling that they were the only ones who could help her now.

Dance Card

1. Waltz ... ... 1.........................
2. Quadrille ... 2.........................
3. Polka ... ... 3.........................
4. Two-step ... 4.........................
5. Waltz ... ... 5.........................
6. Galop ... ... 6.........................
7. Polonaise ... 7.........................
8. Waltz-minuet 8.........................
9. Polka ... ... 9.........................
10. Waltz ... ... 10.......................

PART IV
The Debutante Ball

Behaving with decorum is of the utmost importance, and never more so than on the occasion of a coming-out ball. A debutante must always conduct herself with elegance, grace and charm, and should on no account be seen to romp, especially in the gallop, nor to make herself in any way conspicuous.

From Lady Diana DeVere's *Etiquette for Debutantes: a Guide to the Manners, Mores and Morals of Good Society*, Chapter 20: The Ball – The Debutante's Proper Conduct – Dances – Rooms of Necessary – On the Selection of Music – Decoration of the Ballroom – Duties of Entertainers to their Guests – A Word Upon Partners – The Card Room – The Fancy Dress Ball

CHAPTER TWENTY-ONE

'Lilian is wearing a delightfully dainty *robe du soir* in ivory satin, with black velvet *dévoré* and ivory tulle,' trilled Madame Lucille. 'Note the beautiful hand-embellishing and the exquisite glass bead trim.' She swept her hand towards Lil's gown, and then simpered at the ladies through her lorgnette.

Lil stood perfectly still, frozen in the attitude of a Greek statue, which was generally about all that was required of a Sinclair's mannequin. Madame Lucille – not her real name of course – Lil happened to know that she was really called Ethel, and hailed not from Paris, but from Preston – always said that it was important for the mannequins to think calm thoughts while they posed, but Lil's thoughts on this particular afternoon were not in the least bit serene. Instead, her mind was working energetically, thinking over the events of the previous few days – their visit to Veronica, the encounter with Mei Lim and the trip to the East End, the meeting with Susan, all that they had learned about Lord Beaucastle and the jewelled moth – and Emily's fate perhaps most of all. Nonetheless, she tried to shape her face into a suitably tranquil expression, while the ladies in attendance peered at her and muttered to one another in low voices.

'To complement the evening gown,' Madame Lucille went on, 'Lilian is wearing a scarlet silk sash, and silk slippers.'

All at once Lil became aware of a flurry happening in the doorway. A young lady rushed in very late, and without a word of apology to anyone pushed herself in and took an empty seat in the front row, where her large plumed hat immediately obscured the view of several people sitting behind her. This was not at all acceptable behaviour at a dress show. '*Well!*' exclaimed one lady in a particularly vexed tone of voice, getting up pointedly to move seats, but the young lady who had been the cause of the fuss did not even seem to notice.

Craning her neck from her fixed position, Lil saw to her astonishment that she was none other than Veronica Whiteley. Her cheeks were red, and she appeared a little breathless, but as always she was holding her head very high and looking as if she thought she had more right to a front-row seat than anyone.

'Turn around please, Lilian. You will see that the back of this gown is particularly spectacular,' went on Madame

Lucille in a low, soothing voice, attempting to restore order.

But Lil was not listening. Veronica was staring at her, with an expression of great concentration and purposefulness. Was she trying to telegraph some kind of a message? Her eyebrows were waggling meaningfully and she seemed to be mouthing words. She looked at the floor in front of her. Then up at the clock. Was she trying to say *Meet here?* At some particular time? After the dress show, perhaps?

'*Lilian!*' Madame Lucille had become rather sharp, and Lil recollected what she was supposed to be doing. She performed a graceful turn.

'Thank you, Lilian,' said Madame Lucille huffily. 'Now on to our next model,' she went on, as the next mannequin emerged from behind the draped velvet curtains and struck an exaggerated pose, leaving Lil to glide away.

The dress show finally over, the ladies departed, Lil slipped out of the mannequins' dressing room to find Veronica pacing up and down in the now-empty *salon*.

'I didn't expect to see *you* any time soon,' Lil couldn't resist saying.

Veronica had the grace to look embarrassed. 'I didn't know what to do,' she said anxiously. 'I believe I've found out something about Lord Beaucastle. I – I rather think that you might be right. There is something suspicious about him.'

Lil arched her eyebrows. 'As it happens, we've discovered some information that you might be interested to hear too,' she said. For a moment she hesitated, then she said: 'Come with me. We ought to speak to the others.'

Veronica might have been feeling distressed, but she was not so agitated that she failed to notice that Miss Rose was taking her on a most peculiar route out of the shop. Rather than going down the grand, sweeping stairway that the customers used, she instead hurried her down a back staircase, then through a door and out into a stable-yard, where grooms were rubbing down horses and porters were hurrying by with stacks of boxes. It was all rather *rough*, Veronica thought, wrinkling her nose daintily: the men were shouting at each other in coarse-sounding voices; there was the clatter of hooves on cobbles; and she had to lift up the hem of her gown to prevent it trailing in the mud – or worse, she thought, with an affronted sniff.

'Where are we going?' she demanded, but Miss Rose – or Lil, as she had abruptly announced Veronica should call her – did not reply. To her astonishment, Veronica found herself being led into a stable, where Lil insisted she climb a ladder into a dirty sort of attic full of straw. Once there, she found she was expected to sit down upon a hay bale.

'No thank you, I believe I shall stand,' she announced

219

haughtily, intending to impress upon them all – Lil, Sophie and the two boys – that she was not at all accustomed to such places. But when she saw how comfortably they had settled themselves down upon their makeshift seats, she began to regret what she had said, and after a moment or two, she sat down after all, hoping that no one would notice.

It did not take her long to relate what she had overheard at Lord Beaucastle's mansion. 'So, do you believe us now?' demanded Lil, as soon as she had finished.

Veronica was annoyed to feel her face flushing. 'I – I don't know,' she said. 'All I know is that Lord Beaucastle is hiding things. He's up to something – and I don't like it.'

'What do you think he meant about your father's mines?' asked the younger of the two boys, Billy, who had been scribbling in an old exercise book with a stub of pencil all the time that she had been talking. 'What kind of mines are they, anyway?'

'Some of them are coal, and some are iron ore. One is a diamond mine. They're in South Africa.'

'Your father owns a *diamond mine?*' repeated Billy, incredulously.

'It's not a very big one,' said Veronica, a little peevishly.

'Is Lord Beaucastle involved in mining himself?' asked Sophie.

'Not as far as I know. But from what they said, it sounded

like they knew about something special in the mines – some sort of mineral. That man – Henry Snow, the scientist – he talked about doing experiments that were something to do with incendiaries – at least that's what I think he said.'

'Incendiaries?' repeated Lil.

'Weapons that start fires,' explained Billy.

'They talked about needing access to the mines, and I – well, I suppose I wondered . . . whether the mines might be why he wants to marry me,' said Veronica, her words coming out in a rush. She could feel her cheeks burning red now.

The others looked at each other. 'You think he wants to marry you to get his hands on your father's mines to get this . . . mineral, or whatever it is?' asked Lil.

'And make weapons out of it?' added Sophie.

Veronica nodded miserably. 'Henry Snow said something like, "*He hasn't the slightest idea of what they're really worth.*" I think he was talking about Father. Whatever they know about the mines, it's something that my father doesn't.'

'And as your husband, would Beaucastle have access to the mines?'

'Well, perhaps – because I'm my father's heir, you see. So unless Father and Isabel should have a son, when Father dies, the mines will come to me.'

They all stared at her as they took this in. Veronica noticed, to her great irritation, that they were now looking at her with sympathy in their eyes – even that young man who smelled of stables. She couldn't bear them to start feeling sorry for her. 'Look, I don't know anything about this Baron you keep talking about,' she said in a tight voice, 'but Beaucastle's up to something. I don't know if he is the person you think he is, but I certainly don't care for the idea that he's trying to pull the wool over my father's eyes, and is marrying me just to get his hands on the mines.'

'Have you spoken to your father about this?' asked Sophie. 'Or your stepmother?'

Veronica made a face. 'I tried to talk to Father, but he won't listen. He thinks I'm being silly.'

Sophie thought for a moment. 'We know now that the Baron is behind what happened to Emily,' she said gravely, looking around at the others. 'He's dangerous, and we have to do something before Veronica finds herself married to him. After that, if your suspicions are correct, goodness knows what might happen to you and your family,' she said to Veronica.

'We're in a tight spot,' said Joe. 'If the Baron has even half a clue that we know the truth about his real identity, we're all in danger.'

'And we're not the only ones who know, either,' added Billy. 'The Lim family know that the Baron is Lord Beaucastle too. That could surely put them in danger as well.'

Veronica had been listening to all this with a growing sense of foreboding. She was just about to ask who the Lim family might be, when Sophie turned to her. 'We've got some things we need to tell you too. First of all, we know for sure now that Emily did steal the jewelled moth from you at the garden party. But what's more, we've found out more about the moth itself.'

'Or rather the diamond at the centre of it – the Moonbeam Diamond,' contributed Lil.

Between them, they poured out Mei's story as quickly as they could.

'So Lord Beaucastle didn't save the diamond at all. He *stole* it!' exclaimed Veronica. She suddenly felt very cross, thinking of all those times she had listened to his stories of travelling to faraway places and having exotic adventures – shooting elephants and tigers, and finding treasures in strange ruined temples. 'Everyone thinks he's so wonderful!' she burst out indignantly. 'And all the while he's no better than Emily – he's no more than a – a common thief!'

'He stole the diamond from the temple – and then Emily stole it from you,' said Billy, thoughtfully. 'You don't suppose there really could be some sort of curse on the diamond, do you?'

'No! Of course not – that's nonsense,' said Lil briskly.

'Besides, it hasn't done the Baron much harm, has it,' said Joe in his quiet voice.

There was a long pause. Veronica could hear voices shouting and carts rattling by outside in the stable-yard: it all sounded so ordinary. She was suddenly struck by the most unpleasant fancy that if the diamond really could lay a curse upon the person who stole it, then it was surely Emily who had felt the full force of it. Beaucastle seemed to be immune – almost as if he possessed some horrible supernatural power of his own.

She shook the thought away. 'What ought I to do now?' she demanded. 'These people can have their diamond back for all I care. I don't want the horrid thing – but Lord Beaucastle would notice at once if it were gone. Why, he's expecting me to wear the jewelled moth at my debutante ball the day after tomorrow!'

'There's only one thing to do,' said Sophie decisively. 'We simply must find a way to prove without any possible doubt that Lord Beaucastle and the Baron are one and the same. It's the only way to stop him.'

'But what evidence do we have to prove that?' wondered Billy, aloud. He waved his exercise book in Sophie's direction. 'I've written everything down – but there's nothing at all that proves a connection between the Baron and Lord Beaucastle. We can't even prove that he had anything to do with what happened to Emily. It's all just . . . conjecture. Speculation. We need something definite.'

Veronica spoke up: 'Perhaps there might be some sort of evidence in Lord Beaucastle's study,' she suggested. 'I saw all kinds of paperwork in there.'

'That's it,' said Sophie. '*Paperwork!* Accounts, letters. That's exactly the kind of thing we need. We know that the Baron is making large amounts of money from the people of the East End – surely that must be recorded somehow.'

'So we need to get ourselves inside that study and get our hands on those papers,' said Joe speculatively.

'Hang on a minute!' exclaimed Billy in alarm. 'You don't really mean to say we're going to *break in* to the Baron's house, do you?'

Veronica hesitated for a moment. Then she said: 'There wouldn't be any need to break in. Lord Beaucastle is going to be hosting my debutante ball. You could come to the party as my guests – and that would get you inside his house.'

'That's a splendid idea!' exclaimed Lil. 'Everyone will be occupied with the party, and while they are all busy, we can slip through to the study in secret, and find the evidence!'

'But – but what if the Baron gets wind of us?' asked Billy, still looking rather horrified by the idea. 'What if when he sees us, we're recognised?'

'Well, if you're careful, there's no reason he would have

to see you at all,' explained Veronica. 'There are over two hundred people coming, you know – surely you'd be able to stay out of sight in the crowds. Besides, it's a fancy-dress ball, so you'll have to come in costume. That should make it easy for you to disguise yourselves.'

'In disguise again!' said Lil. 'Gosh!'

She was beginning to sound rather excited at the thought of this new plan, but Sophie's face was serious as she worked out the details. 'So we arrive at the ball, just as though we are ordinary guests,' she suggested. 'Once we're inside, we slip away to the study – you can tell us where to find it,' she added, nodding to Veronica. 'Meanwhile, you ensure that Lord Beaucastle is occupied at the ball, whilst we search the study, collect the evidence, and then get it safely away, without anyone noticing.'

Veronica found herself nodding. But there was one problem, she realised, looking around at them. Having Lil and Sophie turn up at her ball would be one thing – especially if they could manage to dress themselves in something halfway decent – but she couldn't see the young fellow with his cockney accent and unpolished manners passing muster at a society gathering. Nor the boy, who, after all, looked scarcely big enough to be out of the schoolroom.

'I'm not sure that you'll *all* be able to come to the ball,' she said hurriedly. 'That is – er – I mean to say, it might look

226

rather odd if I suddenly add a whole lot of names to the invitation list.'

'No problem,' said Joe, sounding more relieved than anything else. 'You two girls go to this ball. Billy and I will be outside on watch, hidden somewhere out of sight. Then, once you've got hold of the evidence, you meet us somewhere. You can tell us where, miss,' he added, nodding his head in Veronica's direction. 'It could be a side door, a window, the coal cellar if it comes to that – anywhere we won't be seen. Then hand the evidence to us, and we'll take it and have it safely away in a jiffy. No one will even know we were there.'

'The grounds are enormous – there are plenty of places you could conceal yourselves,' said Veronica, feeling increasingly enthusiastic about this plan. 'The study is in the East Tower, which is right on the other side of the house, far away from the ballroom, so there won't be anyone nearby. It's on the ground floor and it has big windows.'

'So maybe we could just hand the evidence out to you through the window,' said Lil, clapping her hands. 'Perfect! Then Sophie and I will be able to slip back to the ball and make our exit. No one will ever suspect what has happened.'

'But how will the two of you get into the grounds, if you aren't arriving as guests at the party?' asked Veronica, suddenly looking more anxious. 'There are high walls all the way around, you know. And it will be a terribly *exclusive* occasion – you won't be able to just stroll in off the street!'

'Don't you worry your head about that,' said Joe, grinning back at her in a way she couldn't help thinking was quite unnecessarily familiar. 'We've got ways and means – haven't we, Bill?'

'And once we've got the evidence safely away, we can keep it until Mr McDermott comes back,' Sophie went on. 'If we make sure it's absolutely watertight, he can take it to Scotland Yard – and they might be able to arrest Lord Beaucastle at once.'

'But wait!' exclaimed Veronica, all at once quite aghast. 'Lord Beaucastle is supposed to be announcing our betrothal at the ball, at midnight – and I'll have to accept him! We'll be engaged – and if he is arrested after that, it will be simply dreadful! I mean, I'll be able to break off the engagement of course, but it will be a scandal. I'll be disgraced!'

Lil looked disgusted. 'Is that really what you're worrying about?' she demanded, hands on hips. 'Emily is dead, and the Baron could be planning to bump off your father *and* you once you're married, for all we know – and all you're worried about is what some idiotic society people will think of you?'

'As if *you* could possibly understand!' snapped back

Veronica, annoyed. 'This is important! It's my whole future – I'd never be able to make a good match after something like that. I'd probably end up a spinster!'

'And what's wrong with that, I'd like to know? I'd much rather be a spinster than a complete and utter *ninny*!'

'This isn't helping!' interrupted Sophie sternly. 'You're both wasting time.' She turned to Veronica impatiently. 'Look – you say that Beaucastle is supposed to announce your betrothal at midnight?'

Veronica nodded, looking most affronted.

'Then we need to be sure we get the evidence from his study before then, that's all. As soon as Billy and Joe get the evidence away, we'll let you know – and then you can sham a sudden illness. After all, he can't propose to you if you've been taken home unwell, can he?'

'But how would I do that?' Veronica asked, sounding rather put out.

'Oh, for heaven's sake, use your imagination!' interjected Lil, rolling her eyes. 'Say you've eaten something that disagrees with you. Shut yourself in the ladies' cloakroom and make terrible noises, as though you're being sick. Then recover just enough to be taken straight home in a carriage.'

Veronica wrinkled her nose. 'But how mortifying!' she exclaimed, apparently repulsed by the very idea.

'Well, you can take your choice. You'll either have to pretend to be ill and be jolly convincing about it – or become Lord Beaucastle's affianced bride,' said Lil shortly.

Veronica said nothing for a moment. Then: 'Very well. I suppose I could do that.' Even as she spoke, relief flooded through her. She had felt as though she were tangled in the web of a terrible spider; but now, at last, she could see that there might really be a way out. If the others really could find the evidence, she would not have to marry Beaucastle.

'I do appreciate your assistance in this matter,' she said, feeling rather awkward. 'I will, of course, ensure you are paid well for all you are doing to help me. Would another ten pounds suffice?'

They all stared at her in silence, frowning. 'I could increase the fee,' she went on hurriedly. 'What about twenty pounds?'

'We're not doing this for *money*,' said Billy indignantly, finding his voice at last. He sounded offended. 'We're doing this because we have to stop the Baron. We have to prove who he really is!'

'Oh I – er – I beg your pardon,' Veronica faltered.

'*And* because we want to help you!' added Lil, with decision. It was obvious that even if she did think Veronica was a ninny occasionally, Lil was still determined to fight her corner.

Sophie nodded. 'This isn't a *job*,' she said crisply. 'It's about doing what's right. You don't owe us anything, Miss Whiteley. We're in this together now.'

CHAPTER TWENTY-TWO

It was midsummer's eve in London. The shadows were beginning to lengthen. In Hyde Park the air was drowsy with the scent of flowers.

On Piccadilly Circus, Sinclair's department store was closing. The ruched silk curtains were descending in each of the enormous plate glass windows, signalling that the day's entertainments were now at an end. The last lingering customers were departing, having made their final purchases – a spotted silk handkerchief, a fan, a blue glass bottle of eau-de-cologne. The golden clock in the entrance was chiming, and Sid Parker was sweeping a low bow as he closed the great doors. Upstairs, the salesgirls were totting up the day's takings. In Mr Sinclair's offices, the clerks were calling farewell to one another whilst Miss Atwood carefully blotted her ledger and neatly set away her pens and ink bottles. Mr Betteredge walked through the deserted store, jingling his keys. The corridors and stairways that just a little while ago had been crowded with people were suddenly empty, echoing with new quietness.

But elsewhere, the evening was only just beginning. Restaurants were opening their doors. In the theatres of the West End, the lights were going down and the curtains were going up. Pleasure boats were setting out upon the river. In the great houses of Mayfair and Belgravia, society ladies and gentlemen were dressing for dinner; champagne bottles were bursting open with giddy, delicious pops.

In Sophie's little bedroom in the lodging house, she and Lil were making their own preparations for the evening ahead. At first they had been at a loss to think what they could wear to Veronica's ball: after all, fancy-dress costumes were not something they could find in the mannequins' dressing room at Sinclair's. If Lil was still at the Fortune Theatre, she could have borrowed something from Wardrobe, but the theatre was closed. In the end, it had been Mei and Song who had unexpectedly provided them with a solution.

As promised, Sophie and Lil had returned to China Town the previous day to tell the pair about their plans. Mei and Song had at once insisted that they should play their parts.

'It might be really dangerous,' Sophie had said to them in a low voice. 'What if we're caught and found out? Are you sure you want to run that risk?'

233

Rather to her surprise, it was Mei who answered. 'We know it's a risk,' she said earnestly. 'We understand that better than anyone. We have to be a part of this. Please – we want to *help*.'

Sophie could understand their resolve. Joe had told them about the Baron's stranglehold upon the East End, of course, but it had taken meeting the Lim family to show her what that really meant. The bright lights of the West End, and the golden glitter and glamour of Sinclair's were a thousand worlds away from the dark, dangerous streets of the East End that they had glimpsed from the cab window. No wonder Song and Mei wanted to do whatever little they could to try and push back the dark.

They had talked for some time, and at last had agreed that Song and Mei would accompany Billy and Joe to the grounds of Beaucastle's mansion, where they could act as lookouts. But as it happened, they were able to help much sooner than that. When Lil had mentioned the difficulties they were having finding costumes for the fancy-dress ball, Mei had simply smiled and slipped away, returning with two Chinese outfits, which she had borrowed from the nearby Magic Lantern Show.

Now, Sophie smoothed the heavy folds of the jade-green satin robe she was wearing. It was a little threadbare in places if you looked closely, but there was no doubt that it was an excellent disguise. Beside her, Lil was scrutinising her hair in the mirror. She had arranged it in a heavy knot, and adorned it with a cluster of red silk flowers. Her crimson robes were belted with a wide, gold-embroidered sash, and she carried a matching fan. Her cheeks were flushed with anticipation and her dark eyes were gleaming. In the brightly coloured costume Sophie thought she looked even more glamorous than usual.

Sophie felt rather more awkward in her outfit. The green robes were a little too long for her, but there had been no time to alter them, so they trailed behind her on the ground when she walked. She had tied up her hair in a bun too, but rather than Lil's pretty ornament of flowers, her head was entirely covered by a pointed straw hat that concealed her hair and kept her face in shadow. They had agreed it would be wisest for her to keep her face hidden – since the Baron had seen her more than once, she was the most at risk of being recognised – but the result did not make her feel exactly elegant.

Now, she reminded herself that she was not going to the ball to look elegant. She was going to find the evidence she needed to prove the Baron's true identity, and to stop him once and for all.

She settled her hat more securely into position, feeling suddenly nervous. It had been easy to make this plan when they had been safely in the hayloft at Sinclair's, but now the evening of the ball had arrived, the very notion of going inside the Baron's own house seemed like madness.

She found her heart was racing faster as she glanced up at the clock and saw that it was almost time for them to leave. She tried to breathe calmly: whatever else happened, she must not lose her head. She found herself thinking of Papa, and at once felt better. After all, this was rather like one of the military campaigns he always used to tell her about, sometimes in wearying detail. In spite of everything, she suddenly smiled. She would be the captain leading a mission into enemy territory: that was the way she should think about it.

'Are you ready?' she asked Lil, as she picked up her fan. 'Do you remember everything?'

'Of course,' said Lil. Her face was more serious than usual, and there was a most determined light in her eye. 'It's simple enough.'

'Well it may not be nearly as simple as we're hoping,' said Sophie. 'We have to find our way to the Baron's study without anyone noticing us, and the place is bound to be full of servants. We're going to have to be very careful. Just make sure that you –'

Lil grimaced. 'I know – I know. *Make sure that I don't draw attention to myself.*' She giggled. 'Honestly, Sophie – you really are frightfully predictable sometimes.' She tucked her arm affectionately through her friend's and gave it a reassuring squeeze. 'Come on, let's go. It's time we were on our way.'

Veronica stood as still as a doll while her maid dressed her. On went her camisole, edged with the finest lace; then the delicate silk stockings; then her stays, made of pink coutil and heavily boned to push her into the swan-like shape that was so fashionable. Her maid's small fingers worked deftly, fastening the metal clips and adjusting the lacings. Mechanically, Veronica stepped into the rustling silk petticoat: her maid lifted it carefully, and fastened the tapes around her waist.

Normally, she would have been absorbed in the process of dressing for a ball – and this one more than any other, since it was her own coming-out. This evening though, she barely noticed what her maid was doing. She felt as though she were floating outside her own body. Ordinary things did not seem to matter very much: even when Isabel had scolded her about her unauthorised trip to Sinclair's, the words had seemed to fade away into nothing. 'Going off by yourself, in a *cab*? Whatever would people think? Imagine if Lord Beaucastle heard about it. Goodness me, you might be seven years old instead of seventeen. And what *is* that stuck to your skirt? It looks like bits of *grass*!'

Now, she stood numb as her maid carefully helped her on with the gown itself: a lovely, frothy concoction that had been made for her with great care by the dressmaker. She was going as a shepherdess in a frock of white silk and taffeta, with bows on the bodice and at the elbows, a low square neck, and tiny buttons all up the back. With it she wore a bonnet that perfectly framed her face, and tied in a large bow just under one ear. When she and Isabel had settled on the costume, she had thought that nothing could be more charming: now she just felt silly, a little girl playing dress-up.

'Oh, Miss Veronica! You look perfectly beautiful!' exclaimed her maid. Veronica said nothing. Her breaths felt shallow in the gown's tightly laced bodice. It was almost time.

Her hair had already been arranged in a careful cascade of curls falling over one shoulder; the bonnet was in place; now all that was left was to put on her jewels. She would wear pearl earrings, the pearl-and-diamond necklace that had been her coming-out gift from her father, and pinned to her shoulder, the jewelled moth.

She tried to repress a shudder as the maid fastened it on to her gown. Even as she did so, Isabel bustled into the room, dressed in what was her dressmaker's approximation of Roman garb: a grandly draped satin gown with a low neck that perfectly showed off her ornate diamond-and-ruby necklace.

'Well, Veronica dear, you do look a picture!' she exclaimed, tweaking a curl of Veronica's hair into its proper place. 'Just make sure you behave yourself with decorum this evening,' she added, more sharply. 'Be attentive to Lord Beaucastle – but not too attentive. Let him see you dancing with some other eligible gentlemen. Veronica, are you *listening*? This is a terribly important night.'

Her last words hung in the air as she swept away again. Veronica gazed at herself in the looking glass: the girl in the frilly shepherdess frock looked like a stranger.

'Will you take me with you, miss, when you're married to Lord Beaucastle?' asked her maid suddenly, from behind her, in a timid voice.

Veronica turned round and looked at her in surprise. 'Of course I will,' she said awkwardly. Then she muttered in a lower voice: 'But I wouldn't be too sure that I'll be marrying Lord Beaucastle, if I were you.'

'But of course you will, miss,' said the maid comfortingly, as if she thought Veronica was merely nervous. 'Everyone downstairs is saying so. He's holding the ball just for you, isn't he? You'll be Lady Beaucastle before you know it, just you see.'

CHAPTER TWENTY-THREE

Mei sat at the tiller of the little dinghy, watching the city vanish behind them. They were only a little way west of Chelsea, but as the river curved away from the centre of the city, the landscape was becoming gentler, greener. As they plashed slowly along, Mei realised that her stomach was fluttering with a peculiar mixture of apprehension and fear, and what might almost have been excitement. It seemed so strange to find herself here, in the rickety old sailing boat that belonged to Uncle Huan, heading up the river towards the Baron's manor house, under cover of dusk.

They had already taken down the sails, well before their final approach to the house; now, Song turned and gave her a grin, from where he was sitting beside Joe at the oars. For a moment, she felt something of the same sense of conspiracy she remembered from their childhood adventures. Since her visit to Belgravia, and their discoveries about Granddad, everything had changed. Now, they were in this together – equals, Mei thought.

It had been together that they had convinced Mum and Dad to let them sail the boat along the river that night. Billy had come up with the idea of approaching Lord Beaucastle's mansion from the river: they knew that the gardens ran right down to the water's edge, and with everyone's attention fixed on the guests arriving, it had seemed the perfect way to slip into the grounds out of sight, and without having to tackle the high walls. Mei and Song had at once offered to take them there in Uncle Huan's little dinghy, which he had long ago taught them both to sail.

'It's the least we can do to help,' Song had said. He had fought their case long and hard.

'But you stay in the boat, mind!' Mum had agreed at last. 'You can take them where they need to go – and then you come straight back home!'

'You can trust us to take care, Mum,' said Song, managing to avoid admitting that they had no intention of coming straight back home. Billy and Joe would be going into the grounds of Lord Beaucastle's mansion – and Mei and Song were going too. Mei felt a sudden thrill of pride to think that they were continuing the work that Granddad had started so many years ago.

Joe had stopped rowing. 'I think this is it . . .' he murmured. 'We're here.'

Mei gazed up at the house that lay before them in the twilight. Her exhilaration faded: foreboding rose up in her chest.

If she had thought that Belgrave Square was impossibly grand and elegant, the manor house was something else altogether: an enormous building of grey stone with arched Gothic windows, and a round tower at each corner. It stood in a large expanse of meticulously landscaped grounds, with trees clustering around it. The gardens were bordered on all sides by tall stone walls, but in the distance, they could see great gates opening to admit a string of carriages and motor cars. A faint trickle of music carried over to them on the still evening air: the party had already begun.

'We have to find the East Tower!' hissed Billy from where he was sitting in the prow of the boat. 'That's where Veronica said the study is.'

'Keep your eyes peeled for somewhere to land,' whispered Joe, as the boat moved silently onwards through the water.

As Sophie and Lil stepped over the threshold of Lord Beaucastle's mansion, bright lights and music greeted them. They were standing in an immense and beautiful hallway: the marble floors and chandeliers made Sophie think at once of Sinclair's, but this was no public building made for anyone to enjoy. It was absolutely a private residence: a footman scrutinised their invitation cards carefully. Lil held hers out to him, between her gloved fingertips:

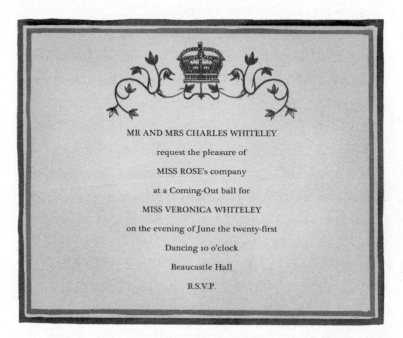

MR AND MRS CHARLES WHITELEY

request the pleasure of

MISS ROSE's company

at a Coming-Out ball for

MISS VERONICA WHITELEY

on the evening of June the twenty-first

Dancing 10 o'clock

Beaucastle Hall

R.S.V.P.

The footman nodded them onwards. They began ascending a staircase, following a number of elegant ladies and gentleman wearing expensively made costumes in sumptuous silks and velvets. Sophie began to feel that she and Lil would stand out at once in their simple Chinese robes. Perhaps Lil was thinking the same thing, for she had become uncharacteristically quiet, twitching her skirts and fiddling with her fan.

'We ought not to look too dazzled,' whispered Sophie. 'We'll give the game away.'

Lil grinned, a sudden spark of mischief igniting in her eyes. She at once affected a look of languid disdain: 'What a very *small* and *inconvenient* hall,' she sniffed, in perfect imitation of the haughty society ladies who came into Sinclair's.

In spite of herself, Sophie giggled, then hurriedly tried to resume a straight face. Two more footmen swept open an ornate door, and they found themselves at the top of a long, sweeping staircase, which led down into an elegant ballroom already thronged with people. Below them, like figures on an elaborate musical box, they could see dozens of couples, dancing a waltz. There was every kind of costume imaginable: Sophie glimpsed pirates and *pierrots* and princesses; a dashing cavalier dancing with Cleopatra; Marie Antoinette accompanied by Robin Hood.

On the brink of the staircase, a stout, grey-haired man dressed as Julius Caesar and a younger lady in a flowing Roman-style gown were welcoming each new guest as they arrived. At their side, Sophie saw Veronica, dressed all in white.

'That's Veronica's stepmother!' hissed Lil. 'I saw her at

the tea party. And that man with them must be Veronica's father. They're greeting everyone!'

They found themselves swept towards Veronica's family. Sophie began to panic: they would have to greet Veronica's father and stepmother, just like all the other party guests. They would have no idea who Sophie and Lil were – surely they would question why two strange girls were attending their daughter's debutante ball? They might tell them to leave; they might summon one of the footmen, or worse still, Lord Beaucastle himself, she thought. He was, after all, the host – so why was he not here, greeting the arriving guests as well?

But Lil was already talking: 'How do you do, Mr and Mrs Whiteley?' she said, smooth as cream. 'I'm Lilian Rose, and this is my – er – my sister, Sophie. Mrs Whiteley, it was delightful to meet you at the charming tea party at your lovely home last week. It's so kind of you to invite us this evening.'

'Charmed,' said Mrs Whiteley in an uninterested voice. Sophie realised that she was not really listening to Lil: she appeared to be looking over both of their heads at the group of guests who were coming down the stairs behind them – evidently important society people. Sophie felt a wave of relief wash over her. Veronica had been right: there were so many guests here that their presence would scarcely be noticed.

'Capital!' exclaimed Veronica's father, giving them

both a vague smile, before turning to greet a gentleman behind them.

Veronica took advantage of their distraction to lean towards Sophie. 'You need to go through the door in the right-hand corner of the ballroom,' she whispered. 'It will lead you to the East Tower. And watch out for the butler – he's always sneaking around and spying.'

Sophie gave the smallest of nods, trying to keep her face neutral as if they were merely exchanging pleasantries. Then Veronica turned to greet the next group of guests, and Sophie and Lil passed on, down towards the ballroom.

'Your *sister*?' she whispered to Lil, disbelievingly, as they slipped past the dancers and moved towards the side of the room where French windows led out on to a terrace. 'No one could possibly believe that! We don't look the tiniest bit alike!'

Lil shrugged. 'I was improvising! Actually, I thought I did jolly well,' she added serenely.

Yet *another* footman handed them each a dance programme – a small white card listing every dance, and a space beside each to write in a partner's name using the tiny pencil attached to the card with a piece of ribbon. Lil examined hers with interest, looking around her at the dancers and the orchestra, but Sophie was already scanning the crowds for the Baron. She could see no sign of him, but nonetheless, she was keen that she and Lil should stay out of sight. She looked around for a corner where they could watch and wait, to be quite sure that the Baron was safely occupied in the ballroom before they went looking for his study. But before they could slip unobtrusively out of the way, a hearty voice boomed out suddenly from behind them.

'I say, Miss Rose! How splendid to see you here!'

The two girls spun around in alarm. A young man was bounding towards them across the ballroom with the enthusiasm of a puppy. He was dressed in an exotic costume complete with a cape and a purple silk turban. Sophie guessed he was supposed to be Aladdin, or one of the characters from the *Arabian Nights*, though the costume looked a little odd in combination with his fair hair and well-scrubbed pink cheeks.

'Oh, juggins,' murmured Lil in a low voice. 'It's Mr Pendleton!'

Sophie knew that Mr Pendleton was a wealthy young gentleman, one of the 'stage door Johnnies' who had haunted the Fortune Theatre when Lil had been performing there. He had proved an unexpected asset in their last adventure, when he had taken Lil to lunch in the Marble Court Restaurant, allowing her to observe a secret meeting being carried out by one of the Baron's top men.

'How jolly to see you,' said Pendleton now, in his loud,

carrying voice. 'It's been too long! I say, I hope you don't mind me saying so, Miss Rose, but you do look simply marvellous in your costume! I'm afraid I look an awful fool in mine, but you've got to join in with the spirit of the occasion, eh?' To Sophie and Lil's horror, a number of people standing nearby were looking over at them, but Pendleton, quite oblivious to their discomfort, went on talking just as loudly as ever: 'I s'pose your dance card is already full to bursting, but I'd be tickled pink to have the pleasure of a dance.'

Lil looked at Sophie, not sure what to say, but Pendleton had already seized her dance card, and was enthusiastically writing his own name in half a dozen spaces. Sophie shrugged: for Lil to refuse a partner would certainly seem rude, and might risk drawing even more attention to them.

A moment later, Mr Pendleton was leading Lil towards the dance floor, talking all the while: 'I must tell you, Miss Rose, all about my new horses. A simply splendid pair. I'd love to take you for a drive in my carriage some time . . .'

Sophie watched him depart with some relief. Whilst Lil was dancing, she could concentrate on locating the Baron. The ballroom was filling up with people; some were dancing, whilst others strolled arm-in-arm through the glass doors that led out on to a little terrace. She looked around her curiously, but a footman gave her a strange look. Apparently it was not the done thing for a young lady to be wandering around the ballroom alone. She spotted a group of debutantes sitting with their chaperones, clutching their dance cards and looking hopefully at passing gentlemen. She went over to them and quietly took a seat in an unobtrusive spot where she thought that she would blend in.

Beyond, on the dance floor, she could see the occasional flash of crimson as Lil was steered around by Mr Pendleton. There was still no sign of the Baron, but from where she sat, she had the advantage of being able to overhear the gossip of the young ladies and their chaperones.

'This is *quite* an affair,' a stately elderly lady dressed in rustling black was saying, in tones that suggested that she did not altogether approve of it. 'Beaucastle certainly knows how to do things in style,' she added, a little resentfully.

'Whoever would have thought that he'd take a fancy to Veronica Whiteley?' said another lady from behind her feathered fan. 'Such a peculiar match!'

'Alice, don't be a nitwit,' said the elderly lady, dismissively. 'The girl will come into an enormous fortune one day. There's nothing in the least peculiar about that.'

'But Lord Beaucastle of all people doesn't need to marry money!'

'One thing you should understand about wealthy men, my dear, is that however much money they have, they *always* think they need more of it,' the elderly lady said briskly before changing the subject abruptly: 'I see that Charlotte Montague is here tonight. How very unseemly! She ought to be in mourning, not gadding about at balls.'

'But Emily was only her second cousin, Mama.'

'I don't care if she was. It's entirely unsuitable, with poor Emily hardly buried. Why, when I was a girl, she'd have been in black for six months!' She made another sudden change of tack. 'Who is that dark girl, dancing with Eliza Pendleton's boy? She's quite the beauty – who is her family? She has a look of Lady Hamilton about her.'

'I don't know, Mama. I don't believe I've ever seen her before.'

'I know her, Grandmama!' A younger voice joined the conversation. 'Her name is Miss Rose – I met her at Veronica's tea party last week and then she came to call on me.'

'Rose?' The voice was very sceptical now. 'I don't believe I know anyone by that name. Is she just out?'

'Oh yes, and she's an awfully good sort!'

'Really, Phyllis,' came the other lady's voice, sounding irritated now. 'Can't you at least *try* to talk in a more ladylike manner? You should say: "She is very pleasant" or "Her company is delightful."'

To Sophie's immense relief, just then the dance came to an end, and she saw that Lil, with some apologetic gestures, was managing to extract herself from Mr Pendleton. Sophie slipped out of her seat and hurried over to her.

'Any sign of him?' asked Lil, at once.

Sophie shook her head.

Lil sighed. 'Like an idiot, I told Pendleton that I couldn't possibly dance and leave you sitting on your own, and now he's gone to get one of his chums to come and be your partner. We ought to slip off before they come back.'

Sophie nodded. 'We have to find the Baron. He must be here somewhere, but we need to be sure. We can't risk wandering about the house unless we know he's occupied.'

Together, they moved off through the crowds. Sophie spotted a secluded corner quite close to the doorway that led towards the East Tower, and nudged Lil – but Lil was looking up in surprise at two smart gentlemen standing close by, drinking champagne.

'Well I never! It's Miss Rose, isn't it? Our enthusiastic chorus girl from the Fortune?'

'Why – Mr Mountville! And Mr Lloyd!' Lil exclaimed in astonishment. 'How do you do?'

Like a number of the gentlemen in attendance, the pair were not wearing real costumes. Instead they were dressed in ordinary evening attire and carrying brightly coloured carnival masks. The taller of the two, whom Sophie couldn't help noticing was extremely handsome, was looking at Lil with an amused expression. 'Whatever are you doing here, my dear? This isn't exactly a chorus girl's usual haunt.'

'Oh, society balls are where I spend all my evenings,' said Lil loftily, looking as though she was rather enjoying herself.

'Who's your friend?' asked the other gentleman, who wore spectacles and had a neatly curled moustache.

'This is Sophie,' explained Lil. 'Sophie, this is Mr Mountville and this is Mr Lloyd. I worked with them at the Fortune Theatre.'

'And are you an actress too?' asked Mr Mountville.

'No, I'm afraid not,' said Sophie, politely, shaking their hands.

'And I thought all the girls wanted to be on the stage these days,' said Mr Lloyd, with a comical shrug. 'Well, Miss Rose, hope you'll come and see us to audition for our new show in a couple of weeks. Seeing you here tonight makes me think that you could be just the person for the part of Arabella in *The Inheritance*.'

Lil clapped her hands and gave a little exclamation of excitement. 'Of course I will, Mr Mountville,' she said. 'I should simply love to play Arabella!'

Sophie smiled too, pleased by this unexpected turn of events. She nudged Lil with her elbow to remind her that it was time to move on, but Lil simply grinned back at her happily, completely misunderstanding her meaning. Bubbling over with excitement, Lil plunged into conversation, asking the two gentlemen all about the play and the new theatre. They, in their turn, seemed amused and charmed by her company. One or two other people connected with London's theatre set came over to join them, and before long, Lil was the centre of a chattering group. Sophie found herself standing on the fringes, simmering with frustration.

Sophie could not believe how quickly Lil had become distracted when she knew that they only had until midnight to find the evidence. Well, she would simply have to track down the Baron, and then head for the East Tower by herself, she thought, in a burst of irritation. She plunged away from the group, into the crowd, but almost at once she found herself almost bumping right into a man striding in the opposite direction. She glanced up instinctively, and turned to ice. The man was already turning away from her, but she had seen immediately who it was. Even if she hadn't recognised him, she would have known it by the way everyone in the crowd was glancing over at him curiously. It was Mr Edward Sinclair!

She darted towards a secluded corner she had seen in the shadow of a large potted palm. Her heart was racing. Why hadn't they guessed that Mr Sinclair would be here? He was always invited to all the most exclusive society occasions. But if he saw her or Lil, he would be certain to recognise them, whether disguised or not. From her corner, she watched breathlessly as he went over to join a circle of gentlemen who were standing right in front of the East Tower doorway, each of whom shook his hand. As the crowds moved and shifted, she caught a glimpse of one of the gentlemen's faces, and realised to her astonishment, that it was the very man she had been looking for – their host, Lord Beaucastle, the Baron.

She stifled a gasp. She knew that the Baron hated Mr Sinclair – and yet here he was, shaking Mr Sinclair's hand in a cheery fashion, clapping him on the shoulder, offering him a cigar. Even from here, she could see that his congenial manner was nothing like the cold, severe way she had seen him behave in private. She stared at the pair from her corner, fascinated. Neither of them had made any concession to the fancy-dress theme, and the black-and-white of their evening clothes stood out starkly amongst the bright satins and velvets and brocades of their companions. But whilst Mr Sinclair held a black domino mask that perfectly complemented his sleek, elegant evening dress, the Baron did not carry a mask at all.

But then, he was already wearing a mask, Sophie realised suddenly. It was simply that his was invisible.

Lil came hurrying over to her.

'I say,' she began, earnestly. 'I'm awfully sorry. I completely lost track of time. It was too ghastly of me. I just got so dreadfully excited when they said I should audition for the new show.'

'He's here,' said Sophie. '*Look*. And he's talking to Mr Sinclair, of all people!'

Lil followed her gaze. 'But – but they're standing right beside the door to the East Tower,' she realised, her face falling. 'We'll never be able to slip through to the study if they stay there!'

'Surely they can't stand there all night,' said Sophie. 'They'll have to move on eventually. They'll have to dance – or go to supper – or –'

'But we don't *have* all night. We've hardly any time at all. Veronica should be here – it was supposed to be her job to keep him busy and out of our way!'

But Veronica was still welcoming guests as they arrived. She showed no signs that she would be coming down into the ballroom any time soon, and the circle of gentlemen showed no signs of moving. Sophie and Lil looked at each other uncertainly.

'Maybe there's a way we could distract his attention away from that side of the room . . .' mused Sophie. 'What we need is some sort of a diversion.'

Lil's eyes brightened with sudden excitement. Recognising the look all too well, Sophie spoke hastily: 'No, *you* can't be the diversion! You need to help me find the evidence.

And Mr Sinclair would recognise you. We'll have to think of something else.'

Lil glanced around the room, evidently hoping that inspiration would strike. As she scanned the crowd, two young ladies caught sight of her. They waved and then hurried over. The smaller of the two, who was dressed charmingly as a Harlequin, seized Lil's hands.

'Miss Rose!'

'We wondered if we'd see you here!' exclaimed the other, who had yellow hair and was wearing a fairy outfit.

'Do you know everyone at this party?' muttered Sophie crossly under her breath. 'Whatever happened to *not drawing attention to ourselves?*'

'How jolly to see you again,' Lil said cheerfully. 'This is my friend Sophie Taylor. Sophie, these are Miss Chesterfield and Miss Woodhouse.'

'Do call me Mary,' said the smaller girl, grinning at Sophie. 'And this is Phyllis.'

'Why are you tucked away all by yourselves over here, and not dancing?' asked Phyllis. 'Miss Rose, I'm sure you ought to be the belle of the ball!'

Lil gave Sophie a thoughtful look. 'I say – Mary, Phyllis, do you think you could help us with something?' asked Lil suddenly. Beside her, Sophie looked rather alarmed.

'Help you?' repeated Mary, in confusion. 'Whatever do you mean?'

At that moment, Mr Pendleton appeared. 'Jolly good, here you are,' he said, well pleased with himself. 'We've been looking for you everywhere.'

'Oh – Mr Pendleton!' exclaimed Lil. 'Well, perhaps you can help us too.'

'And this is Hugo Devereaux,' announced Mr Pendleton cheerfully, gesturing to the young man accompanying him. 'Hugo, this is the delightful Miss Rose and –' he looked uncertainly around at the other three young ladies.

'Oh, never mind all that introductions nonsense now,' said Lil, wafting her hand at him in impatience. 'We need you all to help us.'

'Lil – just wait a minute –' began Sophie, not feeling at all sure about where this was leading.

'Don't fuss,' said Lil, boldly. 'No one else is going to help us, are they? Desperate times call for desperate measures. *She who hesitates is lost*, and all that.' She turned briskly to Mary and Phyllis. 'We have to create a diversion. Sophie and I need to get through that door over there, right where Lord Beaucastle and Mr Sinclair are standing, and *no one can know where we have gone.*'

'Why?' asked Phyllis, utterly baffled.

Lil looked a little uncertain. Somehow she didn't think

there was much chance that any of them would believe that Lord Beaucastle, their generous host, was in fact a notorious villain. She plunged in as best she could: 'There's something fishy going on here at the ball – and Sophie and I have to get to the bottom of it. We can't explain now; we haven't time, but we need your help. Will you trust us for now? We can explain everything later – but first we need to find a way to distract everyone so we can get through that door without anyone noticing.'

'Something *fishy*, you say?' repeated Mr Pendleton, in an unnecessarily loud voice, looking around him curiously, as if he half-expected to see a halibut appearing out of the air.

'*Sssshhh!*' exclaimed Sophie urgently.

'This is secret – and *important*,' Lil admonished him sternly. 'Look, will you help us or not?'

'I don't see why not,' said Mary, with an amused shrug. She looked as if she thought the whole thing was part of some kind of jolly prank. 'It sounds more interesting than mooning around waiting for someone to ask you to dance, at any rate.'

The others nodded too.

'So, what do you think would get people's attention?' Sophie asked them, feeling very relieved that they seemed to be going along with Lil's idea without asking too many questions.

'What would make them all turn around and stare?'

'Being loud or boisterous or unladylike,' suggested Mary promptly.

'Drinking too much champagne?' contributed Hugo Devereaux, gamely.

'*Romping*,' added Phyllis in a meaningful voice.

'Ladies swooning?' went on Hugo.

Pendleton just looked confused.

'Swooning!' exclaimed Lil. 'That's it! Perfect – you're a genius! Phyllis, you swoon. You look like a swooner to me. Mary, you'll have to react to it as dramatically as you can. You know, "*Oh my goodness, Phyllis has swooned, how perfectly dreadful!*"' Lil adopted a high, affected tone of voice. 'Do you think you can do that?'

Phyllis looked anxious. 'But *how* will I pretend to swoon?' she asked.

'Oh, that's easy as pie,' said Lil. 'Just go all limp and fall over. It's frightfully simple. You won't hurt yourself a bit because Mr Devereaux here will catch you.'

'But – but – what if we get into trouble?' asked Phyllis hesitantly.

'Oh come on, Phyllis, buck up,' said Mary. 'It's just a lark. And besides, no one can possibly say it's unladylike.'

'It's *awfully* ladylike,' agreed Lil. 'The gentlemen will love it. A damsel in distress and all that. If you can stage a quick recovery, then I daresay your dance card will be full up for the rest of the evening!'

Phyllis looked appeased by this; and as for Hugo Devereaux, it did not escape Sophie's notice that he appeared rather pleased to have the opportunity to catch a swooning Phyllis.

'What should I do?' asked Pendleton, eager to be of assistance.

'Oh just be fearfully worried. Chafe her wrists and call for smelling salts, that sort of thing.'

'When should we do it?' Mary asked eagerly.

Lil opened her mouth to say that now was as good a time as any, but Sophie interjected hastily, 'Give us time to position ourselves a little closer to the door first. Then – off you go.'

She couldn't help feeling some misgivings as they slipped through the crowd, but a few moments later, Mary's voice rang out quite convincingly: 'Oh heavens! Phyllis, are you ill? Someone fetch a doctor!' Even Lil looked as though she thought Phyllis had done rather a nice job of the swooning. And as for Mr Devereaux, you would have thought that catching ladies was something he did every night of the week. Mary was throwing herself into her dramatic reaction with gusto, whilst Pendleton hovered next to her, trying to manufacture an anxious expression and only succeeding in looking vaguely perplexed.

All around them, people turned to stare. Two footmen hurried over to provide assistance. Mr Sinclair looked around, startled. Beaucastle left their little circle and strode in Phyllis's direction. In the commotion that resulted, no one noticed the two young ladies in Chinese costumes as they slipped through the door and out of the ballroom, into the hallway beyond.

CHAPTER TWENTY-FOUR

Sophie and Lil tiptoed down a long, wood-panelled passageway. In contrast to the crowded ballroom, the corridor seemed deathly silent. The sounds of the party faded behind them. Now the only noise was the shuffling of their feet as they hurried along the parquet floor, very loud in the stillness. It seemed as if the whole house were holding its breath.

'Veronica said to follow the passageway around, and then eventually we'd come to the library,' murmured Sophie, not daring to raise her voice.

Sure enough, after they had gone some way further, they found themselves standing before a heavy wooden door. They glanced at each other nervously, and then Lil gave the door a tentative push. Rather to their surprise, it swung immediately and silently open.

They were standing on the threshold of an enormous, lofty room. It was filled with books, and yet it was like no library either of them had ever seen before. It had high, arched ceilings, and the walls were panelled in dark wood, elaborately carved, making it look like the hall of a medieval king. Two large chandeliers hung from the ceiling, sending out blurry pools of light, but leaving the corners of the room shrouded in dark shadow. In spite of the summer evening, heavy damask curtains were drawn across the window, blotting out the view of the gardens.

Sophie noticed that there was a golden figure positioned in each of the four corners of the ceiling, each with an arm outstretched: from where the girls stood, the statues seemed to be communicating an obscure kind of warning to stay back.

But it was not only the figures that made Sophie hesitate in the doorway. This room reminded her of the study in which the Baron had once held her prisoner. That had been in another house, far across London, but she remembered it with sudden, sharp vividness: the greenish light, the slippery feeling of the leather sofa, the whispering tick of a hundred clocks. There were clocks here too – looking around, she saw an immense grandfather clock, and a beautiful golden wall-clock, richly enamelled – but that was not all. The room held a treasure trove of extraordinary objects.

Together, they crept forwards. Sophie took in half a dozen different things in a single glance. There was an enormous emerald beetle pinned inside a glass case. Beside it were half a dozen butterflies in a rainbow of colours, their dazzling wings spread to the size of one of her own hands. A fan of ornamental swords and scimitars was displayed upon a panelled wall, arrayed like a peacock's tail. An exquisite Book of Hours had been set out on a carved wooden stand, as though someone had been examining it only moments ago: its pages were open to a design of a curving serpent that seemed to be devouring its own tail.

'Look! That door over there must lead to the study!' exclaimed Lil suddenly, her voice echoing out in the silent room. She tugged on Sophie's arm.

Sophie forced herself to stop gazing around and followed Lil to the door in the corner. It stood ajar, leading directly into the room that Veronica had described to them: Lord Beaucastle's study.

As in the library, the study walls were panelled and the furniture was all of heavy wood, but Sophie was struck immediately by a change in atmosphere. This was a conspicuously ordinary room – it could have belonged to any wealthy man. The books on the shelves were bound editions of Dickens that looked as though they had never been opened; the paintings on the wall were dull hunting scenes. There was even a bust of a serious-looking gentleman on a wooden pedestal beside the door. Probably one of Lord

Beaucastle's ancestors, Sophie thought. The room struck such a contrast with the library that she began to feel even more unsettled. There was nothing here that spoke to her of the Baron – no sign of his strange sense of showmanship. It was a room that seemed to have no personality at all.

Although the room was unoccupied, the lamps were lit and the curtains were drawn; a tray with decanters of sherry and port had been set out on a table. Sophie sucked in her breath anxiously – someone might return at any moment.

'We'd better make this as quick as we can,' she said.

But Lil had already begun. She was turning over the few items that lay on the desk. Veronica had said that she had seen it covered with documents, but now there was only a telephone, an inkstand, some blotting paper and a box of monogrammed calling cards. The only thing that looked at all unusual was a curious jade paperweight with strange carvings on it. Lil picked it up and turned it over. It was in the shape of a snake, or possibly a sort of dragon.

Sophie began looking through a tray of letters. Her heart was thumping in her chest. If they were to be discovered now, searching the Baron's own study, she did not even dare to imagine what might happen to them. Her ears were pricked for even the tiniest unfamiliar noise, but all she could hear was the sound of Lil sliding drawers open and shut again.

Her hands were trembling as she leafed through the

papers. They seemed to be ordinary correspondence: letters from Beaucastle's steward about his estate; a note from his banker about some shares. Here and there was something scribbled in the angular, confident handwriting that she took to be the Baron's own, but nothing in the least bit unusual or incriminating.

'There's nothing here,' whispered Lil, sliding a drawer shut.

'Nor here either,' murmured Sophie in disappointment. 'It's all perfectly respectable. Invitations, calling cards . . . nothing at all out of the common way.'

'Wait – what's this?' said Lil. From the drawer, she took out a thick document and handed it to Sophie. The words SOUTH RIDGE were printed across the front of it in bold letters.

'It must be one of Veronica's father's mines,' said Sophie. She opened the report and flicked through. It was a report, detailing locations, depths, yields. It was certainly strange that Lord Beaucastle should have this information. It seemed cold and calculating to have so meticulously researched the property of his bride-to-be and her family, but there was nothing actually *wrong* about it.

She was still looking at it curiously a few moments later, when Lil closed the last drawer in exasperation. 'There's nothing else here,' she said. 'It's all just . . . *ordinary*.'

Sophie looked up from the report, her brow furrowed.

'We should have known he would be too clever to leave anything where it could be easily found,' she said, shaking her head. 'There must be somewhere else he keeps his documents – somewhere secret, like that old derelict house.'

'So what now?' asked Lil.

'I don't really know,' sighed Sophie. She took off her hat for a moment, and wiped her forehead, feeling suddenly weary and desperately disappointed. After all their efforts to get here, all their promises to help Veronica, it was unbearable that they would be leaving empty-handed – without the evidence they had been so confident of finding.

'There *must* be something here,' said Lil stoutly. 'Surely there must!'

Sophie went over to the window, and looked out through the gap in the curtains into the growing darkness. It was awful to think that Billy and the others were out there in the garden, waiting for them hopefully – and all for nothing. Behind her, she was conscious of Lil still moving up and down, examining books on the bookshelves and peering behind paintings, almost as if she expected some clue to be hidden behind them, as in one of Billy's detective stories. But in her impatience, Lil became careless: she brushed against a vase and it tottered alarmingly. She lunged to catch it, but in doing so knocked against the wall, making the oil paintings rattle.

Sophie spun around, a warning on her lips, but the words froze. As Lil bumped the wall, something extraordinary happened. The wall – the whole wall – had actually nudged backwards. *It's not a wall at all*, Sophie realised in astonishment. In fact it was a hinged partition, separating the front part of the study, with its calling cards and sherry decanters, from another space altogether.

Together they pushed the partition back a little further. Beyond was a large room, furnished in an entirely different style again. This was in every sense a practical, working space, full of the signs of purposeful activity. A solid workbench stood in the centre, set with a microscope, a set of brass weighing scales, a sheaf of documents, glass flasks, and a row of test tubes in a rack. There were no oil paintings here: instead, the walls were covered with blueprints and diagrams. A writing desk, cluttered with maps and papers, stood beside a set of shelves crammed with books – no gilt-edged, leather-bound novels now, but row after row of hefty reference books and ledgers.

There was a furtive crackle in the air – the room seemed heavy with secrets. The slightly burnt, metallic, chalk-dust smell made Sophie feel a little dizzy. 'It's not just a secret room,' she whispered. 'It's a secret *laboratory*.'

In even more of a hurry now, they squeezed through into the hidden room and resumed their search. Lil raced towards the writing desk, whilst Sophie turned to the documents lying on the workbench. They seemed to be plans of some kind. The jumble of letters and numbers she encountered were as unreadable as hieroglyphs to her, and yet she couldn't help but examine them closely. When they had last encountered him, the Baron had been working with secret codes – what was his new preoccupation? Could he really be planning to use strange minerals from Veronica's father's mines to create some sort of new and deadly weapon?

She turned to a second stack of papers – and to her surprise, she found that instead of more hieroglyphs, she had in her hands a stash of birth certificates, marriage certificates and property deeds. They belonged to a whole series of different people, she saw, her brow furrowing.

'Look!' hissed Lil suddenly, interrupting her. 'I've found his appointment book!'

She came hurrying over with a black, leather-bound volume, and together they bent their heads eagerly over the pages. At first, they saw nothing but notes about balls and dinners, calls to pay and appointments at the bank, but after they had looked through several pages, Lil pointed to something. The word *Shoreditch* was written against a Tuesday, and underscored twice. A week later, on a Thursday, it was *Whitechapel*.

'Places in the East End!' she whispered excitedly.

'It's still not enough,' said Sophie, shaking her head. 'He could have any reason to be there – legitimate business, or some sort of charitable work.'

But even as she was speaking, an entry caught her eye. It was recent – the Wednesday just passed.

$$PX \int \frac{\partial P}{\partial B} dB + \int \frac{\partial P}{\partial C} dC + \int \frac{\partial P}{\partial M} dM$$

(A.4)

(A.5)

$$= v_0 \frac{\sqrt{c^2 - v_s^2}}{c + v_s \sin \delta}$$

$$= -c^2 v_0 \frac{v_s + c \sin \delta}{(c + v_s \sin \delta)^2 \sqrt{c^2 - v_s^2}}$$

$$\partial_{PB} = \frac{\partial P}{\partial B}$$

$$R = L_0 \frac{c^2 + v_s \sin \delta}{\sqrt{c^2 - v^2}}$$

$$dP = \frac{\partial P}{\partial B} dB + \frac{\partial P}{\partial C} dC + \frac{\partial P}{\partial M} dM$$

$$\frac{v_s \sin \delta}{1 - v_s^2}$$

89

$$\frac{d^2}{d\phi_3}$$

Wednesday 11 June 1909	
Time	Event
11.00am	Mallock, Savile Row
2.00pm	Luncheon at the club with R
7.00pm	Mitila Sygsmue Oemn
8.45pm	Dinner at Fitzmaurice's
10.00pm	York House Ball

'I say,' said Lil, staring at the 7.00 p.m. appointment. 'What a strange name.' She looked up at Sophie. 'You don't think it could be . . .'

'A *code!*' finished Sophie. She thought again of the Baron's fascination with codes and ciphers, and the way he had kept all his most critical communications secret. 'If it's in code, it must be something important! But how do we work it out?'

Lil stared at the page for several moments, and then back at Sophie. 'You know how to work it out, silly,' she said suddenly. 'It's easy. *It's the code that I used when I wrote the note about your birthday tea.*'

Sophie gaped back at her. 'But – it can't be!' she exclaimed.

'It is!' said Lil, her eyes growing wider by the second. 'Look at it!'

Sophie tried to remember how the code had worked. You read every second letter starting with the first, she recalled – and when you came to the end, you started again. 'M – T – L – S,' she began. 'But that doesn't make any sense at all!'

Lil shook her head vigorously. 'It isn't every second letter this time. It's every *third* letter. Look!'

She pointed to the letters as she spoke. 'M – I – S – S – E – M – and now we've run out of letters, so we go back to the beginning again – I – L –'

'*Miss Emily Montague,*' breathed Sophie. 'And Wednesday

is when she went missing!'

'It's proof!' burst out Lil, forgetting to whisper now. 'It's proof that he killed her!'

For a long moment, they stood silently staring at the appointment book, but then Sophie shook her head, as if to snap herself out of her thoughts. 'This is important – we should take it,' she said. 'But we still need more. Something that proves without question Beaucastle's connection with the East End and the Baron's Boys.'

'What about account books?' suggested Lil. 'Look – there's a whole row of them here.'

She took one from the shelf and handed it to Sophie. It was filled out in careful handwriting that did not match the scrawl in the appointment book. Here and there she caught sight of some of the addresses: *Whitechapel Road*; *High Street, Shadwell*.

'I think this might do it!' she exclaimed in excitement. 'Let's take it! And a couple more – there are so many that he mightn't notice these are missing.'

Lil grabbed two more books from the shelf, and then they swiftly slipped out of the secret laboratory and back into the study.

Outside, in the grounds of Lord Beaucastle's mansion, tempers were beginning to fray. It seemed like a very long time since they had left the boat, and there was little for them to do but watch and wait in the shadowy gardens. There was no one in sight. They could hear a trickle of music from the brightly lit house, and see the distant comings and goings of carriages and motors, but in the safety of the trees, all was dark and silent. After an hour or two, everyone was becoming a little snappish when at last Lil's signal – three owl hoots – came quavering through the darkness.

Joe shook his head: 'I hope no one else heard that,' he murmured. 'It sounds more like someone being strangled than anything else.'

'You stay here on watch,' said Billy to Mei and Song. 'If you see anyone coming, do the owl hoot. We'll get the evidence and meet you back here.'

Joe and Billy slipped cautiously through the dark towards the East Tower. The call came again, but even without it, it would have been easy enough for them to find the window at the base of the tower. Yellow light was spilling out on to the grass.

'Did you find anything?' Billy whispered, as soon as he caught sight of Sophie and Lil.

Suddenly everyone was talking at once in low, excited voices:

'Did you get here safely?'

'Did anyone see you?'

273

'Are Mei and Song all right?'

'Here's his appointment book. And these are some of his accounts – they've got lots of East End places listed.' Sophie passed the books through the window to Billy, who took them excitedly.

'Read a bit out,' suggested Joe.

Billy opened one and, squinting in the light that came from the window, began to look down the page: 'There's a list of names,' he reported. 'Payments made, payments received. Let's see . . . *Arthur Smith, 110a Whitechapel Road, £10 6s 2d. Or Mrs O'Grady, High Street, Shadwell, £5 10s.'*

'Ma O'Grady!' exclaimed Joe in excitement. 'She runs a gaming house down by the docks. That's one of the Baron's places, for sure.'

'*Mr George Black 15s . . . Mr James Lee, 12 Hollywell Street, 14s 6d.'*

'James Lee – that's Jem!' exclaimed Joe, forgetting to whisper in his astonishment. 'The fellow I used to work for – leader of the Baron's Boys. This is it – this is the stuff you need!'

They grinned at each other in delight. 'We've done it – we've really done it!' squealed Lil.

'But now you have to get them away from here – and quickly,' said Sophie.

'We will,' said Billy. 'But why don't you come with us?

Don't risk going back to the party.'

Lil looked tempted, but then Sophie shook her head. 'No – we have to let Veronica know we've got the evidence, remember?'

'And don't forget about Phyllis and Mary – and Mr Pendleton,' remembered Lil, with a giggle. 'They'll be wondering what happened to us.'

'Keep those safe overnight,' said Sophie to Billy and Joe. 'Somewhere under lock and key, if you can. Then let's meet at Sinclair's first thing tomorrow and decide what to do next.'

The boys nodded seriously, and Sophie felt a wave of relief sweeping over her. All they had to do now was go back to the party, say goodbye to Veronica and the others, and then go home, as though they were ordinary guests. Even if a servant glimpsed them in the passageway, it would be easy to say that they had merely got lost. She felt a thrill of pride to think that they had actually done it – they had actually managed to get the evidence that McDermott and Scotland Yard could use to prove the Baron's real identity, once and for all.

'Wait a minute,' she said suddenly, an idea striking her. 'Let me fetch some of those papers I saw as well. They might be important – and the more evidence we have the better.'

She slipped quickly back into the secret room and pulled out a few sheets from the sheaf of scientific papers she had seen on the workbench. She might not be able to make head or tail of them, but perhaps someone would – and they might turn out to be important. She folded them up and stuffed them in her pocket, and then hurried back, closing the partition behind her.

Meanwhile, Lil was scrutinising the bust that stood beside the door to the study. 'I say – do you think this is meant to be Beaucastle himself? It doesn't look much like him,' she said, prodding its nose disrespectfully.

But Sophie did not hear her. As she picked up her hat from where she had left it on the study desk, her gaze fell on an old photograph that stood in a carved wooden frame, and suddenly all her lightness swept away.

The picture was of two military gentlemen, smartly attired in dress uniforms hung with medals, and with swords at their sides, standing with a young lady dressed in a light-coloured gown in the fashion of fifteen or twenty years ago, complete with large, and what must then have been very stylish, puffed sleeves. All three were smiling at the camera. Although much younger, it was quite clear that the man in the centre was Lord Beaucastle. But it was not the Baron that made Sophie stop and stare. To her disbelief, she saw that the man at his side was her papa.

What was more, the young woman who stood on his other side was her mother.

Her heart somersaulted painfully in her chest.

'Lil –' she said urgently.

But the voice that replied was not Lil's.

'Good evening, Miss Taylor,' said a horribly familiar voice. 'This is an unexpected pleasure. Still playing at being the Lady Detective, I see?'

Horror swept over Sophie as she looked straight up into the face of Mr Cooper.

He was dressed as a butler, in a neat black tailcoat, and he looked quite different from when she had last seen him – his face was thinner, he had shaved off his beard and now wore a small moustache – but the one-time Sinclair's store manager was quite unmistakable. He was standing in the doorway, one hand on the door handle and a revolver poised in the other.

'Unfortunately for you, I'm afraid that my master doesn't care very much for snoopers.'

Sophie stood as if frozen to the ground. Mr Cooper was Lord Beaucastle's butler – the one that Veronica had warned them about! She could scarcely believe it. As her thoughts raced, he stood watching her with a cold smirk on his face. 'I could call him,' he said thoughtfully. 'Or perhaps I could just deal with you myself. The music from the ball is loud enough that I daresay no one would hear a gunshot. And after all, it seems fitting for me to be the one to bring your little investigation to an end.'

He looked at her mockingly and raised the gun, pointing it straight at her.

CHAPTER TWENTY-FIVE

Everything seemed to happen very quickly. From the window, Billy gave a yell of horror. Mr Cooper glanced up in surprise, and as he did so, Lil emerged from behind the door, clasping the bust of Lord Beaucastle in both hands, and smashed it defiantly over his head. The blow was a hard one: Cooper crashed to the ground. The revolver went off, firing into the air, shattering some of the crystals in the chandelier that hung above the writing desk. The noise was impossibly loud.

Lil dropped the bust, her eyes wide as she gazed at Cooper, prostrate on the floor and groaning feebly.

'Oh . . . *I say* . . .' she muttered.

Sophie began to breathe again – but her relief was only momentary. 'Quickly!' she cried. 'We have to go!'

She grabbed Lil's hand, and dragged her to the window. Billy and Joe helped her through, and then Sophie followed, bundling the skirts of her gown up in her hand.

Mei and Song came running towards them from between the trees. 'What happened?' demanded Song. 'We thought we heard a shot!'

'You did!' said Sophie, breathlessly. She could still scarcely believe what had happened, but there was no time to pause now, not even for a moment.

'It looked like he was really going to shoot you!' exclaimed Billy.

'I reckon he would've, too, if it hadn't been for what you did,' said Joe, giving Lil a glance that was even more admiring than usual, if that was possible. 'That was a cracking great wallop you gave him.'

'Oh *golly*,' said Lil. 'Do you think he'll be all right?'

'Don't waste your sympathy on Cooper!' exclaimed Billy crossly. 'Haven't you forgotten what happened at Sinclair's? He'd have happily finished us all off if he'd had the chance!'

Lights were coming on in the windows of the East Tower, and they could hear the sound of raised voices. 'Come on – we need to go!' said Joe, urging them forwards into the trees, away from the house. But it was already too late.

'I can see them!' yelled a voice from the window. 'They're outside in the gardens!'

A door somewhere banged open: there were footsteps on the gravel, figures coming towards them in the darkness.

'Split up!' called Joe urgently, and they scattered.

'Quick – get the evidence away!' called Sophie over her shoulder to Billy. He was carrying the appointment book and one of the account books, while Joe had the two others. She saw him nod and veer off into the trees, with Song racing after him.

'What now?' cried Lil.

A surge of energy swept through Sophie: They must not lose the evidence now, after they had worked so hard to find it. 'We have to draw them away from Billy!' she exclaimed. 'It's like in the ballroom – we have to create a diversion!'

Lil darted forwards. 'I know how!' she cried. 'Follow me!'

At the back of Lord Beaucastle's manor house, twenty or more carriages and motor cars stood in the stable-yard, waiting until their owners were ready to leave the ball. Their drivers were sitting sociably together, enjoying the mugs of ale that two kitchen maids were passing around. There was a festive mood in the air: music from the ball was spilling out of the open door, inspiring a stable boy to swing round one of the maids in an impromptu dance.

'You ought to see the spread they've got in there,' the other kitchen maid was saying to Mr Pendleton's driver. 'A whole salmon! Roast chicken. Ham and tongue and game. French rolls. Blancmange – you've never seen the like.'

'Ah well, Lord Beaucastle knows how to give a party,'

said a wheezing old groom, proudly. 'Anyway, it's a special occasion, ain't it?'

'That's right,' said Perkins, the Whiteley's driver, nodding sagely. 'Young Miss Veronica's debut. Her maid says she'll be engaged to your Lord Beaucastle before the night is up.'

The maid opened her mouth as if she was going to say more, but her attention was caught by something happening across the yard. A young man was running towards one of the carriages: a glossy black affair pulled by a beautifully matched pair of chestnut horses. Mr Pendleton's driver looked up from his glass of ale in astonishment.

'Hey you!' he called out. 'Get away from there! That's Mr Pendleton's carriage. Whatever do you think you're doing?'

But Joe had already hopped up into the driver's seat. Lil pushed Mei up beside him and he flung out an arm to steady her. Then Sophie and Lil leaped inside the carriage and slammed the door.

'Don't have a fit, guv'nor,' Joe called saucily from the driver's seat. 'I'm just taking 'em for a little spin.'

Joe clucked his tongue and had started the horses before the driver had chance to take more than a step towards them. Astonished, the driver dropped his glass and shot forwards, the rest hot on his heels.

'Hey! Stop! Stop, thief!'

But it was too late. In a great clatter of hooves, the carriage was rattling down the sweeping driveway. Not realising what had happened, but seeing Mr Pendleton's carriage coming, the gatekeeper had already opened the gates, and a moment later, the carriage had swept through and out on to the road beyond.

Mei clung to the seat, white-faced and terrified, as the carriage shot forwards. Beside her, Joe was flicking the reins and murmuring comforting words to the horses as they paced along the road, leaving the Baron's house behind them.

'Well that was a right old fuss, wasn't it?' said Joe, giving her a hesitant smile. 'But with any luck we'll have given your brother and Billy a good chance to slip away without being seen.'

'Will – will they follow us?' asked Mei, her voice tremulous.

'I reckon they will, but we've got a bit of a head start on them,' said Joe. 'Besides, this pair are tip-top – fine horses, they are.'

He settled back in his seat, but Mei could not relax. The thought of Song, left behind in the dark, made her feel sick with fear.

'What about Song and Billy?' she gasped out. 'What will they do now?'

'Don't fret,' said Joe, in the same quiet way he spoke to the horses. 'They'll be safe and sound in the boat by now.

All they'll have to do is sail back along the river. They'll be toasting their toes in front of the fire before you know it.'

His voice, with its familiar cockney sound, was strangely comforting. Mei found herself beginning to breathe a little more easily.

'So where to now, modom?' Joe asked her jokingly, touching his hat as if he were a polite chauffeur and she was his passenger.

There was only one place that Mei wanted to go. She knew exactly where Song would head just as soon as he could. 'Let's go back home – to the shop,' she said eagerly.

Joe hesitated. In spite of his attempts to reassure Mei, he was feeling anything but calm himself, and the thought of going back to the East End gave him a sharp stab of fear in the way that nothing else had tonight – not even taking Mr Pendleton's carriage from right outside the Baron's manor. Mind you, it wasn't as though that was exactly stealing. Lil had been very adamant that this Mr Pendleton – whoever he was – wouldn't mind them 'borrowing' his fancy carriage.

'I don't know if that's such a good idea,' he said gently to Mei now. 'I know we said we'd meet back at your place in China Town if we got separated, but the Baron's Boys, well . . . the East End is their territory. If we get out there and they're on our tail, they'll have the upper hand, for sure.'

'But I know somewhere *perfect* that we can hide the

284

carriage,' said Mei earnestly. 'It will be quite safe and they'll never know. Besides,' she added, after a pause, 'where else could we go?'

For a long moment, Joe found himself thinking of the wonderful comfort and peace of the Sinclair's stable-yard. Right now, it seemed hundreds of miles away. But Mei was right: they could not turn up there in a carriage that to all intents and purposes was stolen. What was more, it would undoubtedly be the first place that Cooper would think to look for them.

He'd already resolved that it was time to stop running away. So he gathered himself: now was the moment to put his fear of the East End aside, once and for all. 'Right then, milady,' he said. 'To China Town we go.'

Lil and Sophie slumped back against the comfortable padded seats of Mr Pendleton's carriage.

'First you're almost shot – and now here we are in a stolen carriage,' gasped Lil in awe. 'What an evening! Not that it's really stolen of course – I mean, Pendleton would have lent it to us, if we'd had the chance to ask. It was rather a good idea of mine, don't you think?' she went on, peering out of the window as they trotted along at a brisk pace. 'I just hope Joe and Mei are all right up there.'

Sophie said nothing. Her mind was working feverishly

as she tried to make sense of all the extraordinary things that had happened to them. She thought of the secret laboratory, which must be where the scientist Veronica had mentioned had been carrying out his experiments on the mineral from the mines. Could the papers she had taken show how it could be used to make an incendiary weapon? She took them out of her pocket and gazed at them, but the numbers and letters remained an unknowable jumble. She remembered that when she had overheard the Baron and one of his companions discussing their plans when she had encountered him before, they were talking about wanting to kick-start a war, and how it would make them rich and powerful. Creating a new and deadly weapon was exactly the kind of thing that would help him to do that. Had Emily somehow stumbled on the laboratory and learned what was going on there? Could that have been what she had used to try and blackmail the Baron?

The horses were going faster now. Lil knelt up on the seat for a better view. 'I say, there's a motor coming up behind us!' she exclaimed. 'We're being followed!'

'Is it them?' asked Sophie, scrambling up beside her.

The carriage lurched to the side as Joe sent them flying around a corner at a rapid pace. It was evident that he was going as fast as he dared, trying to lose their pursuers. But the motor car swerved out behind them too, its bright lamps burning like yellow eyes. The horses were going even faster now, and the two girls had to cling to their seats to prevent themselves being bumped about the carriage. They clattered over the cobbles of a back street, then out again on to a road, weaving between the motor cars and carriages that made London's roads so busy even at this time of the night, then out into another back street. Joe was deliberately taking a twisting route, trying to throw off their pursuers, but the yellow lights were still behind them in the dark. Over the noise of hooves on the cobbles, Sophie could hear the engine roaring.

Then there came a sharp crack, and a pinging sound. A horse whinnied in fear.

'Was that – a *shot*?' breathed Lil. 'They're shooting at us?'

As they looked at each other, horror sweeping over them, another shot rang out, and the stolen carriage rattled onwards, carrying them faster and faster towards the East End.

'Miss Whiteley, my dear. I hope you are having a delightful evening?'

Veronica rose anxiously to her feet from where she had been sitting, talking with some of the other debutantes. She had hardly glimpsed Lord Beaucastle all evening: now here he was, holding out a gloved hand. Instinctively, she glanced around for Sophie and Lil. She hadn't seen them for hours.

It was already after eleven – surely they must have found what they needed by now?

'Would you care for a stroll on the terrace?'

Veronica swallowed, and accepted Lord Beaucastle's arm, trying to smile.

'What a very beautiful night,' he said companionably as they stepped together through the glass doors that led from the ballroom out on to the magnificent terrace. 'A perfect midsummer eve, don't you agree?'

Veronica managed to murmur something about how beautiful his gardens looked.

'I'm delighted to hear you admire them. They will be your gardens soon, after all.'

Veronica felt herself blushing. There were one or two other couples also strolling on the terrace, taking advantage of the warm evening, but Beaucastle led her away from them, down into the gardens. He pointed things out to her as they went: first a magnolia tree that he said was magnificent in the springtime; then a particularly fine marble statue; then a climbing rose that smelled delicious in the evening. Gallantly he plucked a flower and handed it to her.

'Miss Whiteley, I am afraid I have brought you out here under false pretences,' he said, after they had been strolling for some minutes. 'I wanted to take the opportunity to have a talk with you in private.'

She looked up at him, taken aback. It was not yet close to midnight – surely he couldn't be going to propose to her already?

He had stopped short on the gravel path, and gently turned her around to face him.

'I have heard some news this evening that I find *unsettling*,' he said in a rather different tone of voice. It was sharper – colder – the voice she had heard talking to Henry Snow through the study door. 'I don't wish to alarm you, but my butler has discovered two intruders in my study. Two young ladies – or perhaps *ladies* is not quite the right word for them – who were guests here at this party. They took advantage of my hospitality to sneak into my private quarters and help themselves to my property – and took it upon themselves to attack my butler when they were exposed. What do you think of that?'

Veronica felt ice-cold. Had Sophie and Lil been captured? 'That – that's terrible,' she stammered out helplessly.

Beaucastle nodded. He was not smiling now. 'But what troubles me most, Miss Whiteley, is that I have met these two particular "young ladies" before,' he went on, fixing her with a searching expression. 'And so, I think, have you.'

Veronica gazed back at him, her eyes wide, uncertain what he meant. Had he recognised Sophie and Lil from the day they had seen him at Belgrave Square? Would she need to construct some sort of story about what they had been doing there? Her heart thumped frantically.

'I don't care for insubordinate girls,' said Beaucastle in a slow, meaningful voice. 'Young ladies ought to know their place. Don't you agree, Miss Whiteley?'

Veronica managed to stammer out that she did agree, of course.

'You'll have to be more careful about who you befriend, my dear,' said Beaucastle, returning to his usual avuncular tone, tucking her arm back into his, and leading her back in the direction of the house. 'You mustn't let unscrupulous people take advantage of you. But don't be anxious,' he added, patting her hand. 'I'll take care of this. And once we are married, I will ensure you are always well looked after.'

Instead of returning to the ballroom, Beaucastle led her around to the front of the house. His glossy black motor was waiting on the driveway: a uniformed chauffeur behind the wheel. As they approached, he turned his head, and Veronica was shocked to see that he was not Beaucastle's usual chauffeur at all, but the scientist, Henry Snow.

'They are travelling east – towards Limehouse,' Snow said shortly. 'We're headed to the docks.'

'Very well then,' said Beaucastle. He patted Veronica's hand once more, then detached his arm from hers and opened the door to the motor.

'Where are you going?' gasped Veronica.

'I have a matter of business to take care of,' said Beaucastle, coolly. 'That inconvenient incident that I mentioned to you needs to be dealt with properly – and I've decided that I must handle it personally this time. I am sorry to leave you without a host, my dear, but I am sure you will manage admirably. Remember what I said, and do not worry. I'll be back very soon. After all, when I return, we have an engagement to celebrate. Drive on!'

The motor rumbled off into the night, leaving Veronica standing all alone on the empty driveway.

At long last, the carriage jolted to a halt. Sophie breathed out a long, wavering sigh of relief. They had lost the motor car some time ago: whizzing out into the city's brightly lit main streets amongst the traffic had prevented any more shots being fired, and by dint of some clever driving, Joe had at last managed to shake off their pursuers.

Someone jumped down from the driver's seat, and after a moment they heard the sound of a heavy door sliding open. Then the horses were moving forwards, slowly this time. After a few moments, the carriage came to a standstill.

'Where are we?' whispered Sophie.

Lil was peering out of the window. 'I say!' she exclaimed. 'We're inside! I think we're in some sort of a warehouse.'

The door of the carriage opened, and the two girls found Mei and Joe looking in at them. They looked rather pleased with themselves.

'Well, I don't think much of *you* as a coachman,' said Lil, as she accepted the hand Joe was holding out to her. She laughed, but the sound was trembly. 'You had us bumping about all over the place!'

Joe grinned as he helped her to jump down, but Sophie saw that he looked drawn and exhausted. 'Look, you should just be glad that you were safe inside and not up top, with bullets flying at you,' he said, in a voice that was trying hard to remain light and teasing. 'Not like Mei, here. She's a proper trouper,' he added, then let out a long gust of breath. 'I never thought I'd be relieved to see the East End again,' he said. 'But this was a smart idea of yours, all right.'

Mei, still very pale, looked pleased at this. They were in an unused warehouse, not far from the docks. There were some empty wooden crates stacked high in a corner, and the four of them quickly piled them in front of the doorway, so that anyone who looked casually through the doors would have no idea that a carriage and pair were concealed inside.

'We can slip out of the side entrance. The shop is only a couple of minutes away,' Mei explained.

'What about the horses?' asked Sophie, as Joe unhitched them from the carriage.

'We'll have to fetch them in the morning,' said Joe. 'Mei says this warehouse isn't in use, so they'll be perfectly safe until then. I'm only sorry we can't get them some food and water. They've certainly earned it.'

'We can come back later and bring them some,' said Mei. 'But let's go now. I want to get home to Mum and Dad and see if Song is there.'

Mei hardly dared say quite how desperate she was to get home. The thought of it made her knees weak. She took in deep lungfuls of the air, breathing in the smell of smoke and the river, as they crept through the deserted warehouse, up some stairs, and then out on to an iron walkway that ran across the street, connecting the two warehouses on either side.

But as Lil stepped out on to the walkway, Joe pulled her suddenly back, gesturing to them all to be quiet. Below, Mei saw to her alarm that half a dozen men were going by on the street: a couple no more than boys, but the others big, tough-looking fellows. She knew at once by the swagger of their walk who they were.

'The Baron's Boys,' Joe whispered, almost to himself. His attempt at cheerfulness had vanished: now his face was grey with fear.

'What are they doing?' whispered Lil.

Joe shook his head. They waited until they were sure

the men had passed before they slipped over the walkway in a silent row, like a game of follow-my-leader through the shadows. They stayed quiet and watchful for the rest of the short walk to China Town.

As soon as they stepped through the door of Lim's shop, the bell jangling behind them, Mei felt flooded with relief. The wonderful scent of home enveloped her. Mum came running out to greet them, squeezing Mei into a tight hug.

'Mei! Thank goodness you're safe. And your friends too – come through into the back room. You must be hungry and thirsty,' she said, closing the door behind them and bolting it. 'Some of the others are here – they want to talk to you.'

The back room seemed much smaller than usual. To her astonishment, Mei saw that it was crammed with their friends and neighbours: Mr and Mrs Perks; Mrs Wu and her son, his arm bound up in a sling; Ah Wei; Mrs O'Leary from the baker's. What were they all doing here – had they been having another meeting, in the middle of the night?

'Where's Song?' demanded Dad at once.

'We got separated,' explained Lil. 'He's with our friend Billy. They'll be making their way back here too, in the boat. We think they'll be back soon.'

'Did you find it? The evidence?' Dad asked eagerly.

Joe took out the two account books and laid them on

the table. 'It's all in here,' Sophie said. 'They're account books. We took them from a secret room at the Baron's house. Billy and Song have another, as well as the Baron's appointment book.'

A whisper of amazement went round the table. The people of China Town looked at them in awe. Dad was shaking Joe's hand, and Mei glowed with pride at what they had done.

'Sit down, sit down,' said Dad, moving people down along the table to make space as Mum set down some cups and the old blue-and-white teapot. 'We've been discussing all this – and we wanted to talk to you –'

Suddenly, there came a hammering on the shop door and a low, angry voice called: 'Open up! We know you're in there!'

'The Baron's Boys!' gasped someone.

Sophie leaped to her feet in horror. 'They found us? But how?'

Joe was already peering out of the kitchen window. 'There's a fellow in the yard. They're all around the house!'

Dad looked from him to the faces of the others around the table, and back again. 'We'll deal with this,' he said. 'You should get away.'

'But how can we?' asked Lil, her face pale.

All at once, Mei knew what they should do. 'I know a way!' she burst out.

Leaving the others behind in the warm back room, Lil and Sophie hurried after Mei up the steep, creaking flight of stairs. Joe seized the account books and followed. They could hear yelling behind them.

'Open up this door now! Or we'll set the place ablaze!'

There was a crash as a window smashed in the shop. A wave of sick panic swept over Mei, but she pushed it back, and shoved open the door to Uncle Huan's room.

'We can't hide up here!' exclaimed Joe, looking around him in confusion. 'They'll find us in seconds!'

'We aren't hiding,' said Mei, closing the door behind them. 'We're going up and out.' Even as she spoke, she was pulling out the stool, and clambering up to open the window. A moment later she was out on the roof.

'Hurry!' she exclaimed.

Downstairs, they could hear the sound of raised voices. 'I don't know who you're talking about,' Mum was saying boldly. 'What time of night do you call this to be knocking on decent people's doors, breaking their windows? Explain yourselves!'

Lil was the next to spring up on the stool. Her long gown was not exactly designed for climbing, but she was tall and strong, and with Mei lending a hand from above, she quickly managed to clamber out and on to the rooftop. Sophie followed, and then Joe handed up the account books before the three girls together helped haul him up too, closing the window behind them.

For a moment, they paused, taking in the landscape of jagged roof tiles and crooked chimney pots.

'By gum . . .' Joe found himself muttering. He had hoped never to see the East End again, but he'd certainly not expected to see it from this angle. He was struck by the unexpected beauty of it: the fragmented lines of rooftops, broken here and there by a church spire. In the far distance, the lights of the City twinkled.

Ahead of them, Mei was already picking her way deftly along the roofs, sure-footed as a mountain pony.

'How did you know about this?' asked Lil, following her.

'Song and I used to play up here sometimes, when we were little,' she said breathlessly. 'We weren't supposed to, of course, but we did anyway. There's a way we can get down – come on.'

Joe suddenly noticed that Sophie wasn't going anywhere. She was holding on to a chimney stack, her face pale.

'What's the matter?' he said, hastening over.

'I – I'm afraid of heights,' she murmured. 'Don't tell the others.'

Joe looked up to where the other two were already scrambling ahead. 'All right, but you'll have to come with me,' he said. He took hold of one of her hands. 'You've handled far worse, and that's the truth. I'm not so keen on this either, if I'm honest. But I reckon maybe we can get through it together. Just follow me, and hang on – and whatever you do, don't look down.'

Grimly, Sophie unpeeled herself from the chimney stack. She was the captain, the leader of her regiment, she reminded herself: it was her job to keep her head. She couldn't possibly give up now. Her palms were sweating as she inched cautiously along, trying not to look down. Before them, Mei went on confidently, not even hesitating when a loose tile clattered to the ground in front of her. They went along one more rooftop, and then at last it was time to descend – first down an iron ladder on to a flat roof, then down again.

There was no sound but their footsteps.

'Are they behind us?' whispered Mei.

Joe looked up at the rooftops. 'No,' he whispered back. 'It looks like we've dodged them.'

'What about Mum and Dad?' said Mei in a small voice. 'And Shen and Jian?'

Sophie felt guilt wash over her. The last thing she had wanted to do was to get the Lim family in trouble, and now they had brought the Baron's Boys to their very door. What if they did set the shop on fire – or worse?

'You ought to go back,' she said. 'Make sure your family are safe. We'll be fine from here.'

Mei shook her head. 'No,' she said stubbornly. 'You don't know the best way to go.'

They were all very sober as they slipped and slid their way down to the ground again, and crept across a yard zig-zagged with lines of washing. They went through a broken gate and out into the alleyway. 'Look,' said Mei, a note of triumph creeping into her voice. 'We've made it!'

'That's what you think, little girl.'

A man with broken teeth leered down at them from the alleyway. He was carrying a piece of iron piping.

'Guv'nor!' he called out into the darkness. 'I've got 'em!'

CHAPTER TWENTY-SIX

At Miss Veronica Whiteley's debutante ball, the festivities were still in full swing. Many of the guests had not even arrived until just before midnight. The band had struck up a merry polka, and several groups of young people were gathered at the supper table.

Amongst them were Mary, Phyllis, Mr Pendleton and Mr Devereaux, who were tucking into plates of lobster salad with gusto. Phyllis had been enjoying herself immensely since staging her swooning fit. Miss Rose had been quite right: as soon as she had 'recovered', a number of young gentlemen had hastened over to see if she was feeling well enough to consider a waltz later in the evening. The truth was, though, Phyllis preferred the company of Mr Devereaux - or Hugo, as he had insisted she must call him. He had proved himself a divine dancer, not to mention a rather good sort. Seeing her the centre of attention amongst a host of eligible young men, even Grandmama had not intervened. In fact, Phyllis saw, glancing across the room to where the Countess was holding court at another table, she looked as if she were having as much fun as Phyllis was herself.

Only Mary looked a little unhappy.

'What's the matter?' Phyllis whispered under her breath.

Mary shrugged. 'I'm probably being silly,' she whispered back. 'But I can't help wondering what happened to Miss Rose and her friend. It's been *hours*.'

Phyllis bit her lip. 'Gosh,' she said. 'I suppose you're right.'

'And where is Veronica, come to that?' went on Mary. 'I haven't seen her for an age – nor Lord Beaucastle either. When is the big engagement announcement going to take place?'

'It is rather odd . . . do you think we ought to look for them?'

'Look for who?' boomed Mr Pendleton, overhearing them.

'*Ssshhhh!*' hissed Mary crossly. 'Good heavens, Mr Pendleton, you're awfully noisy. For Miss Rose and her friend, of course. We're worried they might be in some sort of trouble,' she added in a low voice.

'In trouble?' repeated Mr Devereaux. 'But surely all that about being in danger – it must have been some sort of a joke, mustn't it?'

'I'm not so sure any more,' said Mary seriously. She got to her feet. 'Let's see if we can find them.'

The four of them left the supper table, and went through

the ballroom and up the stairs into the empty hallway, where there was no one to be seen, but for a footman passing by with a tray of glasses.

'Perhaps we should try outside,' said Mary, heading for the door.

But even before they could step out of the house, a white-clad figure came hurtling through the doorway.

'Veronica! There you are! Goodness me, whatever is the matter?'

Veronica clasped hold of Phyllis in desperation. 'It's Miss Rose and Miss Taylor – Lil and Sophie!' she burst out. 'I think they are in terrible danger! He's gone after them – I don't know what he's going to do!'

'Whatever do you mean?'

'*Who* has gone after them?'

Veronica didn't answer any of their questions. Her eyes had suddenly lit up at the sight of Mr Pendleton. 'You have a new carriage, don't you, and a fine pair? You told me all about them at Mrs Balfour's ball! Quickly – we have to go after them – now! To the East End – Limehouse. I'll tell you everything on the way!'

'To *Limehouse*?'

'Yes, that's right, but we must hurry – there's no time to lose!'

'But – but Veronica – you can't just leave your own

coming-out ball!' said Phyllis, aghast. 'Whatever has happened, we can't go dashing off in a carriage. Not on our own with two young gentlemen! Why, we haven't even a proper chaperone. It would be a scandal – it would be –'

'Oh shut up, Phyllis!' stormed Veronica. 'This is far more important than any of that. Something really terrible could be happening to Lil and Sophie – and it would be all my fault.'

This announcement led to an explosion of questions. Then, finally, Mr Pendleton boomed out: 'Wait a minute! You say Miss Rose is in danger?'

'Yes!' exclaimed Veronica impatiently. 'That's exactly what I'm saying!'

'Well in that case it's perfectly simple,' said Pendleton. 'We must rescue her at once. Now, where's my carriage?'

But no sooner had they got to the stables, than Mr Pendleton's coachman came rushing up to them. He was holding his hat in his hands and looked most agitated.

'Oh, Mr Pendleton, sir, I'm so terribly sorry, I can't think how it happened!'

'What is it, man?' asked Pendleton, looking alarmed.

'It's your carriage, sir – it's gone. *Stolen!*'

Sophie, Lil and Mei stood in a small, shivering group at the end of the dock. They had been herded there by the Baron's Boys: some half a dozen men who were now standing around them in a semicircle, holding sticks and clubs. Joe had tried to put up a fight, but had suffered for it: a long trickle of blood was running down the side of his face. Now his arms were pinned back by the man with the broken teeth – Jem, the man Joe had once worked for – and another of the Baron's boys. He looked desperately over at the three girls.

'Well, well, well, so here we are again,' said Cooper, strolling up to the girls, a smirk on his face. His eyes were gleaming with enjoyment, and he was weighing his revolver in his hands as if he was deciding what to do with it.

'Watch out for her,' he said to the Baron's Boys, jerking his head in Lil's direction. 'She's the one I have to thank for this rather nasty headache. It's put me in something of a temper.'

He held the revolver close to Lil's face. 'You know, nothing would give me greater pleasure than to pull the trigger and finish you and Miss Taylor off here and now. Your antics at Sinclair's inconvenienced me considerably. Sadly for me though, the master has decided that he'd like to deal with you himself.'

A murmur ran through the Baron's Boys.

'You – you mean he's coming here?' asked one of the men holding Joe, looking astonished.

'That's right, Mr Lee. He's going to be paying us a visit any moment now. So you all better make sure you're on your best behaviour,' said Cooper, looking round meaningfully. 'The Baron is coming.'

The men glanced at each other, visibly surprised and nervous. 'Just for them kids?' Sophie heard one of them muttering. 'But – he never turns up for no one!'

'What on earth shall we do?' whispered Lil in Sophie's ear, taking advantage of their momentary distraction.

'I don't know,' said Sophie desperately. 'Could we swim for it?' she asked, glancing across at the murky waters of the river.

'We can't leave Joe,' said Lil. She was staring miserably at him, as he struggled helplessly in the arms of the Baron's Boys.

'No talking,' said Cooper, looking at them both sternly. 'Another peep, and your friends here will wish you'd never opened your mouths.'

Sophie's stomach twisted sharply. This had all been her idea, she realised, more guilt rising up like a sickness inside her. She had been the one who had said they should go to the ball; she had been the one who had wanted to find the evidence; she had been the one who had suggested creating the diversion so that Billy and Song could escape. The thought that perhaps they had got away safely with some of the evidence was the one thing she had left to cling to.

But even that word, *evidence*, seemed weak and silly now

– something from a childish game of playing at detectives. How could they ever have been foolish enough to think that they could really help topple a man like the Baron? He held all of the East End in the palm of his hand – and they were nothing more than a couple of shop girls. She had tried to be someone else – to emulate her father and be the captain, taking her troops bravely into battle. Yet in the end, this was where she had led them. To the edge of the docks, late at night, facing down a revolver. Beside her, Mei was weeping quietly.

'He's here!' came a voice from the edge of the circle. The group parted at once, and beyond, Sophie caught sight of an expensive motor car pulling up. The chauffeur got out and opened the door, and then the Baron emerged. In his immaculate dress suit and neat gloves, he looked completely out of place in the murky lamplight of an East End dockside. He seemed mildly bored, like someone on his way to attend a not particularly interesting social engagement. He paid no attention whatsoever to the gaggle of Baron's Boys, who were silent, bowing their heads respectfully. Instead, he addressed Cooper.

'Good heavens, Freddie. This is all rather uncivilised, isn't it? There's no need to be quite so brutish. Can't someone give that little girl a handkerchief?'

Without waiting for a reply, he turned abruptly to face

Sophie. 'Good evening, Miss Taylor,' he said, sweeping her a low bow. 'So we meet again.'

In spite of everything, Sophie couldn't help thinking how strange it was to hear him address her directly. She realised that she hadn't ever heard him say much at all – only the few brief words that she had overheard in the box at the theatre. Then he had been clipped and authoritative, almost curt: now he seemed more expansive.

As she stared, she realised that he was staring back at her just as keenly. 'I would appreciate it if you could give me back what you took from me,' he said coolly, after a few moments had passed.

'We've already got them, sir,' said one of the men holding Joe, looking excited. 'Tommy. Bring the books.'

A weaselly little man dashed forwards and presented the Baron with the two account books that they had already taken from Joe.

'Not those,' said the Baron, coldly. '*She* knows what I mean. The papers you took from my laboratory, if you please.'

He looked back at Sophie again, and this time it was like a flash of electricity. It felt as though he was seeing into the very core of her. Then he did something that she had not expected. He laughed.

'It's a shame, really, that it has come to this, but you and your little *band of comrades* have inconvenienced me twice now, and I can't let that sort of thing continue.'

To her utter astonishment, he leaned forwards, quite close to her. 'You're like him, you know,' he said in a low, intimate voice. 'Not in colouring, perhaps, but the way you hold your chin up. That arrogant look in your eye. I'd know you were his daughter anywhere. You think you're a little bit better than everyone else, don't you, just like he did? But I don't see much of her in you. She was the prettiest girl I'd ever seen. No – not pretty – that's too weak a word. She was beautiful.'

Sophie gaped back at him. Her blood was pounding in her ears. He was talking about her parents: how had he known them? How could he say these things to her?

'But enough talk. Give me back what I came for.'

In her pocket, her hand found the folded sheets of paper. She took them out slowly, stepping backwards as she did so until she was separated from Mei and Lil by several feet, standing right beside the edge of the docks, beside the dark river water.

'Do you mean these?' she snapped out suddenly, taking even herself by surprise. 'These bits of paper? Why are they so special that you'd come all the way down here to get them back?' She held out her hand: the papers were above the water now.

'That's quite enough. Hand them over.' His voice was sharp, suddenly less easy.

'I'll give you them if you tell me why they're so important,' she said.

'My dear, you are hardly in a position to bargain,' said the Baron, but to her surprise, the chauffeur had darted forwards.

'*Why they're so important?*' he spat out. 'You don't even know what you've got! That formula is going to *change the world*. Do you have the first idea what a weapon that powerful will be able to do?'

'No,' said Sophie, standing fast. 'And I don't much want to, either. Maybe I should just throw them in the river now and be done with it.'

'Think carefully,' said the Baron in his smooth voice. 'Whatever you may believe, you're not a detective. You're not the heroine of a sixpenny novel. You're a girl. A silly, ignorant *little girl*.' He took a step closer. 'A little girl all alone. No one to come looking for you. No one who cares. Not since dear Papa passed away, anyway.' He paused: he was so close to her now that she could feel the warmth of his breath. 'Have you ever wondered how he died?'

A little gasp escaped Sophie's lips, but he had already turned away as he continued: 'My point is that no one will mind very much if you wash up in the river tomorrow. Not like Miss Montague – her accident caused quite a fuss – but girls like you disappear in this city *every day*. Do you really think anyone will notice one more?'

Seizing his opportunity, he turned back, wrested the papers from her grasp, and handed them to the man in the chauffeur's uniform, who clasped them possessively to his chest.

'Thank you,' the Baron said quietly. 'That wasn't so difficult, was it?'

To Sophie's horror, he reached into his jacket and pulled out a long, sheathed knife, with an ornate handle shaped like a twisting dragon. She made a last desperate effort to dart away, but Cooper grabbed her immediately and pulled her back. The Baron removed the knife from its leather case and began slowly polishing the blade.

'Now . . .' he said in a leisurely voice. 'You're all going to learn a lesson about what happens when you cross me. Which one first, I wonder? This little girl? Or the lovely young lady perhaps? Hold on to her tightly: she's stronger than she looks. Miss Taylor, I believe I'll save you until last.'

Joe managed to break away from his captors, and tried to dart towards Beaucastle, but Jem caught him again and gripped him savagely, half choking the life out of him. 'Your turn next,' chuckled Jem in his ear. 'Or maybe he'll let us deal with you ourselves, if we're lucky. Bye bye, Joey Boy.'

Joe could see Lil gazing at him in distress. He felt desperation wash over him: surely there had to be something else, something more that they could do. But before he could think or move or act, something extraordinary happened.

'*Mum! Dad!*' screamed Mei.

Racing along the docks towards them were the people of China Town. They were carrying what at first glance looked like weapons, but as they came closer, it was clear that they had armed themselves with anything they could find – shovels, rakes, rolling pins. Mrs Lim shoved her way roughly through the throng, and rushed up to Mei, wrapping her arms protectively around her daughter.

'Enough!' she cried furiously, looking round at the men. 'We've had just about enough from you. You want to hurt them? Well, you'll have to come through all of us first.'

The Baron looked startled. 'Who on earth are these people?' he murmured low to Cooper. But Sophie was close enough to hear.

'That's Lim's daughter-in-law,' Cooper hissed back.

For a moment, Sophie thought she saw the Baron's face whiten. This was what he had always worked so hard to avoid, she realised suddenly. He had kept himself so carefully hidden from the people of the East End for so long. But he had already recovered himself. He gave a short laugh. 'This is a delightful touch of local colour, but I'm afraid it's rather misguided,' he said, addressing Mrs Lim directly. 'What exactly do you intend to do? My men have revolvers and knives and clubs. Your . . . *people* have kitchen utensils. I admire your bravery, my dear, but I'm afraid this is a fool's errand.'

But even as the words were out of his mouth, a horn was heard honking loudly and persistently. To Sophie's astonishment, she saw another motor car pull up: the doors were flung open, and out sprang two young men dressed in silk robes and turbans. They were accompanied by three young ladies, one of whom appeared to be wearing fairy wings, another in a frilly white dress and beribboned bonnet.

'*Miss Whiteley?*' choked the Baron.

'Stop!' shrieked Veronica. 'We know everything!'

'Mr Pendleton!' cried Lil, in amazement. 'Mary! Phyllis!'

'Don't worry, Miss Rose! We've come to rescue you,' announced Mr Pendleton in a thunderous voice. He leaped forwards, Mr Devereaux close at his heels.

'Let go of them, you brutes!' screeched Phyllis, in a voice that no one could say was at all ladylike.

As if her cry had been the match igniting a fuse, suddenly chaos seemed to explode in all directions. One of the Baron's Boys aimed a blow of his club at Mr Devereaux, who ducked nimbly and put the skills he had learned at his boxing gymnasium to good use by dealing the fellow a smart punch to the nose. Together, Mary and Phyllis were raining blows upon Henry Snow, whilst beside them Mr Perks wielded his spade with unexpected vigour. 'That's what you get for taking my pub from me!' he was heard to yell, as he advanced upon a particularly burly Baron's Boy. Mei clung to her mother, frozen with astonishment, as Mr Lim leaped into the fray, sending two of the Baron's Boys crashing to the ground with a single, forceful kick.

'I didn't know Dad could do *that*!' exclaimed Mei breathlessly.

'He learned kung-fu from the monks when he was a boy,' said Mrs Lim, as she pulled Mei away. 'But it's been a long time since he had cause to use it.'

Meanwhile, Ah Wei could be seen smashing Jem over the head with his iron frying pan, forcing him to release his grip on Joe, who at once ran towards Lil.

'What is going on here?' yelled Cooper angrily, reaching for his revolver.

But before he could draw it back out of his pocket, there came a dazzling flash of bright light that fixed them all dazedly for a long moment. Then everything was moving again, louder and more chaotic than before. There was the shrill blast of a whistle and the clang of a bell. There was the roar of an engine, and then there were people, policemen, spilling everywhere. Cooper let go of Sophie in panic, and she fell to the ground.

'Stop right there! You're surrounded!' yelled a voice.

Sophie gaped upwards. Above her, the Baron stood

motionless, before shooting her a distinctly poisonous look. It was the first time he had looked at her with any expression that was not coldly triumphant.

'You said I was silly and ignorant – and maybe you were right,' she found herself choking out. 'But whatever else I am, I'm *not alone*.'

'Really, Miss Taylor,' he hissed back sharply, 'I'm wishing I had simply let Freddie put a bullet through you when I had the chance.' He looked at her contemplatively. 'Still, I can't deny you're cleverer than I gave you credit for. I daresay we'll meet again. For now – *adieu*.'

He swept her another exaggerated bow, then there came a sharp pinging sound, and the whole place was plunged suddenly into darkness.

'He's shot out the lights!' someone cried out.

More shots rang out above her, and Sophie instinctively flung her hands over her head. She heard Lil scream again, and in the dim light, she groped blindly towards the sound. She stumbled to her feet, sliding on the cobbles. Then someone else screamed, and then she heard Joe's voice quite close, yelling: 'Get a light!' She struggled towards him, but all at once hit something very hard, so hard that stars danced before her. She fell back to the ground again, dazed – there was a scuffle and a splash – and then all at once, light returned, and she saw that Joe and Lil were standing beside her.

'What's happening?' she asked, groggy and disorientated. They were at the edge of the docks: across the river, a small dinghy was moving very fast over the water. In it was the Baron.

'He's getting away!' called voices. 'Quick, after him!'

But Joe and Lil weren't looking at the boat. They were both looking gleefully down at the man who was bobbing up and down helplessly in the dark water. 'Help!' he called out. 'I can't swim!'

Joe's face was cut and swollen, but his bleeding lips were cracked into an enormous smile. 'You only went and knocked him right in the river,' he said delightedly, nodding to the figure in the water – and Sophie realised that it was Mr Cooper.

By now, Sophie had gathered her wits enough to see that all around them were uniformed policeman, several of whom were gripping struggling members of the Baron's Boys. Mr Lim was shaking hands with one policeman whilst Veronica stood and watched as another hauled away a downcast Henry Snow. Best of all, running towards them across the docks were Billy and Song. They looked tired but delighted.

'Miss Taylor,' said a very familiar voice from above her.

Sophie looked up to see none other than Mr McDermott leaning over her. He held out a hand. 'Let me help you up.'

PART V
The Supper Party

An impromptu supper party may be quite a delightful occasion. I speak not, of course, of the formal banquet supper at a ball – that is a much more formidable affair, with its ornamented cakes, oyster patties, and champagne cup. Let us consider instead the simpler pleasure of gathering together around a small supper table at little notice. The remains of the chicken might be fricasséed, a savoury omelette prepared, to be followed by tarts, cakes, cheese and biscuits. Such a cosy gathering is the perfect setting for a tête-a-tête between intimate friends.

Lady Diana DeVere's *Etiquette for Debutantes: a Guide to the Manners, Mores and Morals of Good Society*. Chapter 14: Supper – Appointments of the Table – Impromptu Suppers – Ball Suppers

CHAPTER TWENTY-SEVEN

There was quite a party in Lim's shop that evening. There were so many people that they could not all be fitted into the back room, but instead spilled out on to the shop floor, where Ah Wei had set out a feast of dishes from the Eating House along the counter. Mary and Phyllis helped Mrs Lim to hand around mugs of tea, whilst Mr Devereaux rushed out to fetch the two bottles of champagne that by happy chance he had in the motor. Meanwhile, Shen and Jian were watching the goings-on from the upstairs landing, well pleased by the unexpected late-night activity – and delighted that Mum and Dad had not even noticed that they were out of bed. They were even happier when Mei slipped up the stairs to bring them a plateful of tasty morsels from Ah Wei's spread.

In the kitchen, Song was at the stove, cooking up another batch of his now-famous dumplings.

'I say, these really are jolly good,' exclaimed Mr Pendleton, attacking a second plateful with enthusiasm. He was so busy tucking in that he merely nodded when Mei explained to him that his fine new carriage and pair were waiting for him not far away in an abandoned warehouse.

Meanwhile, Sophie, Lil, Billy and Joe were sitting around the kitchen table, talking furiously. Veronica was with them, sitting in a chair beside Billy. Her white dress was bedraggled now, and she looked somewhat sheepish – but still very pleased to be part of the group.

'Tell us what happened after we split up,' Lil demanded eagerly.

Billy looked up from his case notes, which he had been busily updating. The dog-eared exercise book was now almost full. 'Well, we managed to get back to the boat and then we set off down the river,' he began. 'But it was awful not knowing if we were being followed – and having no clue about what had happened to the rest of you. We weren't sure of what to do – but then I remembered that there was one other person, apart from Mr McDermott, that we could trust to help us.'

'Who?' asked Joe, frowning.

'Mr Sinclair, of course,' said Billy with a grin. 'After what the Baron tried to do to Sinclair's department store, we knew that he would help us. But still, we felt a jolly pair of fools ringing the bell to the Captain's private apartments, I can tell you.'

'But he wasn't at home!' exclaimed Sophie. 'He was at

the ball – we even saw him talking to Lord Beaucastle!'

'That's right, he wasn't – but Mr McDermott was there waiting for him! He'd got your letter and come home straight away. He'd just got off the boat train from Paris, and he'd gone to your lodgings, but of course you weren't there – so he came to Mr Sinclair.'

'Golly – what a stroke of luck!' exclaimed Lil.

'As soon as McDermott saw us and heard what we had to say – well, he went into action at once,' Billy went on. 'He was on the telephone in two seconds flat – and it was scarcely more than five minutes before some fellows from Scotland Yard arrived in a motor car and whizzed us off to the East End to find you.'

It was just then that Mr McDermott himself appeared in the doorway. He nodded to Song, at the stove, and then came over to where they were all sitting at the table. He took the empty chair beside Sophie. 'I've just spoken with Scotland Yard,' he explained. 'I thought you would all like to know that they have confirmed that the documents you obtained are more than sufficient to prove Lord Beaucastle's connection with a whole host of illegal activities in the East End. He's a wanted man now.'

'That's wonderful!' Lil exclaimed, as a buzz of excitement ran around the crowded kitchen. 'We did it! We proved who the Baron really is!'

'Well, in one sense you're quite right, Miss Rose – but I'm afraid that you're wrong too,' said McDermott enigmatically, as he gratefully accepted a mug of tea from Mei. 'Unfortunately, I'm afraid that things have proved a little more complicated than we expected.'

'What do you mean?' asked Sophie in surprise.

'It looks as though the man that everyone knew as Lord Beaucastle may not, in fact, have been Lord Beaucastle at all,' McDermott announced, taking out his pipe. He turned to Veronica. 'Miss Whiteley, what can you tell us about Beaucastle's background and family?'

Veronica thought for a moment. 'He was the second son,' she remembered. 'He didn't get on very well with his father, and went off to join the army when he was young.'

'Oh yes, that's right!' said Mr Devereaux, pitching in. 'He was something of a traveller, wasn't he? Always full of all sorts of tales of places he'd been.'

'Frightfully dull stuff, if you ask me,' added Mr Pendleton, looking around to see if there might be any more dumplings ready yet.

'A traveller, indeed,' said McDermott, lighting his pipe and settling back into his chair. 'The story goes that he went abroad with his regiment when he was a very young man. He severed all ties with his father and elder brother, and no one heard from him again for a number of years. In the

321

meantime, the old lord died, and the elder son inherited the estates, but then he died too, just a few years later, without leaving an heir. By all accounts the family lawyers had to go to all sorts of lengths to track down the second son – there were even rumours that he had died abroad – but eventually they found him. He came back to London, where he inherited the whole Beaucastle fortune. By that time, he had been away for over fifteen years.'

Sophie was frowning. 'Do you mean to say,' she asked slowly, 'that the man who came back wasn't the real Lord Beaucastle?'

'That's exactly it, Miss Taylor. The evidence now suggests that he was in fact an impostor – someone impersonating the second son in order to claim the title and fortune.'

'But – that's impossible!' exclaimed Billy. 'Surely people would have realised that he wasn't the same man!'

'Remember that the real Beaucastle was little more than a boy when he left – and he would likely have been changed a great deal by army life,' said McDermott. 'Fifteen years is a long time.'

'But he would have had to provide proofs of his identity, wouldn't he?' asked Song shrewdly, as he dished up another plate of dumplings. 'He would have had to convince the family lawyers that he was who he said he was.'

'And apparently he did provide proofs – convincing

ones, too,' said McDermott, taking a dumpling from the plate and blowing on it to cool it a little. 'Likely they were forged papers, such as a birth certificate.'

'Like those papers I saw in the secret room!' Sophie remembered. 'I saw a whole sheaf of them – there were birth certificates, marriage certificates, all kinds of things. They were all different identities – different people!'

'So he was just shamming all the time?' exclaimed Mr Devereaux in disgust. 'I say, what a frightful cad!'

'So we haven't discovered who the Baron is at all!' said Sophie. 'He wasn't Lord Beaucastle – that was just another mask . . .'

She felt utterly crestfallen. She had been so sure that they were exposing the truth, but it was nothing more than another piece of the Baron's theatre. Everything they had done had been for nothing.

'That may be true,' said McDermott. 'But it doesn't mean that what you have achieved is not of enormous value. Thanks to you, we have managed to arrest a dozen of his men, not to mention two of his closest associates – Freddie Marvell, the butler, sometimes known as John Cooper, who has eluded us once before, and Henry Snow, the scientist who worked with him. They are all going to have a good deal of useful information to give to my colleagues at Scotland Yard.'

'You'll have a job to get the Baron's Boys to tell you

anything,' said Joe, thoughtfully. 'But I hope you'll lock 'em up and throw away the key. It's no more than Jem and the rest deserve.'

'We shall see,' said McDermott thoughtfully. 'I believe that "the Baron's Boys", such as they are, will cease to exist as of tonight. The Baron has fled – their leader and most of the gang are behind bars – what use is their loyalty now?'

'China Town won't have to worry about them any longer,' said Song, grinning at Mei.

'That's right,' said McDermott. 'But what's more, together you have torn down the carefully constructed identity that the Baron has spent years refining and perfecting. You have lost him access to some tremendous assets – the Beaucastle fortune and estates, an influential position in society, which he has no doubt used to his own personal advantage – and the chance to secure the Whiteley mines for his own. All that is gone now. He'll never be able to appear as "Lord Beaucastle" again.'

Sophie suddenly looked over at Lil. 'That's it!' she burst out. 'That's what Emily Montague discovered. The secret she found out on the day of the garden party, the day that she stole the jewelled moth. She must have learned that Lord Beaucastle wasn't the real Lord Beaucastle.'

'Golly – you're right!' exclaimed Lil. She looked at McDermott. 'Miss Montague's maid told us that Emily had found out a big secret about Lord Beaucastle that she planned to use to blackmail him. I suppose he couldn't risk the truth getting out – especially when he was so close to becoming engaged to Miss Whiteley, and to getting his hands on her father's mines.'

McDermott nodded. 'You may well be right,' he said. 'The mines, by the way, seem to be a particularly interesting business, and you were spot on in your assessment of the Baron's plans. It seems that, with Mr Snow's help, he had identified that a particular rare mineral could be used to create very powerful incendiary weapons – explosives unlike anything we have seen before. This mineral is only found in a very few places, notably your father's mines, Miss Whiteley. He determined to take control of the mines and use the mineral to manufacture deadly weapons, which could then be sold to governments around the world – at quite a price, of course. Happily for you and your family, Miss Whiteley, he won't have that chance now.'

'But what will happen about the mineral?' asked Billy, curiously.

'I suppose that is up to Mr Whiteley,' said Mr McDermott. 'I am sure he'll be contacted very soon by Scotland Yard's scientists. Personally I hope that it will prove to have the potential to be used for purposes other than warfare.'

Veronica nodded slowly, but across the table from her,

Joe was frowning. War and weapons did not interest him much; but what did puzzle him was the Baron's behaviour. 'What I don't understand is why he came to the East End tonight,' he said. 'All right, so the Baron – whoever he really is – he finds out that the real Lord Beaucastle has died, and sees an opportunity to fake it and claim his fancy title and great big fortune. He manages to pull the wool over the lawyers' eyes, spends years pretending to be Beaucastle and enjoying all his money. At the same time, he's running his rackets out of the East End, taking special care to protect his Lord Beaucastle identity and make sure that there's no chance of anyone making a connection between him and the Baron. He plays it safe for so long – so why did he risk it all by coming to the East End tonight, just to get hold of those papers?'

'A very good question,' said McDermott. 'My guess is he was getting anxious. He's a clever fellow – he must have known that Scotland Yard were on his tail. Since what happened at Sinclair's in the spring, they've been tightening their net around the Baron. I myself had been in Paris, following a trail that pointed to a link between the Baron and someone high up in society on Scotland Yard's behalf. And then of course, poor Miss Montague had already come close to uncovering his most closely guarded secret.'

'It's not that I can't see him wanting us at the bottom

of the river, where we couldn't tell anyone what we'd discovered,' said Joe. 'But why not let his Boys deal with us, and stay safe at Miss Whiteley's party?'

'I think it was because of *you*, Sophie,' said Lil, suddenly. 'He spoke as if he *knew* you.'

'Or if not me, then my parents,' said Sophie soberly; and she told them about the photograph she had seen in the Baron's study.

McDermott forgot all about his pipe. 'A photograph of your parents? Are you quite sure of that?'

'*Sophie!*' exclaimed Lil. 'Why didn't you tell me? You didn't say anything about a picture!'

'Well, what with getting shot at, and clambering over rooftops, and being held at knifepoint by the Baron, there wasn't exactly a great deal of time!' Then she went on in a different tone of voice: 'Besides, it's just so strange. I don't know what to make of it at all . . .'

Her voice trailed away, but at that moment, Mr Perks came through the door, carrying several jugs of ale he had brought from the Star Inn, Mr and Mrs Lim and the others following behind him. Whilst the ale was being poured out, and more food was being passed around, Mr McDermott took the opportunity to turn to Veronica.

'Miss Whiteley, I managed to reach your father on the telephone. I've told him that you – and Miss Woodhouse and the others – are quite safe and sound.'

'Thank you, Mr McDermott,' said Veronica, in rather a small voice. She sighed unhappily. 'I suppose he was awfully angry. I've disgraced myself, I know. Running away from my own debutante ball! My reputation will be utterly ruined!'

'Well, I have to admit that he did sound rather – *distressed*,' said Mr McDermott carefully. 'And I believe it was your stepmother I could hear in the background? But his first concern was for your safety.' He paused for a moment, contemplating her, then went on: 'I also managed to have a few words with Mr Sinclair, who happily was still at the party. He undertook to explain matters a little further to your father and stepmother. I am sure that he will be able to convince them that what you did was not at all disgraceful – but in fact extremely brave. I cannot think of many debutantes who would head into the night to rescue their friends from a notorious East End criminal.'

'But – but debutantes aren't *supposed* to be brave,' wailed Veronica. 'They're supposed to be prim and proper!'

Across the room, Mr Devereaux was jovially accepting a glass of ale from Mr Perks. 'Oh I don't know,' he said, hearing this. 'That's all a bit old-fashioned, isn't it? Speaking for myself, I'd much rather dance with a jolly girl with a bit of pluck than a prim miss without a word to say for herself – wouldn't you, Pendleton?'

'Too right I would, old bean!' said Pendleton, waving his glass of ale enthusiastically and gazing at Lil so admiringly across the table that Joe sat up in his chair, looking alarmed.

'Besides,' added Mary to Veronica, 'imagine how much worse things might have been. Why, you'd have been engaged to a criminal by now! Just think what everyone would have said about that.'

'Gosh,' agreed Phyllis. 'That's right. We could have been toasting your betrothal at this very moment. Thank goodness we're here instead – and anyway, I think this is just as jolly as a ball.'

'And so it is!' said Pendleton. He turned to Lil: 'But it's a dashed shame that we never got any more dances. I say . . . might I escort you to a dance next week? There's going to be a party at The Ritz on Friday – perhaps you would do me the pleasure of accompanying me?'

Lil grinned. 'Thanks awfully for the invitation, Mr Pendleton. It's very kind of you to ask. But I'm going to be rather busy for the next few weeks practising for my audition for Mr Lloyd's new play – and besides, I think I've had enough of high society for a while.'

Next to her, Joe swigged his ale casually, trying not to look too relieved.

Across the table, Veronica found that Mei was sitting beside her. All at once, she remembered that she was still wearing the jewelled moth. With some difficulty, she unpinned it from her shoulder.

'I think this belongs to you,' she said, holding it out.

Mei took it in awe, holding it in cupped hands. She looked over at her father. 'The Moonbeam Diamond!' she breathed.

'What will you do with it?' asked Billy, curiously.

Mr Lim leaned over, and gently lifted the moth from his daughter's hand. He raised it up to the light, where it glinted brilliantly. 'It's truly a beautiful piece of work,' he said thoughtfully. 'But for us, it's the diamond that matters. If you are really willing to give it up, we should like to have it removed and to return it to the temple.'

'But – but wouldn't you rather sell it?' asked Veronica in astonishment, looking again at the many signs of poverty she saw all around her.

Mei shook her head. 'Of course not. It's special – we couldn't do that.' For a moment, she hesitated. She had never really thought about what would happen once they got the diamond back. She had supposed they would keep it, so that it would protect them. But she saw that Dad was right. The diamond should be returned to the monks, as Granddad would have wanted. Besides, she reflected, looking around them, it had been the people of China Town and their new friends, in the end, who had protected them from the Baron's Boys – not a magic jewel.

'But how will you get it to the monks?' Billy was asking with interest.

'On his last voyage to China, my brother brought back word that the monks had begun to rebuild the temple in our old village,' explained Mr Lim. 'He should be able to return it to them. Perhaps I might even go with him. It would be good to see our old home again.'

'If we take out the diamond, then you could have your brooch back,' Mrs Lim said to Veronica, more practically. 'I'm sure a jeweller could replace it with another stone. It's such a fine piece.'

Veronica shook her head. 'Oh no – I don't want it back. I don't want to see it ever again,' she said, eyeing it mistrustfully. She knew that the moth would always remind her of Lord Beaucastle – or the Baron, as she supposed she ought now to call him – and of Emily Montague. She shivered. 'You keep it,' she said hurriedly to Mei and Mrs Lim. 'Maybe you could sell the other stones. They must be worth something. And if you don't want the money, then perhaps you could use it to help the other people here, after what the Baron did.'

Mei smiled at her in surprise, and Veronica found herself grinning back.

*

They were all still there in the early hours of the morning, no one wanting to be the first to bring the celebration to an end. The champagne bottles were empty now, but there was still tea in the pot and Mrs Lim was talking about the different ways they might use the money raised from the sale of the jewelled moth to help the people of China Town. Mr Lim and Mr McDermott were discussing the possible voyage to China, whilst Billy scribbled down a few last notes in his exercise book, which now had a title boldly inscribed upon its cover: CASE NOTES: THE MYSTERY OF THE JEWELLED MOTH.

Across the room, Mary and Phyllis were feeding the green parrot with sunflower seeds, whilst Song was talking enthusiastically to Mr Pendleton and Mr Devereaux about the West End's best restaurants. Meanwhile, Joe, who had drained his glass of ale rather quickly, had made up his mind to say something to Lil.

'Er . . .' he began awkwardly. 'I know you said you were going to be busy with your audition practice and all, but well – if you need a break from rehearsing, *wouldyouliketotakeawalkalongtheriverwithmeoneevening?*' he burst out all in a rush. 'We could get an ice, or something like that?' he added uncertainly.

Lil looked at him. Her dark eyes were sparkling with mischief. 'Just you and me?' she asked.

He nodded, his cheeks beginning to flush red.

'Well . . .' she said, looking cheekier than ever. 'I think that sounds rather nice.'

Sophie smiled to herself. From where she was sitting at one end of the long table she was aware of the conversations going on all around her, but had no desire to join any of them. It was very late, and she was beginning to feel very sleepy. It had been such a peculiar evening, she reflected, as she stroked Mei's white cat, which had jumped up on to her knee and was now purring happily in her lap. She supposed that tomorrow everything would go back to normal, just as it had after their last adventure. They were done with being detectives.

Yet all the same, she felt sure that she had not seen the last of the Baron. She thought of what he had said to her on the dockside, just before he shot out the lights. This time she knew that he wasn't going to forget about her anytime soon, and not just because she had exposed him. Rather unwillingly, she turned her mind back to the mysterious photograph she had glimpsed in his study: the Baron as a young man, smiling alongside the unmistakable faces of Mama and Papa. The very thought of her father being mixed up with someone like the Baron was so awful that she pushed it away at once. It surely couldn't have been that they had known him – that they had ever been friends?

*

Sophie was still thinking about the photograph several days later, back in the Millinery Department at Sinclair's. The store was as busy as ever. She saw that a little crowd of debutantes had gathered to examine a new display of the very latest hats from Paris.

'I say, isn't the news about Lord Beaucastle fearfully shocking,' one girl was saying, as she tried on a hat with a big green bow. 'Papa says it's an utter disgrace.'

'I heard that he was just about to become engaged to Veronica Whiteley,' said another girl, raising her eyebrows.

'Oh no, that was just a rumour,' said the first girl authoritatively. 'I heard that all the time Veronica had been secretly engaged to Hugo Devereaux. They ran away from her coming-out ball together.'

'No you've got it all wrong!' exclaimed the girl in the frilly gown. 'It's Phyllis Woodhouse who is secretly engaged to Mr Devereaux. My sister saw them together in his motor!'

Sophie turned away to hide her smile, just as the cheeky porter appeared beside the counter. 'Parcel for you, Miss Taylor!' he announced, handing her a small square packet, wrapped in brown paper and tied with string. 'Sending you presents now, your young gentleman?' he teased as he went on his way. 'He must be getting serious, I reckon.'

Sophie laughed and shook her head at him, and then

turned her attention to the parcel. To her astonishment, when she had untied the string and pulled off the wrappings she found the Baron's face looking up at her – and there beside him, her mama and papa. It was the framed photograph from the Baron's laboratory! With it, she found a brief note.

Dear Miss Taylor,

Scotland Yard have completed their examination of the secret laboratory at Beaucastle Hall. They will be retaining most of the material there for further investigation, but I thought you might like to have this. I have no further information to offer you about the photograph, but you will see there is an inscription on the reverse, reading Cairo, 1890.

Yours respectfully,

Anthony McDermott

Cairo, 1890! Sophie knew her papa had travelled a good deal – but he had never once spoken about Egypt. What on earth could it all mean?

But even as she stood there at the counter, staring at the photograph, a lady that she recognised slightly came hurrying over to her. She had a very purposeful expression on her face.

'I'm sorry to bother you,' she began, sounding rather anxious. 'I'm Eleanor Jenkins. I work in the Toy Department. You are Miss Taylor, aren't you?'

'Yes – I'm Sophie Taylor,' said Sophie, hurriedly wrapping the brown paper back around the photograph.

'I hope you don't mind me coming to you like this,' said Miss Jenkins, looking more worried than ever. 'I know you're busy, but I wanted to ask for your help at once. It – it's urgent, you see.'

Sophie was confused. Had there been some problem in the Toy Department? She couldn't quite see how she was going to be able to help. Seeing the expression on her face, Miss Jenkins hesitated. 'You are the young lady who solves mysteries, aren't you?' she asked. 'You and Miss Rose – you're the detectives?'

Sophie gazed back at her in surprise for several long moments. Then she nodded decisively. 'Yes that's right,' she said. 'Tell me, Miss Jenkins – what can we do to help?'

AUTHOR'S NOTE

Today, London's Chinatown can be found in the heart of the West End, but during the 1900s it was situated in the East of the city. From the mid-1880s, Limehouse was home to a small Chinese community. Most of its residents were sailors, working out of the London docks, but there were also some families, like Mei's in this story.

It wasn't until the 1930s that the Limehouse Chinatown began to decline, as a result of the slump in shipping. Many of the so-called 'slums' in the area were torn down, and much of Limehouse was then destroyed in World War II during the Blitz.

After the war, a new Chinatown began to develop in Soho, where it continues today. Few traces now remain of this lost East End Chinatown, but you can still spot the tin dragon sculpture at the end of Mandarin Street, close to Westferry station, which marks the location where it could once be found.

ACKNOWLEDGEMENTS

A very big thank you to all at Egmont for all their support for Sophie, Lil and the gang. Special thanks to the brilliant Hannah Sandford and Ali Dougal for editorial wisdom, afternoon teas and intrepid boating excursions. Thanks also to publicist extraordinaire Maggie Eckel, designer Benjamin Hughes and all those who have been part of Team Jewelled Moth.

Enormous thanks to extraordinary illustrator Júlia Sardà for her incredible artwork. Hearty hurrahs for Louise Lamont – a truly marvellous agent and friend. Three cheers for all the wonderful booksellers who have given such amazing support for *The Mystery of the Clockwork Sparrow*.

A toast (in ginger beer, of course) to all my fellow authors in the Crime Club, most especially Mystery-Girl-in-Chief Robin Stevens. Special thanks to Katie Webber for being one of this book's first readers (and spotting embarrassing mistakes), for incomparable levels of enthusiasm, and for always being KWebb to my KWoo.

Finally, a huge thank you to my friends and family, most especially my parents for all of their support and for being my biggest fans – not to mention the fashioning of hats and designing of luggage labels! And thank you to my mum for saying that this one is 'even better than the last'.

Biggest thanks of all to Duncan, for everything.

SINCLAIR's

Sophie and Lil will return
in another thrilling adventure:

The Mystery of
THE PAINTED DRAGON

When a *priceless painting* is stolen,
our dauntless heroines find themselves
faced with *forgery, trickery and deceit*
on all sides! Be amazed as the brave duo
pit their wits against this *perilous puzzle!*
Marvel at their cunning plan to unmask
the villain and prove themselves
detectives to be reckoned with –
no matter what dangers lie ahead . . .

Coming February 2017